COME TO THE OAKS

The Story of Ben and Tobias

Bryan T. Clark

COME TO THE OAKS—The Story of Ben and Tobias

Copyright© 2017 Cornbread Publishing Inc.

Published by: Cornbread Publishing
Fiction / Gay & Lesbian / M-M Romance / Historical

Cover Art by: Kristallynn Designs
Cover content is for illustrative purposes only and any person depicted on the cover is a model.

First Edition: May 2017

ISBN-13: 9780997056235
ISBN-10: 0997056231

DEDICATION

To Irene 1909-1995:
Kind and spunky, you were light years ahead of everyone else in your progres-
siveness. As vibrant as the Cardinal, you charmed us all with your presence.
Leaving Kentucky for love, you taught us that love has no boundaries.

Slavery in Kentucky

Come to the Oaks is a fictional romance novel; it is not meant to depict actual events involving slavery in America. The language in this book is a reflection of the times in which the story is set.

The following information is intended to give the reader a better understanding of American slavery during the 1800s:

In 1807, the United States Congress outlawed the importation of slaves. This law took effect on January 1, 1808.

In 1833, the state of Kentucky prohibited the importation of slaves into the state for sale. However, because of the lucrative nature of the slave trade, slaves continued to be brought in illegally and bought and sold.

In 1865, following the end of the American Civil War, slavery was abolished in the United States.

Tobias's journey to America takes place during the year of 1845.

PROLOGUE
Warren County, Kentucky
March 10, 1845

"Bitterly cold" didn't begin to describe the temperature in the six-by-six-foot cell, which reeked of a horrifying mixture of bile, urine, and ammonia. If not for the icy draft streaming through tiny holes in the damp, dilapidated walls, the stench would have surely suffocated its dweller. The outer wall's main purpose—keeping those imprisoned within apart from the world outside—had the effect of locking in the cold.

In the back left corner of the gloomy cell, in a tight ball on the dirt floor, a thin nineteen-year-old slave lay motionless. His name was Mamadou Masamba, and he was the proud son of Babatunde Masamba.

Babatunde Masamba had been a West African healer with divine knowledge of herbal medicine. Right now, however, Mamadou's lineage meant little to him.

A tiny ray of sunlight stretched into the cell from a small barred opening in the cell across the aisle. Days ago, Mamadou's eyes had adjusted to his dim surroundings, which had contained him and four other young boys for the last week. The darkness covered him like dirt over his grave, seeming to forebode his future. Mamadou was not ready to concede that he would die in this tiny dark metal box.

Cold beat at his skin, and the little bit of clothing he wore could do nothing to protect him. His lips tingled against chattering teeth—yet another sign that he was unfamiliar with such cold. He had never been in temperatures below a cool sixty degrees. The freezing air reminded him how drastically his life had changed in the blink of an eye. He was far from his homeland, and the scent of fresh air had long ago disappeared from his senses.

Mamadou was just entering the prime of his life. He had been preparing to learn the trade of his father, passed down from his grandfather and his great-grandfather before that. As long as Mamadou could remember, he had studied with his father, followed him from village to village to treat the wounded, the elderly, and the dying. During their walks through the mountains, his father had often said, "My son, you will be the greatest healer, highly revered and respected across all lands. But be patient, for it is all timed." Never had there been a moment in his life during which he thought his destiny would be anything else—until now.

Fire flared up through Mamadou's memories. Smoke was everywhere, and his entire village was burning. People were screaming; cries for help came from all around, and he could do nothing. This was where the life he knew had ended.

Carried across the ocean in the belly of a ship, for months he had lain, bound in chains, amongst one hundred and twenty other slaves. They were men, women, and children. Most of them were sick, and some were already dead. The stench of the ship and that of the room that now imprisoned him—these things would certainly be his death. It was a death for which the spirits had not prepared him.

On this bitter and grey morning, the auction house was especially quiet. Through the low moans and cries of other slaves around him, he could hear voices laughing and talking on the other side of the wall. The tenor of their speech was slow and much more cheerful than the coarse voices of the white men on the ship—those animals who had beaten and tortured him and his people.

He tucked his chin into the pit of his arm, trying to breathe warmth into his own skin. His breathing, too shallow to give him any comfort, expelled much of what little life he had left. He hadn't moved in hours, maybe in days, having long ago lost any sense of time. Drifting in and out of consciousness, he heard the sound of footsteps as they came to rest in front of his cage. Then came the faint metallic click of a lock turning. Mamadou drew a breath. This, he thought, would be the last breath he ever took. He resigned himself to death; perhaps some part of him even welcomed it.

1

Shivering, Ben used the back of his freezing hand to wipe the chill from his runny nose. He was cold down to the bone and, to make matters worse, his back and neck were so tight that he believed he might never stand up straight again. Shifting his light brown, watery eyes over to his pa, who was driving the wagon, he wondered how the man could be unruffled by the icy wind blowing off the backs of the two chestnut mares that pulled them along.

The icy March conditions were of no concern to Master Emmett Lee or to the horses that had been quietly pulling the oversized wagon since dawn. As for Ben, he would have given anything to be back in his warm bed, waiting for the smell of fried eggs and morning coffee to waft through the house.

"Well, now, that took as long as a month of Sundays," Ben mumbled, as the little town of Myrtleville, Kentucky came into sight. The muscles in his jaw were tight from hours of clenching his teeth. He counted the wagons that had already arrived on the two streets that came together to make Myrtleville. The dirt intersection, being the town's square, would also be the site of this afternoon's slave auction.

"You've had your feathers in a ruffle since we left this mornin'," Master Lee said with a scowl. Never taking his deep-set eyes off the muddy road, he finessed the reins ever so lightly. The tiny wrinkles at the outer corners of his eyes deepened. "You ain't said but two words this whole trip. Now—do you think the sun is rising to hear you crow?"

Ben's breath caught at his father's callousness. "No, sir." He turned his head slightly at the gruff tone of Master Lee's voice. It wasn't what pa said; it was *how* he said it that told the nineteen-year-old to button it up. Rolling his weary eyes, Ben struggled not to show any other reaction. The few words that Master Lee spoke to Ben these days usually only reminded Ben of his pa's disappointment with him. Most times, it was best to say nothing back.

Shifting his one-hundred-and-forty-five pound body onto one butt cheek, Ben eyed the general store, which was coming up to their left. Inhaling deeply through his nose, he blew a cloud of vapors from his mouth—a sure sign of how cold it was and of his frustration. As he shifted yet again, he knew that his rump had borne all it could take. At five feet and eight inches, he'd been gifted with his mother's high cheekbones, which were a constant burnt rose color regardless of the temperature of the air. His slightly curly hair, the color of honey, touched the back of his collar, setting off his warm chestnut eyes and long, dark eyelashes. However, his milky pale complexion, dotted with freckles across his nose, was what drew the boy so much admiring attention.

Master Lee slowed the once-fancy wagon as they entered town. Ben took the slower gait of the horses as an opportunity to adjust his behind on the splintered wooden bench. He steadied his eyes on the townspeople.

"The auction's at noon. I'd like to pick up the grain before then and look at a couple of those milking cows they're selling off. If I can get two, that would be best." Master Lee pulled back on the reins, slowing the two mares to a walk. As he looked at his son, his lips tightened and the corners of his mouth tilted downward. Born in a little cabin in the backwoods of the Louisiana swamps to parents as poor as any slave, Master Lee had a hillbilly accent that would forever mark him as just that, no matter how rich he became.

Ben reached down into his front pocket and pulled out the gold, ornate pocket watch he had received for his sixteenth birthday. Glancing at the crystal, he reviewed a mental checklist of the things his father had instructed him to pick up down at the general store and trading post. What Ben wanted was black licorice with a nice hot cup of coffee. The black licorice sold at the general store had been on his mind for two days.

"Need you to be down at the square before the auction starts. If I can get a fair price for two or three negroes, should help to get the fields planted early when this cold lifts."

Negroes. He said it as if he was talking about a cow, ox, or chicken, Ben thought. The woman who had bathed him as a child was a negro. The women who cooked, cleaned, and smiled at him throughout the day were all negroes. Why his father—no, not just his father, but every white male he knew—referred to negroes in the same tone they would use for a barn animal was something he couldn't comprehend. It was as if everyone was saying the sky was green, while he saw, as clear as day, that it was blue. There were many reasons why Benjamin Nathanael Lee felt alone in this world, but the foremost was, without a doubt, his sensitive, kind spirit. He valued all life, regardless of the color of its skin.

"Benjamin, are you hearin' anything I'm saying to you, boy?" His father's unrefined voice echoed in his ear, shaking him back into the present. "Now, don't be pussyfootin' round. I'd like to be back at the plantation by nightfall."

Ben rolled his eyes. He knew of no one else in Kentucky who referred to his farm as a plantation. This was his father's attempt to sound as rich and fancy as those families in the Deep South. His choice to wear his burgundy double-breasted frock coat this morning clearly indicated his message: that he was a man of wealth.

"If we intend to clear any kind of a profit this year with the price of corn falling, we're goin' to have to make every dollar count today. You hear me, boy? I thought by bringing you along today, you can learn somethin', take an interest in running the business." The *business*—otherwise known as the Oak Grove Plantation.

Melancholy swept through Ben, causing him to drop his gaze. He knew that, as an only child, he was expected to follow in his pa's footsteps. The farm was to be his someday; he would marry and raise his family on the very land on which he had been born. He had watched for years as his pa had skillfully maneuvered to become one of the richest and most powerful businessmen in Warren County. Ben knew how his pa made every dollar count: he was cheap when it came to spending money on anything other than himself. Listening every morning to his pa discuss business with Dexter, the farm's white overseer, Ben had a pretty good grasp of the fact that the family's wealth was not as it appeared.

The fifty-acre farm that Master Lee had inherited from the family of his wife, Clara, was tucked back into the rolling hills of Warren County, Kentucky. Clara's grandfather, Major George Manson, had originally built the farm over a hundred years ago.

Master Lee himself, being the son of a sharecropper, didn't come from money. However, by the age of twenty-five, he had scraped enough money together to invest in a start-up lumber mill in Kentucky. The other four slick investors in the endeavor promised that, within a year, it would be a huge success, and young Emmett would be one of the richest men in Warren County.

The lumber mill never materialized. This was because several states, including New York, abolished slavery followed by the race riots in Cincinnati in 1827. Two of the investors thought that their planned work force of slaves might be in jeopardy and pulled out of the deal. It was that summer that Emmett met Mr. Samuel Manson, a potential investor.

Though Mr. Manson declined to invest in Emmett's mill, it was through him that Emmett and Miss Clara met. Initially, she found Emmett ill mannered and too short. However, under the unmistakable persuasion of her father, she and Emmett were married less than a year later. Their one and only son, Benjamin Lee, followed exactly nine months, to the day, after their wedding. When little Ben was born, following a long, intense labor, Clara realized that bearing children was a chore she'd rather have skipped.

Ben's parents had been married going on twenty years now, and they were widely considered one of the wealthiest couples in the county. At the ripe old age of nineteen, Ben wanted none of his parents' perceived wealth. He loathed everything about the farm: the abuse, the smell, the lavish lifestyle built on the backs of other human beings. He had heard it a thousand times: "Negroes are not humans, they're livestock, and they're dangerous if you turn your back to 'em. You don't walk behind a horse, and you don't turn your back on a negro." These words were no truer now than they had been the first time his pa had said them.

Master Lee's tiny hands pulled back on the reins as his bold, round body leaned back, drawing the wagon to a halt in front of the trading post and the auction house. The trading post was a mecca of everything anyone would ever need, including the imported goods increasingly demanded by the wealthier customers.

Ben tossed his black velvet hat over his head and tilted the brim downward slightly as he prepared to disembark from the wagon. After four hours of riding next to Pa, he was ready to put some distance between himself and his old man. This was about as much as Ben could take, in one sitting, of pa and his egotistical point of view on everything.

"Remember, boy, be right here before the auction starts." Master Lee glanced at Ben, and his eyes narrowed. Cold and rigid, they displayed his skepticism.

"Yes, pa." Ben turned his focus on a couple strolling arm-in-arm in front of the wagon. They were a man and wife, he imagined, walking in their own world. City slickers in fine clothing stood out in Myrtleville like a donkey in a herd of horses. His eyes followed the couple, especially the man. He was tall, with long, thin legs and wide shoulders that captured Ben's full attention. Ben tucked a long strand of his hair behind one ear as the couple rounded the corner.

"Don't be late!" Emmett climbed down off the wagon, making the entire thing rock.

Ben climbed down and stood behind his pa. He watched as Emmett loosely wrapped the horse's reins around the hitch post. Waiting for the perfect moment to ditch his pa, Ben was standing with his back to the street when a sudden, loud thud behind him drew his attention across the wide dirt street. Turning his head slightly, he saw someone loading a wagon in front of the general store. Looking closer, he saw a negro girl sitting on the back of the wagon as two people loaded it with dry goods. *Time for that licorice*, Ben thought to himself as he spotted the low-hanging sign of the general store. With a mumbled goodbye, he took off across the road.

"Hey, Benjamin Lee," called a low, deep voice from the other side of a wagon. Looking over the wagon's top, Ben saw it was his one-time schoolmate Jonnie Johnson with his pa. They had just finished loading several large sacks of grain onto their wagon next to the young negro girl.

As young boys, Ben and Jonnie had been joined at the hip. During their early schooling, both being introverts, they had found comfort in one another's silence. At the end of Ben's seventh grade year, Emmett had decided that his son was educated enough and pulled him from school. Ben remembered the discussion around the breakfast table one morning, his mother begging Emmett to allow Ben to continue with his schooling, to go north for a formal education. Emmett wasn't having it. He reasoned that education hadn't helped anyone in his family put food on the table. Ben was to stay there, learn the farm, and help with the business.

"Oh, hello, Jonnie. Mr. Johnson." Ben's eyes moved from the small negro girl over to Jonnie and then to Jonnie's father. Not at all like Ben's parents, Mr. Johnson was always scruffy and dirty. His overalls were soiled and tattered as if they were the only pair he owned. Nevertheless, in Warren County, even the poorest families had one or two slaves.

"Been a while." Jonnie's smile stretched across his face. "Pappy, you member Benjamin Lee? Folks own the Oak Grove farm over in Warren." Jonnie moved around the wagon to greet his friend.

They shook hands, and Jonnie's dry, rough skin drew Ben's attention to the other boy's hands. They were hands of a laborer, callused and scarred. His jagged fingernails were caked with dirt. Ben looked up into Jonnie's hollow eyes. A rush of sensations tingled through Ben's body as he scrambled for something to say. Avoiding eye contact gave him the second that he needed to gather his thoughts, brushing away the many memories, seemingly from a lifetime ago, that played out in his head. "It's good to see you. You look good. Fit as a possum eatin' a sweet 'tater," Ben lied.

Jonnie's eyes stayed locked on Ben. His Adam's apple bobbed gracefully in his neck as he swallowed. He was now at least three inches taller than Ben and probably twenty-five pounds heavier. "I seen you and your pa pull up. You in town for the auction?" Jonnie finally broke eye contact. "Got this nigger girl. Plan to do some breeding." The pitch of his voice made the words sound more like a declaration than a simple account of his morning.

"I see. We have supplies to pick up as well." Ben looked at the goods on Jonnie's wagon, seeing all they had purchased, including the girl. Sitting motionless in the wagon, she looked to be maybe eleven or twelve. Ben gave her a nod, and she lowered her head. Hearing Emmett's booming voice behind him, Ben turned around to see his father greet two gentlemen. Then Ben turned back to Jonnie.

In the split second during which he had looked away, Jonnie had changed. No longer was he the young classmate who Ben had unknowingly admired, the friend whom he thought of as his equal. Jonnie had aged far more than Ben. His eyes were sunken with dark circles, his hair tossed and dirty. Jonnie's family's wagon even paled next to that of Ben's family. What Ben had thought of minutes ago as his father's old tattered wagon was actually the most impressive carriage in town. The realization that he was now so different than his friend caused heat to rush to Ben's face. His cheeks burned, as a feeling of loneliness settled in his belly.

"Whatcha in the market for?" Nervousness flickered across Jonnie's face.

Ben tried to push down his own insecurity with a forced but unbending smile. "Pa's looking to purchase two or three field hands." As the words rolled from his lips, those field hands seemed like an abundance compared to the money Jonnie's pa had most likely spent on their slave girl.

"Been over to the auction house yet?" Jonnie's wandering eyes looked over Ben's shoulder toward the auction house.

Ben couldn't help but follow Jonnie's gaze across the street. "No. The males don't go on sale until one o'clock. Headin' over there in a bit."

"Pa, you mind if I take a walk with Ben here? Take him over to the auction house?"

Mr. Johnson gave a tiny nod. Ben knew it was out of respect for his father that Mr. Johnson didn't protest. Turning on his heels, Ben fell into step behind Jonnie as he marched off before Mr. Johnson could say anything else.

They entered the rear of the auction house. Holding the door open for Jonnie, Ben followed him inside. The stench of bile, urine, and sweat punched Ben in the gut, nearly sending him to his knees. He had forgotten how vile the inside of this building was. He held his breath as long as he could before gasping.

Jonnie grinned benignly. His crooked smile revealed a decaying tooth. "This year, there's more niggers than ever before."

Stopping just inside the doorway, Ben stared down a dim corridor lined with steel cages. The eerie quiet raised the hair on the back of his neck. He had come here many times over the years and never liked it, but this time, a disheartening feeling pushed into his soul. The whole notion of selling and trading humans sickened him.

His steps shortened. The first cell he came to held women and children. He refused eye contact, the sight being too hard to stomach, but he knew their eyes were upon him. With each step he took down the hall, deeper and deeper, the sounds of their breathing followed him.

Hearing a cry, he instinctively turned towards the noise. His eyes stopped on a naked, pregnant female. His pa had once told him, "They're tricky. You could get two for the price of one, or she could die giving birth and you end up with nothin'." Ben shook the thought from his head as he turned away.

Jonnie's high-pitched voice reverberated in his ear. "Pa and I was here early this morning. They auctioned them females off. Two hundred got you a real nice one. No whippin' marks, neither. These niggers are straight from Africa."

Africa, Ben thought. *They were illegal.* Everyone knew that, since Congress passed the Act of 1807, it was illegal to bring slaves into the country with the intent to sell them. Yet they did it anyways. A building full of slaves, being sold as if born and bred right here in Kentucky. Everyone knew it was a lie. Ben gritted his teeth as his eyes focused on the ground in front of him. He could feel his chest going in and out. His breathing was heavy.

The cages were crammed. Children and women were separated from the men. Jonnie led him down toward the end of the corridor. "Down here. The bulls are down at the end."

The term "bull" meant a strong, large man. A bull was the most expensive slave of all, a slave used with an ox to plow a field. A bull in his prime could go for a thousand to two thousand dollars, a sum that only the wealthy could pay. Reaching the first of four cages that housed the bulls, Ben saw that the males were again divided, young bulls on one side and bulls in their prime on the other. The men were shackled by their feet, in extra-large chains, to a steel post towards the back of the cage. Ben knew this was for everyone's protection.

"Y'all goin' to bid on a bull? I reckon I could talk pa into stayin' a bit. Like to see what one of these fetch for." Jonnie hammered a stick between the bars, sending an echo through the hallway. He clearly intended to startle the cage's occupants.

Ben studied the men in the cell. He knew that his pa needed at least two bulls to replace the two they had lost last year. One had run away over the winter and was found dead a week later, killed by a mountain lion. Then there was Ole Man Blue, who had up and died in the middle of their field last year when his heart gave out. Scrutinizing the men, Ben told himself to be mindful, staying in the middle of the aisle so they couldn't grab him. Looking through the cold bars, he felt his heart jump when he saw a young male curled up in the corner of the cage. The slave, who was wearing no shirt and only a potato sack for britches, lay in the fetal position, motionless. His skin was dark and shiny, the color of chocolate. His frame was thin.

Stepping closer to the bars, forgetting any notion of a threat, Ben lowered his chin. "Look a here," he mumbled, more to himself then to Jonnie.

"Get up, boy," Ben called to the young slave. The others in the cage moved aside, giving Ben a better view of who he was looking at. "Get up, and come over here so I can see you." The young slave lay there as if dead. Ben wondered if he had even heard him.

"Look at him. He goin' just lay there like an ole dog," Jonnie said.

"Boy, do you hear me talkin' to you? I say getsup!" Ben's voice cracked.

A deep, throaty voice came from another cage behind him. "He can't. Gots the fever from the boat. Might not speak no English neither."

Ben turned towards the voice. Across the way, gripping the bars, stood a large male slave. The man's wild eyes bore into him like a knife. Taking in the man's height, Ben took a step back, closer to the young slave's cell. Unaware that he was leaning on the bars of the other cage, Ben quivered as he looked at the big man. His face paled. Glancing at Jonnie and then back at the big slave, Ben heard the young slave stirring behind him.

As Ben's gaze swept over the young slave once more, a door creaked and light flooded into the hall. It was the auctioneer and Emmett. With them came two other well-dressed gentlemen.

"Mr. Lee, I wanted you to see what will be going up at one o'clock. Give you a chance to see them before the crowd gathers." The group of men marched towards Ben and Jonnie and came to a stop next to them.

Ben watched as the slaves rose to their feet. The young slave that held his attention kept his eyes down. He was beautiful. His frame was long and thin, at least a couple of inches taller than Ben's. Although he was frail, his shoulders were wide. Ben figured he had to be close to his own age.

A feeling from somewhere deep inside Ben took over. His eyes focused on the source of these emotions. Pushing away some of his darker thoughts, he pulled his eyes from the young slave. But he couldn't stop himself. "Pa. This one. I want to buy him for myself." His voice cracked as his own words repeated themselves in his head. *Did I actually say that aloud?* he thought. Emmett continued talking to the auctioneer.

"Pa, did you hear me? This one, I'll take it."

Emmett stopped mid-sentence, a look of irritation crossing his face. "Which one, son?" His annoyance caused the other men to stop and take note.

"There, that one," Ben said, pointing. Unsure why he was asking to purchase the young slave, he felt his chest tighten. *What am I doing?* He was caught between opposing feelings, as a tide of emotions rushed through his body. Uncertainty mesmerized him. His chest squeezed his lungs. His entire body tingled as if he was about to pass out. He knew only one thing for certain: he wasn't leaving without this young slave.

"Naw, you don't want that one." The auctioneer was staring at Ben but clearly talking to Emmett. "The boy is too sickly. Won't make it through spring. Wasn't planning on putting him up for bid." The other gentlemen chuckled at the ridiculous notion that anyone would consider this slave for purchase.

"Pa. You said you wanted me to learn the business. Well, I ain't leaving here without this slave. Get him cleaned up and ready for the auction," Ben commanded, staring down the auctioneer.

That afternoon, Ben was the sole bidder on the young slave, whose name was Mamadou Masamba, #1478. A bid of just under a hundred and a half earned Ben the title of Master. Along with Ben's purchase, Emmett also successfully bid on three new field hands by the names of Obi, Simba, and Rudo. As they began their trek back to the Oak Grove Plantation, neither Ben nor his father had any idea what had come over him in the last three hours.

2

Huddled in the back of the wagon, Mamadou's six-foot frame had been wedged between Obi and Rudo for the last four hours. He tried to shield himself from the harsh and relentless wind while occasionally glancing up to take in the countryside. The moldy scent from the sodden leaves on the side of the trail penetrated his nose. In combination with the familiar smell of moss and fallen, decaying trees, it made him think of home. As much as the fresh air was welcome, the feeling of being alive again meant thinking of the loss of his family, his home, and his former life.

An hour outside of town, Mamadou caught his first hint of a sweet aroma as the wagon passed under a huge, budding tree. His lungs expanded to accommodate the clean air. As he looked up into greenish sunlight diffused through a canopy of trees, for a moment, his world was full of tiny bits of purple and the robust scent from a million blossoms. This was before Simba gave him a nod, signaling him to keep his head lowered.

When the wagon made its way around the last turn leading up to the house, Mamadou caught his first glimpse of the grand mansion through the many oak trees. His eyes grew wide as he stretched his neck over the side of the wagon. He wasn't sure what to make of it, but he knew it was a building of some sort.

The wagon made one last sharp turn and came to a stop by the porch of the giant house. Mamadou lifted his head up over Rudo's shoulders and, for the first time, took a good look at his surroundings. Afraid to speak, he scanned the property and then looked to Simba, hoping for a sign that he wasn't in immediate danger.

Off to the side of the big white mansion, through a picket fence, several women were working in the garden. Though layers of clothing almost completely covered them, he noticed that their hands, necks, and faces were much lighter than his were. He wondered, *Are they African?*

Smoke rose from the top of a small building next to the garden. The scent of whatever was cooking passed his nose and landed in the pit of his belly. Sudden panic captured Mamadou. His heart rate increased, as a vision of fire flashed before him. His entire village was burning, and people were screaming and running. He trembled remembering the sound of gunshots. The white man was everywhere. They were burning his village and capturing his people. He knew this because it had been happening for years in other villages. He had heard of entire tribes being wiped out. Gone in a day. Poachers sold them—shipped them to the new world as slaves. They had come for him and his family.

Mamadou's heart was pounding, and he held a scream inside his throat. Both Rudo and Obi grabbed him and held him down in the wagon before anyone saw his panic. "Calm down. Calm down, boy, before you get us killed," Rudo whispered.

The sound of footsteps running towards them drew Mamadou's attention.

"Massa Lee, Massa Lee, welcome home, sir." The voice grew closer. "We were expectin' you home hours ago. Feared somethin' happen to you."

Out of the corner of his eye, Mamadou watched as an old man— the one who was addressing Emmett—approached the wagon. Mamadou couldn't seem to draw any breath into his lungs. As he starved for air, his vision began to blur.

"Oh, come on, Charlie. You know ain't nothing goin' to happen to me. I'm goin' to outlive you all." Emmett chuckled as the tall negro named Charlie helped him down off the wagon.

Charlie smiled, vibrant and spunky. Mamadou was to learn that Charlie had been born on the farm forty years ago. He shook his head at Master Lee. "I reckon you right, sir. You were a sight for sore eyes when you come round that corner. Mrs. Clara's been pacing the porch the last hour. Thought I was goin' to have to put new boards down by morning just so she could keep pacing."

Mamadou turned his attention back to the massive white structure that stood before him. His eyes followed the large white columns up the side of the building until he had bent his neck all the way back. Dropping his wide eyes back down, he saw a woman step out of the front door, her skin as pale as the moon. Directly behind her came a thin negro woman wearing a long dress and white apron. They hurried down the steps and over to the wagon.

"My dear husband, you are two hours late for dinner. I had the good notion to feed it to the hogs, had Penny not gone through the trouble of making you your favorite." The woman gently kissed Emmett on the cheek before eyeing Mamadou and the others in the wagon. "Dolly, give Charlie a hand there." The negro woman who had followed her from the house rushed to the other side of the wagon.

"Good evening, Mrs. Clara. Might say it's good to see you. Best part of the day, I say." Emmett tipped his hat to the woman as she came to his side. "So, am I to guess there's chicken and dumplings in the house waiting on us?" He smiled as he winked at his son, the young man they called Ben.

Mamadou studied the woman called Mrs. Clara, as well as Charlie and the negro woman named Dolly, who were standing next to the wagon. Charlie was just a little taller than Mamadou but had over a hundred pounds on him. He was not only Master Lee's most trusted slave but also Dolly's husband and the only blacksmith on the property—a skill passed down by his daddy, who had also been born on the farm. Charlie appeared to be on good terms with Master Lee, who Mamadou had realized was Ben's father. *She must be his mother*, Mamadou thought, as he observed the three white people. Who were these other two, who shared his dark skin color? Was this their village? Shifting his eyes about, he caught Ben staring at him. The young man's penetrating stare made Mamadou look down. He had seen that stare several times back at the auction house and again when they were loaded onto the wagon at the beginning of the trip.

"We have less than an hour of daylight left. Let's get these boys unloaded so I can tend to this hunger pain that has been rollin' around in my belly," Emmett said. "Charlie, I reckon these horses deserve a good supper too. They been travelin' all day. Make sure you tend to that as well."

"Come on now, get out that wagon," said Charlie, tapping on the side of the wagon. He held his glare on Mamadou before looking over at the other three. "Come on now. Get up!" He waved one of his large hands for Mamadou and the others to get out. Using his other hand, Charlie braced himself against the side of the wagon as movement from its occupancy rocked it from side to side.

Mamadou's body was stiff as he moved to stand. He watched as Mr. Lee produced a key from his pocket and handed it to Charlie, who used it to unfasten the locks around each of their ankles. The pressure of the heavy shackles was instantly relieved when they fell from his ankles. Badly bruised and scarred from the wear of the metal, his ankles had not been free of chains in months.

Charlie helped Mamadou and the others out of the wagon, lining them up in front of Mrs. Clara. Lifting her chin high in the air, Clara took note of the four new slaves. Looking at Mamadou, her eyes widened. "What are you doing with this one? He's too small to pull a plow, and he looks sick." She took a step back as if he was contagious.

Emmett shook his head. "That there is Ben's. He done bought his first negro." Walking over, he pulled on Mamadou's bottom lip and inspected his teeth and gums. "Probably overpaid for him as he don't look a damn. Not sure he even talks, but he gots good teeth. Could be worth something someday if he don't die." Emmett looked at Ben and then at Charlie. "Charlie, take these boys and chain 'em up in the potato shed until Dexter can have a look at 'em in the mornin'."

Clara abruptly called out to Charlie. "Stop! Not the boy. Have Miss Gee-gee tend to him. Dolly, take him to Miss Gee-gee's. He will be no good to any of us if he dies lying in that shed, now, will he?"

Miss Gee-gee, Mamadou would learn, was the oldest slave on the property. Although nobody knew for certain, people thought that she was in her late seventies. This brought her a certain amount of respect from everyone on the property, both free and enslaved. It had been many years since she had last worked the fields; she was now the full-time guardian for the young orphans on the property. Some of these were newly purchased children too young to work the fields, while others had been left behind by the deaths of their parents. Whatever their backgrounds, they all went to Miss Gee-gee.

She raised them until they were ready to move into a cabin housing single slaves of the same sex. Her own cabin was located at the end of the two rows of slave quarters on the property. Slightly larger than the other cabins, it was the only one containing a loft—the children slept there.

"Now, Mama, don't go makin' decisions 'bout my negro!" Ben hollered as he glanced at Mamadou. "I get the say on him, not you!"

Clara rolled her ocean blue eyes and shook her head. "Son, can you humor your mother and try to talk as if you had some schooling and I didn't fail you completely? I shut my eyes, and I can't tell if it's a negro talking or my own flesh and blood."

"Yes, Mama," Ben replied as he lowered his chin.

"So, what exactly is your plan?" Clara's eyes shifted between Ben and his father.

Emmett removed his pipe from his mouth; Charlie had just lit it and handed it to him. "We talked about it on the way home. Your boy has finally taken an interest in the future of this here farm." He appeared to be growing impatient with his wife's query. "He will look after this negro—acclimate him to the plantation. With any luck, we can get him out in the fields in a few weeks."

It was clear to Mamadou they were talking about him. Listening, he stood motionless for what felt like an eternity. Submerged in fear, he began to sway. He felt as if someone was choking him.

Clara guffawed, her arms folded. "Dolly, take the boy so Mr. Lee and his son can come inside and stop being foolish." Clara was, for the most part, a kindhearted woman, but Emmett often tried her patience. Pale and chubby, with sandy grey hair that was thinning, she had deep wrinkles across her forehead that she had long blamed on Emmett.

To Emmett, Clara was the apple of his eye. He had told her when they first married that she was too pretty to be living in the country on a farm. As a consolation, he said, he was going to build her the grandest home in the state of Kentucky. He had done just that, building a house that mirrored the southern Greek revival architecture of the Deep South.

Dolly did as instructed. Taking Mamadou by his hand, she escorted him back down the road, away from the house. Looking over his shoulders, he saw that Ben and his mother were engaged in a conversation on the verandah.

A month shy of their wedding, Clara's father, Samuel Mason, had dropped dead of a heart attack, leaving everything to his daughter. Emmett's dream of becoming a wealthy man came true. His first order of business was replacing the modest previous home with one that was up to his standards.

A year after the new house was finished, Emmett convinced Clara to buy the twenty-five acre plot next to their land. This expanded the farm to fifty acres, on which they farmed hemp, tobacco, and corn. Fifty acres of rolling hills, farmland as far as the eye could see, and forty slaves, all controlled by one family: this was Mamadou's new village.

"Can you speak?" Dolly didn't turn around to acknowledge Mamadou as she led him down the path. "I'll have Miss Gee-gee take a look at that ankle."

Mamadou looked over his shoulders again to see if anyone was watching them. He was free. For the first time since being in captivity, he wasn't chained or watched by anyone. *Who is this woman? Is she one of them? Would she scream if I ran?* He looked around for an escape route. Which direction would he even go? He had no idea where he was or what might lie beyond the trees, waiting to hurt him. He was too weak, and his ankle to injured, to run even if he wanted to.

"Boy, do you understand English?" Dolly looked at him, waiting for a response. He had a feeling that she wasn't one of them.

"I speak . . . Eng-English." His breathing grew weaker with each step. The two passed near several large oak trees, under which even the soft rustling of the branches made him wary. His sense of hearing and smell were heightened, and the dirt and decomposing leaves made the air feel closed and thick.

"Is you from Africa? How you learn English?" Dolly asked over her shoulder.

Mamadou tried to pick up his step behind her. "I am from Africa. My people, we speak Twi, but I have two tongues. Father and I speak to many people."

"You ain't got but one tongue . . . And whatever you just said, I got two ears, and I still didn't understand you." Dolly's tone was brash. She quickened her step as she led him around the backside of the cabins. Mamadou repeated her words in his head, perplexed as to whether she was a friend or not.

The sun was starting to set. Mamadou could hear various voices, some of which sounded like children's laughter, coming from the other side of the cabins. Between the cabins, he caught glimpses of people moving about. They appeared to be moving freely, just as he and this strange woman were.

Mamadou worked up his courage and asked, "Where are you taking me?" Over the last several months, he had seen what happened to those who asked defiant questions, but he wasn't sure he could walk much further. The pain in his ankle was increasing, sending spikes darting up his leg. He could barely keep up with her, though he feared angering her if he stopped. "May I ask where you are taking me?" His tone weaker this time.

"You goin' down to Miss Gee-gee's. She tend to that ankle of yours and look after you till Massa say you too old to stay there no more." After walking around one more cabin, they reached the one belonging to Miss Gee-gee and stopped in front of her tiny porch. The cabin was little and decaying and had been raised about a foot off the ground.

Over the years, twenty single-room slave quarters had been built on the lower end of the property, down next to the narrow river. Cabin Row, as everyone on the plantation referred to it, as it was built with oaks cut down on the property. Most of the cabins were barely standing and were in dire need of repairs. The tiny cabins were positioned between the master's home, which stood downwind, and the river, thus making it harder for a slave to steal off during the night. Everyone knew negroes couldn't swim, and many runaways proved the theory correct when their dead bodies washed up down river. However, in case the water was not enough of a deterrent, a small negro graveyard lay on the other side of the river, reminding potential escapees where they would end up.

Mamadou could see between the horizontal slats of wood on the side of the cabin. Smoke rose from the chimney, and he could hear movement inside. He gasped in pain as he shifted his weight off his injured leg.

Hearing footsteps sliding towards the door, Mamadou braced himself for what might come. The door slid open, and a petite old woman stepped out onto the porch. Her skin was as dark as his, her face wrinkled and drawn. She smiled at him as she ran her hands down her apron.

Mamadou took a step back, looking at the old woman, her right eyelid drooped down over a greyish white eyeball as she tilted her head just a little to see him. Mamadou took a deep swallow, trying to moisten his dry throat. His breath was racing from the short walk, or was it because of this woman? A million miles from home, in a different world, he was as scared as he had ever been.

Miss Gee-gee held her hands out, palms up, signaling for Mamadou to come to her. Dolly nudged him forward. "Go on, boy. That there is your new momma. She take care of you now." She pushed him again. "Master Ben be around to fetch him in a couple of days."

Mamadou lowered his head as he stepped up onto the porch. Miss Gee-gee gently wrapped his rigid body in her arms and led him inside. Mamadou almost collapsed from the tenderness of her touch. The kindness he felt was like the gentleness of an antelope nestling her fawn: compassion after months of only brutality.

The inside of the cabin was rustic: a single room with wood plank floorboards. Shielded by the lack of windows and the front door that lay askew on its rusty hinges, the interior appeared dark until his eyes adjusted. On the right side of the door sat a rocking chair in front of the stone fireplace. On the left side was a ladder with six steps leading up to the sleeping loft where the children slept. On top of a flat straw mattress was a wool blanket tossed against the wall. Under the loft, another flat mattress lay on the floor.

Many years ago, Miss Gee-gee had given up sleeping on the lower mattress and had taken to the old rocker, which Charlie had made for her. The only other piece of furniture in the cabin was a wooden table used to prepare meals. On it sat two old pots, a couple of tin dishes, and several wooden spoons of various sizes.

The glow from the fire illuminated five children, huddled on the floor and eating from a single bowl. That night, Miss Gee-gee had prepared her usual cornbread for dinner, pouring warm goat's milk into the bowl over the cornbread. The children stopped eating as they looked at Mamadou.

He took in the strange room. Bowing his head, he felt tears forming behind his eyelids. This was the closest thing to normal he had seen in months, yet it was so foreign that it left all of his insides quivering.

A very dark-skinned negro girl sat on the floor in front of the fireplace with the eating bowl in her lap. The remaining four children sat around her and took turns eating from the bowl. She looked at Mamadou and extended the bowl to him.

She introduced herself as Pearl. Barely twelve years old, she had come to the Oak Grove Plantation when she was only two, torn from her father's arms as he pleaded for his baby. Master Lee had traded the neighboring farmer a crate of nails for her. She had been given to Miss Gee-gee to raise until she was old enough to work.

Though Mamadou hadn't eaten in days, what he really craved was water. Approaching Pearl, he looked at Miss Gee-gee for permission. With a slight nod of the head, she gave it, and he took the bowl from the young girl. Using two of his dirty fingers, he dipped into the bowl, scooping up a huge handful of bread soaked in warm milk. There wasn't much in the bowl, but the feeling as it rested in his stomach brought warmth to his entire body.

After dinner, Miss Gee-gee put the children to bed and then used the hot water she had boiled over the fire to bathe Mamadou. She rubbed delicately, cleaning his cuts and bruises from the chains before giving him a fresh nightshirt.

"I find you some clothes in the morning," she told him. Her voice, soft and gentle, made him feel that he was okay. For how long, he didn't know, but for right now, he was safe.

After his bath, Mamadou climbed up into the sleeping loft with the other children and squeezed between them. He laid his head on the straw mattress and closed his eyes. He felt the heat radiating off their little bodies as they huddled together and a tear slid down his cheek before he drifted off to sleep.

3

After several days of mostly sleeping, Mamadou opened his eyes to the sounds of pots clanging below. Though he was not ready to move, the pressure in his chest was gone. He slid a hand up and down the mattress, checking for other bodies. He had woken up several times over the last couple of days to find the little ones next to him moving about. He couldn't remember how many there were, but he did recall the young girl named Pearl. Now, as his eyes took in the ceiling and wooden beams inches above his head, he wondered how far from home he was. Could he ever make the journey back across the big ocean? Then the unavoidable thought crept into his head: was there even a home to return to? The village had burned, and the people had been seized. Had anyone survived, and if so, what must the village look like today? Over the last couple of months, his entire world had spun out of control, a blurred vision colored in with pain and suffering. He didn't want to move; he wasn't ready to get up. As he rolled onto his side, his eyes met those of Miss Gee-gee, who was staring up at him.

"Chile, can'ts fatten you up if you ain't eatin' nothin'. Come on down while it's still hot and somethin' left."

His senses kicked in. He could smell food and saw a skillet of cornbread sitting on the narrow table. Studying the tiny room, he watched as Miss Gee-gee tended to a pot hanging over the fire. Pearl, who was busy as well, paid him no mind as she fussed at the little ones, grabbing them up one by one and sitting them by the fire.

"'Bout time you come on down here and eats something." Miss Gee-gee looked directly at Mamadou and nodded towards the morning meal. "Take a look at that ankle too. Make sure its healin' properly."

As Mamadou slid his legs towards the ladder, he glanced at his ankle. The swelling had lessened, and the pain was half of what it had been a couple of days ago. Slowly, he made his way down and sat next to everyone.

"Y'all introduce yourself to your new brother. We goin' to call him Tobias . . . Yes, that's it, Tobias." Miss Gee-gee handed Pearl two tin plates, each with grits and a piece of cornbread. Pearl passed a plate to one of the boys next to her.

"My name . . . is Mamadou, Mamadou Masamba," his eyes locked onto Miss Gee-gee as he muttered his name.

"I'm Henry." One of the little ones piped up first as he politely took his plate from Pearl.

The little boy next to Henry looked shyly at Mamadou. "I'm Stuart."

Mamadou stared at them both. They were identical. He wasn't dreaming; there were two people sitting there that looked exactly alike.

Miss Gee-gee pointed at the two babies. "And that there is little Harriett and Niles, and you meets Pearl."

Mamadou eyed them all, including the old woman. "Mamadou . . . My name is Mamadou." He looked at Miss Gee-gee as he took a seat on the floor next to Pearl. "My name is Mamadou Masamba." With his tone, he unmistakably corrected his elder.

Miss Gee-gee took another tin from the table, ladled a spoonful of grits into it, placed a biscuit on it, and handed it over to Mamadou. He forgot about the name "Tobias" as he consumed his breakfast.

The two sets of tiny eyes belonging to the twins watched him, and Mamadou watched them just as closely.

When everyone was finished, Pearl took each of their tins from them, stacking one on top of the other. "I'll wash up. You want to come with me?" She asked as she rested her hands on her hips.

"Yes, take Tobias and shows him around. He goin' to be needin' to know right quick. Ain't goin' to be here long before Massa Lee move him where he supposed to be." Miss Gee-gee took the two smaller babies up and placed them on the bed under the loft.

The thought of going outside sent a queasiness through Mamadou's stomach. He knew what slavery was; it occurred in his country as well. He was well aware of the slave trade, the stories of men taking one another for their own possession. Those stories held nothing, though, to what he had endured over the last several months. Surrounded by these four walls, he was protected, safe from whomever it was that held him here. He hesitated before speaking, unsure of what to ask as he had so many questions.

His eyes followed Pearl as she gathered up a pot and a couple of wooden spoons from the table and walked towards the door. His body was heavy as he rose to his feet and stabilized his legs under himself.

The outside air filled his lungs as he took his first step off the porch. Following Pearl to several washtubs next to the river, he watched in silence as she cleaned out the pot, spoons, and tin plates and then rinsed them in the water. Looking over his shoulders, he stared at the row of cabins about a hundred yards from them. It was quiet; no one was around except a few small children and a couple of women.

A year ago, Pearl had been one of those children. Now her responsibilities included tending to the chickens, gathering eggs, stacking tobacco leaves, and looking after her four younger adopted brothers and sister.

As they made their way up the small embankment, Mamadou counted the cabins in his head. "Who lives in all those?" he asked, pointing to the cabins.

"People."

"I mean, who?" Mamadou thought about the words he had used and wondered if he had spoken correctly. He was sure that he had, and as they came around to the front of Miss Gee-gee's cabin, he tried and failed to think of another way to ask his question. Placing the dishes on the porch, they continued their walk up the middle of the two rows of cabins.

Pointing to the first cabin on their left, Pearl said, "That's Mr. Charlie and Miss Dolly. They is married. He take care of the horses around here and makes things. Miss Dolly, she works up in the big house." She then pointed to their right. "That's Mr. Adam and Miss Sarah." Pearl continued listing names that meant nothing to him. When they reached the last couple of cabins, she said, "The boys live in them." Mamadou stared at the three cabins to which she was pointing. They were old and in poor condition, the wood rotted to the point that he could actually see bits and pieces of the cabins' interiors.

Passing Cabin Row, the two entered a larger wooden structure. The smell of burning coal pierced Mamadou's nose, causing him to stop just inside the doorway. His eyes adjusted to the dim room, revealing a man standing over the fire, pounding a metal rod with a large hammer. "Dis here is Mr. Charlie. He makes nails, horse shoes, and all kind of stuff."

Mamadou remembered seeing the man on the day that he had arrived. "He's the man who took the other three men that traveled with me from the auction house. Have you seen them?" Mamadou squinted as the coal dust burned his eyes. "Where are they?"

"Yeah, I see them. They in the cabin with the males. I showed you that cabin already. You need to pay attention." Pearl released a noticeable heavy sigh as her five-foot body stepped in front of him.

Heading back outside, she pointed towards a small building as they resumed their journey. "That there is the ice house."

Mamadou had no idea what an ice house was, and he did not particularly care at the moment. He walked by, barely glancing at it.

"You ain't got no business in there," she warned as she pointed to the ice house before rounding the corner and heading up towards the mansion.

Mamadou had never seen so many buildings made of so many different materials. Comparing it to his village of mud huts with thatch roofs, he became overwhelmed and needed to sit down. "Stop. Can we rest a minute?" Blaming it on his ankle, he took a seat on the dirt.

As he rested, he could see his sister in Pearl. She reminded him so much of Chima, who had been a talker and extremely smart for her age. Facing a sudden mental numbness, he fought to picture her face. Smoke and fire overshadowed most of his memories now.

Pearl continued to talk rapidly, bouncing from one subject to the next as she stood over him. Pointing to several small buildings next to the mansion, she explained the detached kitchen, the smokehouse, and the numerous other buildings surrounding the house.

Like most farms, the Oak Grove Plantation was self-sufficient. Slaves were in the field by dawn every morning and worked until sundown. They were given two ten-minute breaks, which they used to eat lunch and dinner in the fields. At this time of morning, the farm was a working machine, and everyone had a job.

As Pearl was telling Mamadou what she knew about Mr. Lee and his family, Mamadou could see several slaves working in the distance, hauling large bags from a wagon parked next to the field. Looking across the field on the other end, he saw the older man that had arrived with him in the wagon. Yes, it was Simba; he was strapped to a plow being pulled by two oxen and was struggling to hold it upright. There were several women behind him, planting something as they followed him.

Farming was not new to Mamadou. His people had farmed for many generations. What was new to him was the wide-open space of rolling hills in which they farmed and the equipment they were using. Everywhere he looked, for as far as he could see, there were crops. Pearl explained that behind the big house were fields of tobacco and behind those were fields of corn.

To the left of the big house was Master Lee's hemp crop. Pearl told Mamadou that, due to the price of corn dropping, Master Lee was taking out acres of the corn and increasing his tobacco production. As the wind blew, one could see bits of pollen blowing across the rolling hills. These caused Mamadou to sneeze.

Passing by the old feed barn, he asked, "Why did she call me that other name? My name is Mamadou—Mamadou Masamba. I don't know who Tobias is."

Pearl laughed. "You talk funny. Did anyone ever tells you that? You can'ts have no Africa name in America. You goin' to be called something Massa cans remember."

"What does it mean?" he asked as he listened to his own voice, wondering how he sounded.

Pearl frowned. "I don't know, I reckon it don't means nothin'. It's your name."

"All names mean something," Mamadou shot back. "Mamadou stands for 'praiseworthy.' As a newborn, I was examined by my father and found fit enough to be amongst my family. My name is Mamadou," he commanded.

"Praiseworthy—Well, it ain't no mo'," stated Pearl matter-of-factly.

Mamadou thought about what she had said. *Tobias. Tobias,* he repeated in his head, listening to how it sounded. *My name is Mamadou.* After several minutes of silence, he asked, "Who is this Miss Gee-gee? This person that is trying to change my name?"

"Why you ax so many questions? Mind your business, and keep your head down, and you be alright. If not, Dexter takes a switch to you and teaches you to mine your business." As she tilted her head, her neck stretched, and her eyebrows arched as far up as they seemed able.

"Who is Dexter?" The thought of being whipped sent a tremor throughout his body. Over the last several months, he had seen numerous men and women whipped and beaten. Pearl's words rang out in his head. Flashes of flame filled his vision, followed by an immediate sense of panic.

"He the overseer. He sees everythin'. He works for Massa Lee. Knock an apple from a tree when you ain't supposed to, he know and come with his whip to teach you." Pearl sashayed away from him. Tobias watched as her pigtails swayed from side to side; her once-pretty blue dress, now stained and torn, stopped just over her brown ankle boots.

Rising to his feet, Tobias joined her, continuing to take in his new surroundings as they headed back towards the slave quarters. Their clothes, the buildings, the dirt smell in the air: he understood none of it. He longed to see his family again and dreamed of the day when this would happen.

Miss Gee-gee was standing in the doorway of the cabin, holding a straw broom. Sweeping the dirt out of the building, she barely looked at them as they stepped onto the porch. "Mr. Ben come a lookin' for you. He tells me he'll be back in the mornin' for you. Best you rest that ankle."

That night after dinner, Tobias listened as Miss Gee-gee explained to him who Benjamin, Emmett, and Mrs. Clara Lee were. Her voice was weak but clear about the importance of obeying them at all times. In detail, she laid down the rules for life on the farm and the unfortunate consequences should he step out of line. "Remember boy, keep your eyes cast down and don't speak unless spoken to, and always use 'sir' and 'ma'am,' you understand?"

After putting the young ones to bed, Miss Gee-gee sat on the porch, resting on an old cut tree stump turned into a chair. It was the first time she had sat down all day. Tobias and Pearl sat inside by the fire, whispering so as not to wake the little ones.

"They say you come from Myrtleville. That right?" Pearl's chocolate brown eyes narrowed.

"If that's the village I was caged at, than yes. But I don't *come* from Myrtleville, I come from West Africa . . . where I will be returning." Tobias saw by Pearl's expression that his tone may have been a bit sharp, but he didn't care. This was not his home. He didn't care what the old woman had said to him either. Nobody owned him.

"I ain't never been nowhere," Pearl said. "Ain't never been past the gates of this ole farm. This is the only somewhere I got. Tell me about Myrtleville."

"What do you want to know?" Tobias asked.

"I don't know," Pearl replied.

Tobias stared into the fire as he took a moment to think. "I remember when we reached land. They took us off the ship and loaded us onto wagons. The wagons took us to a village, where someone led us into a cold building. Inside were rows and rows of cages. I shared a cage with other men who I did not know. I hollered for my father, hoping he was close somewhere, but he wasn't." Tobias's voice dropped off . . . "Perhaps he did not make the journey. Maybe none of them did." He pushed away the thought that he might be the only member of his family still alive. At the same time, he feared that they, too, were enslaved somewhere. Remembering the young women whom he had seen raped on the ship, he lowered his chin, feeling guilty of wishing death for his sister as a better alternative.

"How long were you there?" Pearl asked.

"Many days, I think. I was sick. They fed us like animals, pushing food through the bars. I continued to grow weaker due to a lack of fresh water and food." Tobias stopped talking as he stared at the flames. The only noise in the room came from the crackling of the fire.

Tobias wiped a tear from his eye, hoping that Pearl hadn't seen it. The glow of the fire dimly lit the room, enough for him to see that she was staring right at him. Tobias cleared his dry throat. "I remember the day they came and got me. I was weak and sick. They wanted me up on my feet. I had seen what happened to the sick, so I struggled with every ounce of muscle that I had left to get up. I feared them dumping me in the wagon that hauled the dead away."

Pearl leaned in. "So den what happen?" she asked impatiently.

"I couldn't do it. Another young man in my cage came to help me. They took us outside and made us stand on a platform. The sun was bright, and I could barely see. I stood at the end and watched as the six men next to me were sold off, one by one. When they came to me, I remember the crowd laughing. I stood there as they laughed. No one bid; they laughed and screamed things about me." Tobias's voice had dropped, becoming inaudible.

"Where was Massa Lee?" she asked.

Clearing his throat, Tobias raised his chin. "Slow down, I am getting to that. I knew I was worth nothing and would probably be put to death when it was over. Then, from the back of the crowd, I heard Ma—Master Lee call out to the auctioneer. The crowd erupted into laughter again, and then I saw Master Lee's son. He pushed his way to the front of the crowd and stood there. Staring right at me, he shouted out his bid, and then doubled it as he faced the crowd. I don't know why he did this. It was clear he was the only one interested in me."

"Do he pay a lot for you? Pearl asked.

"He doubled his bid, and it was still less than half of what they paid for the man next to me." Tobias thought about what he had seen over the last month. He had witnessed so much abuse on the ship, at the dock, and in the auction house. A thickness grew in his throat as another tear slipped from his eye and ran the length of this cheek.

Later that evening, after Pearl had gone to bed, Tobias remained sitting by the fire. He heard singing coming from outside. He told Miss Gee-gee that he wanted to go see who was singing and that he would bring more wood for the fire when he returned. "You be careful in the dark. If Dexter catches you outside the quarters, he thinks you runnin' 'way."

Tobias followed the sounds of the beautiful female voices. His chest tight, he could barely breathe, so running wasn't an option. Finding a small group of women around a fire in the middle of cabin row, Tobias stood in the shadows and listened to their velvety voices.

They were singing songs he had never heard before. Their voices were soft and in perfect harmony, as two young men hummed in the background. Their voices spilled over with both sorrow and hope. Tobias sat outside the group. Listening, he felt a deep loneliness wash over him. Would he ever see his family again?

4

"Tobias! Tobias! Come on out here! It's time to work!" Ben nervously called as he stood on the step of the tattered cabin. Staring at the building's front door, he could actually feel his own heartbeat as it pounded in his chest. His pulse quickened with the sound of movement coming from inside. Ben had waited as long as he could to see Tobias. *Tobias*, he repeated in his head. When word got to him of the name Miss Gee-gee had chosen, he had no opposition to the change. The man needed a name, and Tobias was as good as any.

Shifting his weight, Ben bit his nails as he watched the front door of Miss Gee-gee's cabin open. His worst nightmare had come true. He was a slave owner, like his pa and his grandpa before that. *What happened to me down in Myrtleville?* From the moment he laid eyes on Tobias lying in that cage, his life had been a blur. Had he not been there that morning, Tobias would surely be dead. Aware of the tight fists he had formed with his hands, Ben wiggled his fingers loose to get the blood flowing as he tried to justify what he had done. There was no rational justification for his impetuous behavior.

His entire body tingled, an itch too large to scratch. Rubbing the back of his neck, he thought of the dinner conversation the other night with his parents about Tobias. Ben's pretense of interest in running this farm was as far from the truth as possible.

"I'll start with that boy out there in Miss Gee-gee's place. Fatten him up, make a right nice field hand out of him. Yep, you'll see, pa." The words that had flowed out of Ben's mouth at that table were surprising even to him—surprising in terms of how convincing he sounded. The smile on his pa's face had sickened him. Making a field hand out of Tobias was the last thing Ben wanted to do. *What are you doing?* he had thought, as his knees trembled under the dinner table.

When Tobias stepped out onto the porch, Ben took a deep breath and controlled the exhale that immediately attempted to escape him. Tobias was as breathtaking as he remembered. He had to take another deep breath to clear his airway. "Wells, what you standin' there for? Come on, I ain't got all day." Ben's voice cracked as he fought to sound the part of his father. Wanting to be alone with Tobias, he had turned down any help from his father or Dexter. He had no actual plan, and he couldn't let his father or Dexter see that. "We got some cleanin' to do down in that ole shed, and you goin' to do it. You do know English, don't you?"

"Yes, I speak English—and Twi, my native tongue, but I will use English if this is what you prefer."

"Wha's 'p-fer' mean? You ain't got no need for no other language but English now, boy. You hear me?" Ben's words were forced; they weren't at all what he wanted to say. He watched closely as Tobias stepped off the porch and approached him. Ben wanted to ask how Tobias was feeling, but somehow that was too personal. Dexter or pa would never care how a field hand was feeling, unless of course that field hand was valuable.

Hearing the way Tobias pronounced his words, Ben gazed at him, forgetting for a second that they ought to be walking. "Boy, this the way we talk in Kin-tucky. Now, you watch your mouth!" Ben's heart raced, and he knew that he had to look away from the tall, lanky figure that held his attention. Turning on his heels, he walked out towards the barn.

The two men worked for hours, clearing out the feed that had gone unused over the winter. Tobias moved sluggishly about the barn. Breaking into a sweat, he stopped long enough to slip out of the shirt that Miss Gee-gee had given him, tossing the thin material onto a stack of crates.

Ben couldn't help but notice how the sweat beaded on Tobias's lovely mahogany shoulders. Negroes' various skin tones had always fascinated him. They had many beautiful shades of brown. But Tobias's dark, rich mahogany skin caught his eye the most.

When they took their first break, Ben said, "At this rate, we goin' to be here again tomorrow."

Tobias flashed a look of irritation at Ben, the first real expression Ben had seen on his face. "Well, if you helped a little more and watched a little less, we could have been done." Tobias had finally said more than two words.

Ben was shaken—whether by what Tobias had said or by the way the slave's words put them on equal ground, he was not sure. "Boy, I'm your master, not your friend. Now you can finish all of it by yourself." Ben scanned the front door, ensuring that no one was witness to their conversation, and took a seat on a rotted-out hay bale. He didn't like being sassed, but he couldn't help but chuckle at Tobias's smart tongue. He had never heard any slave talk to his pa in that manner, and if Dexter had heard it, there would have been some lashes coming Tobias's way. For his own good, Ben knew he had to show Tobias that he was the boss and that he would not tolerate sassing. Talk like that would get them both skinned. "Now, you knock off all that sassing, you hears me?"

Tobias looked at Ben. "Yes, I *hears* you . . . sir."

"Well, good, then!" Ben knew he had put an end to his tiny problem.

Over the next three weeks, Ben met Tobias each morning in front of Miss Gee-gee's cabin, eager to spend the day with him. Spending the better parts of his nights devising plans that would put them alone during the day, Ben had never been so excited about each day's work. But Tobias's fiery tongue, he thought, would surely get them in trouble. The last thing Ben needed was pa or Dexter meddling and overhearing a slave sassing him. The problem was that Ben enjoyed the bantering, Tobias's wit, and the sound of proper English coming from a negro.

That morning, Ben had Tobias filling sacks with potatoes that were going to town later in the week. "So how old are you?" Ben asked as he watched the man tie off yet another sack and throw it on top of the growing pile.

"I am nineteen in my homeland but eighteen here, I guess." Tobias reached for another empty sack and curled the top down a couple of times so it would stay open.

"What do you mean, you guess? You're either eighteen or nineteen. You can't be both."

Tobias tossed a handful of potatoes and looked at Ben. "We believe that when you're born, you're already nine months old. Why you don't count the first nine months doesn't make sense to me. You are nine months old when you come out."

"That's why we call it your *birth-day*. The day you were born." Ben stared at Tobias's silky skin as he thought about how the man spoke, picking each word carefully. "Then we are the same age . . . If you weren't so bony, you would be bigger than me. Tell me about where you come from, your ma and pa. Do you know them?"

"Of course I know them! I'm from the Ashanti tribe of the western mountains of Africa. My father was a healer in our village, and my mother tended to my little sister and me. She made baskets with other women in the village. We sold and traded the baskets to other tribes for goods we could use." Tobias moved over and sat next to Ben. "I was to follow my father as he followed his, and his followed his. We lived at the base of a mountain; over many other mountains was the ocean. The Gods chose that land for us because it kept us safe from the rise of the ocean and poachers."

Ben thought about the ocean as he attempted to visualize Tobias's homeland. He had never seen the sea but planned to one day.

"The distance between the ocean and our village kept us safe from poachers who led the kidnappers on their expeditions. My people farmed and hunted for our food. I don't know of this corn you eat here."

Ben was enthralled. "So how do you know English?"

"There are lots of people who speak English in my country. The white man has been trading on our lands for many years. They bring tools, pots, beads, and even guns. My people have never traded directly with them—only through other tribes. We did not trust them. Father traveled to other villages many times, and I often accompanied him with the plan of someday assuming his role. The great chiefs in all the villages speak English as well as their own tongues." Tobias picked up a potato and rolled it around in his hand as if examining it. "Do you speak anything else other than English, Mr. Ben?"

The edges of Ben's mouth bowed, revealing a hint of a smile. "Nope, just plain ole English. That reminds me, stop calling me Mr. Ben. When we're alone, just call me Ben. I never did like no one callin' me Mr. Ben." The use of the term "mister" suggested superiority, and anything that reminded him of his father he surely detested. "When you were born, what did they call you? Tobias ain't no Africa name." Ben's gaze moved from Tobias's eyes to his lips. He wanted to touch them. They were the most beautiful lips he had ever seen.

"My name? My name is Mamadou."

Ben frowned. "What kind of name is *momma do*?"

"Ma-ma-dou. It means 'praiseworthy' in West Africa."

"Mo-ma-do." Ben tried to say it as Tobias had. He was enjoying this conversation far more than he enjoyed watching Tobias work.

A loud shriek pierced the walls of the shed from outside. There was silence for a second, and then more cries followed. They were the screams of women. Jumping to his feet, Ben moved over to the door and slid it open enough to see outside.

Several women were screaming as they gave chase to Dexter, who was riding his old bay mare. Ten feet behind the horse was Obi, the young slave who arrived at the farm with Tobias. He was struggling to stay on his feet. Obi's wrists were tied, and Dexter firmly held the other end of the rope. Ben knew that, if Obi fell, Dexter would drag him to wherever they were going. Fortunately, they stopped at the big oak tree that stood between the house and the slave quarters. This tree was where most slaves received their lashes. *What has Obi done?* Ben wondered as he watched Dexter dismount and tie Obi to the tree.

"Come, come watch what happens to a nigger who tries to run!" Dexter called out to those around him. Grabbing his whip from the side pouch on his horse, he raised his hand and reared back, sending the whip airborne with a thundery crack.

Ben felt Tobias jump when the whip made contact with Obi. *Dear God, what has Obi gone and done?* Similar scenes played out regularly on the farm. This was everything Ben hated about slavery. His heart rate quickened as the hair on his neck rose. He knew what was to come. As the second lash struck Obi, his back split open and blood spattered. Ben turned and grabbed Tobias by his shoulders, pushing him away from the door. "Get back. I don't want Dexter to see us." That was a lie. Really, he couldn't allow Tobias to see the brutality, to witness the cold, demonic ways of his family.

Backing Tobias to the other side of the barn, he tried to block out the sound of the whip. His hands shook as he fought to gain control of himself. Seconds ago, he had been sitting and talking to his— *friend.* The use of the word "friend" wasn't the result of conscious thought; it came as naturally as did the instinct to protect Tobias.

"Don't push me!" Finally having enough of being pushed backwards, Tobias aggressively swiped Ben's hands away from him and took a step back as if ready to fight.

These actions caught Ben off guard. He wasn't trying to hurt Tobias; he was protecting him. Seeing Tobias's fist in a ball, Ben lost his train of thought for a second. He didn't know this side of Tobias, and it confused him. "I wasn't pushin' you. I was tryin' to—" The muscles in Ben's jaw tightened. The truth was on the tip of his tongue, but his heart raced as anger swelled inside of him. "Boy, you have to listen to me when I tell you somethin'." He lowered his voice to a whisper as he glanced over towards the door. "Don't go gettin' your knickers in a—"

"You pushed me!" Tobias cried, looking firmly in Ben's face.

Ben took a deep breath. He was at a loss. He had known such a moment might come. He couldn't allow Tobias to raise his fist to him, yet all he wanted was for Tobias to accept his apology. A sudden thickness swelled in his throat, and he felt his gut failing him as bile filled his mouth. Doubling over, his breakfast of oats and peaches splatted between his boots before he could move his feet. He couldn't look at Tobias as the heaves kept coming. Embarrassed, he drew a breath. "Go on. Skedaddle, let me be!" Listening to the scurrying of Tobias's feet heading toward the door, Ben felt like his whole body was on fire.

Within seconds, the barn was quiet. Ben's world had spun out of control in a matter of minutes, leaving him wretched.

When Tobias reached the cabin, Miss Gee-gee was surprised to see him returning so soon. "Did Mr. Ben let you off early? Pearl's with the chickens. You help watch Harriett and Niles while I gets next door for a minute."

Tobias walked passed her without saying a word. He thought again of his family and whether he would ever see them again. The sound of the whip rang in his ears as he climbed up into his tiny space in the loft and pulled the tattered covers over his head. If the babies moved, he'd hear them from here.

He slept through dinner, and when he woke, the cabin was quiet. His new brothers and sisters were all sleeping next to him, and the fire dimly lit the room. He stared down at Miss Gee-gee as she slept in her rocker. Seeing her petite body quiver with her quilt draped across her lap, he climbed down and quietly placed a small log on the dwindling fire in front of her. The log lit up the room and produced instantaneous heat. With the added light, he saw how weary her face was and thought of his own grandmother.

He had never felt so alone, so lost. Most days, the pain lay at the back of his mind like a steady heartbeat. Other times, it pushed forward, demanding attention. Visions of the village, people screaming—they were as recognizable as Pearl or Miss Gee-gee standing next to him.

He longed for his family. Not until yesterday, seeing so many negroes moving about the plantation freely, had he thought it a real possibility that he would never see his family again, that this was to be his home. He tried to hold back tears as he accepted that slavers must have captured them. He now remembered seeing it with his own eyes, and it played out in his head repeatedly.

In the forest, digging for roots with his father, he had heard shouting and smelled fire. He and his father ran as fast as they could towards the screams. Reaching the village, they found white men and African poachers everywhere. The village had been torched, the villagers driven out of the huts. Poachers had led the kidnappers to their remote village. The day had come that Tobias and his family had feared. Tobias heard his own voice almost as if it belonged to someone else. "Father! Father! What do we do?"

Turning to his right, he realized that his father was no longer there. He had to search the village for his family, he thought. Seconds later, someone grabbed him by the neck and pushed him to the ground. This was followed by a blow to the head. Losing consciousness, he saw his little sister in the arms of a kidnapper, struggling to break free. She appeared to be screaming, but the world had gone silent. Then his eyes closed.

In captivity, he had watched for his family every day, whether he was on the ship, at the auction house, or on the farm.

It was two days before Ben came calling for Tobias again. That morning, the sun had not yet risen, and already the day was showing signs of getting warm. Watching Tobias exit the cabin, Ben stood out front, his shoulders tense as he drove his hands deep into his pockets. "How you doing this morning? Sorry I didn't come for you the last two days. Been sick." Ben cleared his throat, trying to strengthen his brittle voice. Things had been left unresolved between them. He was unsure of whether he needed to address their tussle. He didn't want to fight—he just wanted things to be as they had been before Dexter interrupted them. He waited for Tobias to say something, but the slave was silent. With another deep swallow, Ben glanced around to see who was near. He knew he wasn't supposed to care how Tobias was feeling, but he did. He cursed the day he had convinced his father to purchase him. Happiness and excitement had accompanied Ben during these past weeks with Tobias, and it mortified him.

"What work is needed today?" Tobias stood face to face with Ben, their eyes locked onto one another.

"Um . . . we have to . . . to . . . replace all that wood on the old summer kitchen." Ben took a step back and glanced around again to see who was around.

"Summer kitchen? What is that?"

"We use it when it's hot. Don't want that heat in the house." Ben walked towards the house, listening for footsteps to follow.

"Penny and Corinne been cooking inside all winter. Helps heat the house. Keeps us warm." The presence of Tobias helped lighten Ben's mood. Arriving at the small wooden outbuilding behind the main house, Ben tossed him a hammer. "Let's get these boards off the windows. See what's been living in there all winter."

Tobias took a step back as Ben went to work, yanking a nail out of the first board. "Who is Dexter? Is he kin?"

Dexter was the last person Ben wanted to talk about. "Ain't no kin. Been round since I was a little kid." Ben inhaled, trying to control his breathing.

"No one should ever be beaten like that. Not even an animal." Tobias's voice came from directly behind Ben, catching him off guard. Ben heaved a sigh. Reluctantly, he accepted that he couldn't ignore what had happened the other day.

He tossed his hammer down and took a step to the side before turning. "You're right, Tobias." Pausing, he collected his words. "You have to stop sassing me. Now, I would never hurt you, but Dexter is evil. He won't think twice about takin' a whip to you . . . and I can't have that." Ben hoped he had said enough to appease Tobias. Any more would have surely crossed a line in their relationship. This, whatever it was between them, was foolish. *Tobias can't be a friend. He's a slave, a negro, and it has to stay that way.* Looking up at the other man, Ben's stomach churned at the thought of being unable to keep him safe. Dexter was a cruel man who thought nothing of taking a whip to someone, even a child. Ben had never seen his pa lay a hand on a slave, but he had heard him speak of them as livestock. Pa couldn't be depended upon to keep Tobias safe. For as long as Ben could remember, Ben had wrestled with the ridiculous notion that negroes weren't people. Sure as Cheyenne, they had ten toes, ten fingers, and two eyes that communicated feelings.

Charlie, Dolly, Penny, and his nursemaid Corinne were the kindest people he knew. The four of them had been watching over him since the day he was born, and for this, Ben had a deeper connection with them than with his own kin.

Within a few weeks, Tobias and Ben were nearly finished with the summer kitchen. In their established routine, each day began to mirror the last. Ben was there at dawn to pick up Tobias, like the sun coming up each day.

Thinking of his family constantly, Tobias found some days easier than others. This morning, instead of feeling scared, lonely, or despondent about his situation, he woke up thinking cross thoughts about Ben, Ben's family, and Dexter. All of them had taken him away from his own family. At home, he had seen other tribes that enslaved people, and he had always been indifferent to their actions. It simply was not a practice his people had adopted; they practiced virtue, generosity, and forgiveness, believing these qualities were why the Gods kept them out of the eyes of the poachers. His feelings this morning were turning his entire world upside down, just as the poachers had done on that horrible, unforgettable morning. The thought of wanting to harm his captors scared him. It went against what he had always believed, but he didn't know what to believe anymore.

"You're quiet this morning," Ben said.

Tobias sensed that this wasn't a statement but a question. "Nothing to say." Ben had been nothing but kind to him, but he *was* the reason Tobias was here. This farm—these fields, all of it—was the reason he was here. Even avoiding most contact with Dexter had done little to make Tobias's situation better.

"Are you feeling okay? How is that ankle?" Ben's eyebrows rose as he tilted his head.

"I'm fine." The truth was that his ankle had healed just fine, but now he felt a constant shortness of breath. He had never felt able to catch his breath since arriving on the farm.

"Well, you sure as hell don't sound it. Something's in your bonnet!"

"I don't have a bonnet on." Tobias shook his head and increased his stride. He noticed that when he was outside, especially if the wind was up, his chest felt tight, and he fought to get air down into his lungs. At first, he thought that he had not completely recovered from whatever he had caught on the ship. But now, months later, he knew it was something else—something more serious than a cold.

Reaching the summer kitchen, Tobias circled the building. "I'll finish up this roof today," he announced as he looked for the leather pouch that held his tools.

For hours, the two worked in silence. Finally, Ben broke the standoff. "It's okay if you hate me."

Bracing himself on the roof, Tobias looked down to find Ben looking up at him. "What? What did you say?"

Ben wiped the sweat from his brow with his handkerchief. "I hate myself too. Thought about killing myself. Sure enough be better than inheriting all this. Reckon the Good Lord ain't got nothing decent planned for me no how."

Tobias slid down off the roof. The thought of a person killing himself was inconceivable to him. This was taboo—even to speak of it would anger the Gods and bring misfortune to one's family. "Why would you say that?" Tobias stood inches from Ben's face. Ben's eyes were bloodshot, his cheeks bright red.

"I know you hate me." Ben turned his face away from Tobias.

Seeing two house slaves on the upper balcony of the main house with Mrs. Clara, Tobias walked into the kitchen and nodded for Ben to follow him. His own misery momentarily pushed away, he leaned towards Ben. "I don't hate you. There is much that I don't understand. But I don't hate *you*."

"Why?" Ben's voice trailed off. The two stood in silence for several minutes.

"I think . . . I sense you have lost your way. The reason why you are here, in this world."

Ben lowered his chin. "I don't believe you can lose your way if you ain't never known where you were goin' in the first place. Reckon I've been lost my whole life." Looking back up at Tobias, he arched his left eyebrow. "Do you miss your family?"

"Yes, I want to go home. I want to be with my family. But I don't know if they're alive or if I have a home to go back to." Something about saying it aloud sent a chill up his spine. A wave of emotions built as images of his family floated through his head. He now regretted his earlier judgmental thoughts about Ben. Perhaps it was Tobias who had lost his way, judging someone whom he knew nothing about.

"I can't change this. The world we live in. I don't understand it any more than you. I know another man can't own another. It's wrong, what we're doin' here. To you, to everyone here. It's wrong." Ben reached out and touched Tobias's arm. "I'm sorry."

Tobias looked down at Ben's white hand, which rested on his own brown skin. Ben's light touch caused Tobias to take a deep breath. His world, which had been spinning out of control, slowed. Tobias reached up to wipe a tear from Ben's eye, but Ben pushed his hand away and took a big step backwards.

Using his forearm, Ben wiped his own eyes. "Look at me. Carrying on like an ole lady that fell out a wagon." He moved towards the door. "I could never hurt—" He stopped short as Charlie, leading a mare by her reins, walked passed the front of the building. Not seeing them, the large slave continued towards his shop.

Ben picked up a couple of small pieces of scrap wood and cleared his throat as he tossed them outside. "So tell me about your pa. You said he was a doctor?" He stepped back into the kitchen and slid his butt down the wall, coming to rest on the dirt floor.

Tobias watched as Ben squared his shoulders against the wall and then ran his fingers through his hair. "I don't know that word. He is a healer." Tobias had to force himself to use "is" instead of "was." *He is a healer.*

"So were you rich? You're kind of highfalutin' for a negro. Ain't never met one as smart as you."

Tobias didn't understand many of the strange words that Ben used, but by repeating a word to himself, he was usually able to get the gist of it. "We were not rich. No one is rich. You give to your neighbor what you will not use, and you never take what you don't need. We had everything we needed."

Ben paused for a minute before asking, "Did you have a girlfriend in your town, I mean, village? Were you allowed to have a girlfriend?"

Tobias looked up at Ben, unsure what he was asking. "Girl-*friend*? No, we don't have girl-*friends*. My father *would* have arranged my marriage once he found a suitable family. I would fall in love with whoever he had chosen for me." Although this was true in principle, Tobias knew it was never to be the case for him.

"So you wouldn't even know her? Wow, I would never do that. She could be ugly or skinny."

"It doesn't matter. I would have loved whoever was chosen." Tobias envisioned his own ceremony, a ceremony that would never take place. Lowering his chin, he brushed his palms together nervously. "Has a mate been picked for you?"

Ben chuckled. "No. That's not how it works here. I choose who I like, who I'm fond of."

Tobias looked back at him. "So are you fond of anybody?" He wasn't sure why he had asked this question, but nevertheless he was interested in Ben's answer.

"Nay, not really. Mary, at my schoolhouse, was kind of cute. But I don't see her anymore since I ain't there no more. Ben's head rose. "Have you ever kissed a girl?"

"No." Tobias answered. Hearing noise outside the building, he turned away from Ben and began nailing metal brackets to the wall.

"Can I touch your hair? It looks funny, like a bear."

Tobias laughed as he turned around. He did not see anyone outside. "Sure, if I can touch yours."

Ben stood up and walked over to Tobias. Smiling, he slowly reached up and lightly rubbed the top of Tobias's head. "It's coarse, like a pig!" Ben shrieked.

"A pig!" Tobias envisioned the nasty, wiry hair on the wild boars in their woods. "Stop touching it then." Staring into Ben's eyes, he reached out and ran his hand through Ben's wild, long hair. "Yours is soft, like grass. I like it. It reminds me of my mother's hair." He took note of the red highlights within the mound of brown hair on Ben's head. It was soft to the touch.

"My ma hates it. Always barking for me to cut it. I like it long. One day I'll grow a mustache as well and send her hollering." The two broke out in laughter.

Tobias had just asked about Mrs. Clara when they heard hooves barreling towards them. They scrambled for their tools and resumed working just as Dexter walked in on them.

"Your pa been looking for you. Let this nigger finish up in here." Dexter puffed, catching his breath. "We got a cow calving, and everyone's out in the fields. Need your help."

Tobias knew better than to look at Dexter, but he couldn't stop himself. Their eyes met. Dexter glared back, his eyes locked on Tobias. Tobias blinked and looked away. He had seen that look before. It was the one shared by his kidnappers and the sailors on the ship. His eyes held pure evil, an uncontrolled rage, a place of darkness and death.

Ben quickly tossed Tobias his leather pouch and trailed Dexter out the door. Relieved that Dexter was gone, Tobias covered his mouth and eyes with his hands. He could feel, in every part of his body, that Dexter spelled trouble for him.

5

Lying in bed, Ben listened as the trusted red rooster fulfilled its morning ritual of waking everyone up. For the last five minutes, the crowing had echoed from outside his window, causing Ben to pull his pillow over his sleepy head to drown out the wakeup call.

The high humidity invaded his ten-by-ten bedroom. The light dampness that covered his body was a reminder that summer was approaching. Ben's mind raced back and forth between his plan for today—to take Tobias to the far side of the farm to clear away a beaver dam—and what had happened between them in the kitchen yesterday.

When Tobias had declared that he didn't hate him the other day, it had come as a relief. Ben wasn't sure if could bear that the person he was so fond of hated him. From that moment in Myrtleville, Tobias had commanded his attention. Ben knew that a man couldn't be intimate with another man. Yet this was all he desired. Rolling to his other side, he stretched his mouth open. He realized that he had been clenching his jaw all night; the muscles were tight in his face and jawline.

If anyone knew he fancied a man, a negro, they would surely hang them both while condemning his soul to damnation. *Damnation—but at least we'd be together.* Ben silently laughed at the thought of them being together. The stirring in his gut told him he was being a fool. Shifting again, he listened to the many footsteps that walked past his door and knew that he had to get out of bed.

Ben and Tobias had been working down on the canal for about an hour, making slow progress clearing the dam. Every year, the beavers took to rebuilding their home, stopping the flow of water to some of the fields down on the lower half of the property.

"What does a beaver look like?" Tobias did little to hide his concern as he pulled another tree branch from the twenty-foot stretch of piled branches, mud, and rocks.

"Like a big ole fat rat. With big teeth." Ben laughed, seeing the nervous look on Tobias's face. "And they bite. Rip your arm right off if you let 'em."

Tobias wiped the sweat from his brow as he threw branches up to Ben, who was standing on the bank. Ben wasn't that worried about any of the little beasts actually biting Tobias, though they sometimes defended their homes. If he had to, with his pistol, Ben could put a bullet between a creature's eyes before Tobias ever saw it.

"Before we leave, we got to burn all this up here. If you leave it, those critters will rebuild this whole damn thing overnight. I ain't coming back tomorrow to do it all over again." Ben's eyes traced the length of Tobias's arm, taking in the sheen from sweat and water on his muscular biceps. Ben's eyes then scanned across Tobias's chest. He was gorgeous, no doubt the most magnificent person he had ever set eyes on.

"You? I'm doing all the work," Tobias shouted from below.

Ben pushed the hair out of his face and blew out a heavy sigh. "I'm the supervisor. Making sure you ain't swept downriver if that damn thing breaks. If it breaks, you need to get out of there . . . fast."

Ben pulled his eyes away from the stunning beauty before him to assess the amount of work they had left. He figured that, at any minute, water would start pouring through the opening they had created. Thinking of how the whole damn thing could break, sending debris and water over Tobias, an idea came to him. "Hold on, let me get you a pitchfork." Ben ran back to the wagon, grabbed the fork by its long, wooden end, and rushed back.

Scurrying back to the end of the bank, Ben saw that Tobias had removed his shirt and had tucked the collar down into his britches. Frozen, he beheld Tobias as the man stood knee high in the water, watching it flow over the top of the dam. Tiny beads of sweat on Tobias's shoulders glimmered in the sunlight as not-so-proper thoughts overtook Ben's imagination.

"Are you going to hold that thing or can I have it?" Tobias asked, breaking Ben out of his private moment.

"Oh, um, here." Stammering, Ben extended the handle far enough for Tobias to grab it. As Tobias took hold of the fork, Ben's eyes moved to his dark brown nipples, which rose slightly from his muscled chest. Surprised that, in a short amount of time, Tobias had packed on such muscle, Ben's britches tightened in the crotch.

Sure that Tobias had seen his unmistakable arousal, Ben crumpled over, placing the palms of his hands on his thighs, hoping to hide his protruding bulge. "Back up, and use the fork to knock the rest of it down! Let the rest of it go on down the creek." Ben watched as Tobias thrust the fork down into the muck a couple of times, before the entire dam began to give way. "Okay, move, get out of there. It's comin'. It's about to break."

Tobias scampered up the side of the embankment as the dam gave way, sending the rest of the debris and the imprisoned water down the creek. "Yahoo! We did it!" Tobias whooped as he stood next to Ben, both of them watching the water as it began its descent towards the farm.

"See there? And you didn't even lose an arm. They should see this water before we make it back." Ben tried his damnedest to look into Tobias's eyes and not at his chest. Unfortunately, the moisture that glistened on Tobias's shoulders, neck, and arms dominated his thoughts. The desire to touch Tobias stirred in his belly as his trousers tightened once again. His thoughts would become dangerous if he allowed them to go on. Tobias was not his to touch. But the thoughts kept coming, radiating warmth throughout his body. He knew that masters and overseers often took what they wanted. How they pushed themselves on unwilling people was both immoral and brutal. Still, intense thoughts of being with Tobias remained in Ben's mind. No woman had ever stirred such emotion in him. There were those times with Jonnie, years ago, but they had been kids.

"C'mon. We best be getting back. Been out here long enough." Avoiding eye contact, Ben walked towards the wagon. "I said c'mon, let's go!" He shoved his hands into his pockets and quickened his step.

That night, after supper, Ben lay in the warm bath Corinne had prepared for him. Thoughts of Tobias standing in the water with his beautiful back exposed to the sun, his almond-shaped brown eyes softly staring back at him, made Ben smile. He would never forget the day that he touched Tobias's hair. Once more, Ben's penis began to respond, the tip gradually making its way to the surface of the warm water as it stood at attention. Staring down at himself, he craved Tobias's touch. Blowing out a deep breath, he slowly took hold of himself and began lightly stroking his penis beneath the water. As he increased the tempo with each stroke, his breathing picked up.

Within minutes, Ben exploded onto his fist, sending his seed down around his hand and into the water. He had intended to keep it from spilling into the water, but for that tiny space in time, it hadn't mattered. His chest labored up and down as he quietly caught his breath.

Drifting into a snooze, Ben knew that his desire for another man was not right. He had never met anyone who shared these feelings, this fancy for his own sex, but he had felt this way for as long as he could remember. Nothing in his world seemed to fit.

As a child, Ben had found peace in seclusion, an introvert in the truest sense of the word. Fearing even his own thoughts and the reality that he was somehow different, the notion of hanging himself had crossed his mind more than a few times. Had it not been for Corinne, life might have been too difficult for him to bear. As a child, he had opened his eyes to her in the morning; she had fed and clothed him before bringing him to his mother. Corinne, the sweet negro woman who had sung to him at night, told him stories, and wished him a good night, was more of a mother to him than his own. But now, Tobias had stirred something within him. From the moment he saw Tobias, something had drawn Ben to him.

"Mr. Ben? Mr. Ben, is you all right in there?" The knock on the door startled him. It was Corinne, checking on him.

Splashing about in the tub, he made as if he was finishing up. "Yeah, almost done." Smiling, he laughed at the fact that, though he was now a young man, she was still checking on him. Pulling the plug from the tub, he watched as the water, which had long ago turned cold, drained down through the walls into big barrels that stored water for the family garden.

Gathering up his towel, Ben dried himself before retreating into his room for the night.

6

As he lay awake for most of the night, Tobias struggled to draw in a full breath. His chest felt as if a four-hundred-pound lion was sitting on it. He feared another coughing spell; the pain in his ribcage during the last one had nearly caused him to lose consciousness. He couldn't believe his little brothers were sleeping through his wheezing, coughing, and tossing about as he fought to get comfortable. Sleep—oh, how he wished he was sleeping, but there was no chance of that.

With idle time, his mind raced. He was sure he had picked something up on the ship. Whatever it was that had caused so many of the ship's prisoners to die surely must have infected him. Every time he opened his eyes on the ship, he saw another dead body carried up to the deck. He would never forget those sights. Even at the auction house, he had been sick. He could hardly hold down any of the food they gave him, if you could call it food.

There was a brief time after his arrival at the farm during which he had thought he was getting better, his lungs able to draw a full breath. He had been on the mend until yesterday. While pulling apart the beaver dam, his chest had tightened up. He had gotten so nauseous that he had to take off his shirt to keep from passing out. The wheezing started on the wagon ride back, and by late last night, he had hardly been able to breathe.

Last night, Miss Gee-gee had boiled the roots from a skunk cabbage and told him to first breathe in the steam and then drink the mixture. That had helped for a minute or two. Mumbling something about how he had "the poison" down in his lungs, she had fussed over him, trying to make him comfortable. She clutched the boiling pot over the fire and slowly poured the mixture into a cup. Tobias wondered how old she was and if she was losing her sight in her one good eye. He had no idea what time it was. Glancing over and through a knothole in the wall next to him, he could only see darkness.

"How's you feelin'?" Her weak voice moved about in the dark below him.

"I think a little better—as long as I don't move." Tobias focused on the pain in his chest. *I think I feel better. I'm afraid to move.*

"Let me gets this fire goin'. Make you somethin' to drink. Steam from it might do you some good."

A clatter filled the cabin, and soon a small flame flared up, bringing light into the room. Miss Gee-gee stood over the fire with her stick, ready to poke it again to ensure the fresh wood caught. "You got to learn what to do when you gets in a bad way. The poison, that's what they call it. Gets in your lungs and stops you from breathing. It's in the air. Gets some, others pay it no mind. Seems to like you."

Tobias rolled to his side to see her better. Her back was to him as she stood over the fire, jabbing at it and increasing the light in the room.

"Massa ain't goin' to lets you stay with me much longer. You grown. He move you down with the boys on the other end." Miss Gee-gee wobbled over to the side of the bed and held something up. "This here, you take a little of this here root. Break a little piece, not too much. Boil it down in some water until it gets soft."

"What is it?" Tobias strained to see what she was trying to show him.

"Cabbage root. Grows it in the garden. Save the root. This here will help you breathe. If you got some garlic, mix it in too. Kill up them pin worm you might have."

Pinworms? He had no idea what pinworms were, but the thought of them made him shudder.

The cabin was quiet. Pearl had moved out last week and was now working the fields full time. At age twelve, she was late going to the fields—until Tobias had arrived, her primary responsibility had been looking after the other children in Miss Gee-gee's care. Henry and Stuart were thought to be around age six, and the two babies, Harriett and Niles, were most likely both under the age of two. Tobias had never heard where they all came from, and until now, he had naturally assumed that he was going to stay here and help care for them.

"But who will help you with Harriett and Niles?" Tobias looked down at the top of Niles's head. None of them had moved an inch since they had started talking. Two babies and two boys. Hell, little Stuart was more than enough work for anyone.

"I been taken care of chilins all my life. I manage just fine." Returning to the side of the bed, she handed his tea up to him. "It's hot."

Miss Gee-gee had come to the farm about seventy years ago, somewhere around the age of nine. She had been a beautiful little orphan, curious and with bright hazel eyes. People believed she was from the West Indies due to her long black hair, which she had tied back as a child into a ponytail. In the beginning, Miss Gee-gee could often be seen skipping and singing as she tended to her chores.

Clara's father, Master George, had purchased Miss Gee-gee with the intention of breeding her. However, he also had a liking for young negro girls, and he took to Miss Gee-gee. He had her brought to him nightly in the barn as his wife, Ruth, would never allow a negro in her bedroom.

By age twelve, Miss Gee-gee was pregnant and beginning to show. When Ruth overheard two of her house slaves talking about Miss Gee-gee being pregnant by her husband, she was outraged. She ordered the baby aborted.

For touching Ruth's husband, Miss Gee-gee had been whipped beyond recognition, losing her right eye in the process. As if that wasn't enough, the barbaric abortion had left her with a permanent limp and unable to have children.

Miss Gee-gee was now useless, as she could no longer see well enough to thread a needle and was too slow to work the fields. Master George never forgave his wife for her actions, and although he could never again look Miss Gee-gee in the face, he made it clear that she was never to be whipped again, for any reason. As long as Miss Gee-gee remained on the farm, she would always be safe. Now, Emmett paid little attention to how Miss Gee-gee handled her duties; she never varied from doing what was expected and never took more than she needed.

Tobias knew none of this. To him, she was a sweet, sweet woman who never tired. With the twins stirring about, Tobias rose so they could scoot by. Feeling as if he was about to gag, he erupted into another wild coughing spell that sent hot liquid everywhere.

"What's wrong with you?" Henry asked as he hurried past Tobias.

Stuart followed him. "Ma'am say he got the *poison!*"

"What's that?" Henry skipped the bottom step, jumping and landing on all fours.

Little Harriett cried as Tobias continued to cough and fought to hold onto his bladder. Gasping for air, he doubled over.

When he came to, he wasn't sure how long he had been out. His mind focused on voices coming from outside the cabin, on the porch. Listening, he could tell that one of them was Miss Gee-gee. *Who is she talking to?* The other voice was muffled.

Shortly thereafter, Miss Gee-gee made her way inside. "You 'wake? That was Mr. Ben. He come callin' for you. I tells him you in a bad way this mornin'. Ain't goin' to be much use." She made her way over to the babies, who lay on the lower mattress. Pulling the blanket up evenly over them, she took a seat in her rocker.

Tobias's head was pounding, and he had to pee. Sluggishly, he made his way to the end of the bed and slunk down the ladder. "I have to tend to business," he announced. He attempted to cover his early morning erection as he made his way to the door. Dashing around back, he was thankful for the close proximity of the outhouse to Miss Gee-gee's cabin.

Standing over the hole, Tobias released his bladder. His mind turned to Ben. Pearl had nothing good to say about him. She had called him a . . . What was that word she used? *Beef-headed. That's it, beef-headed. Dumb as an ox.* Tobias laughed, causing his sore ribs to twinge.

He took in a cautious breath, trying to maximize his air intake, and slowly released it. He thought of the men and women from other villages back home who had been enslaved. It wasn't like what he was seeing here. These people, the white men, they were evil—hateful and full of anger. Yet, Ben was none of that. Ben was good to him. Maybe Pearl didn't know him. She herself admitted that she spent little time around the master's son.

Tobias gave himself a good shake and tied up his britches. His entire body hurt. He was slightly relieved, thinking maybe he hadn't caught whatever had taken so many lives on the ship. If he had the "poison," as Miss Gee-gee said, it didn't sound as if he was going to die from it. Tobias thought of turmeric and red bark. His father had boiled them, along with milk thistle, for his patients who couldn't breathe. *I need to get some red bark when I feel better.*

The next morning, Tobias woke to the memory of a dream he'd had. He and Ben had been out somewhere on a wagon. The place wasn't familiar to him at all. He tried to remember what they had been doing and why they were on the wagon.

"How's you feelin' this mornin'?" Miss Gee-gee asked.

Tobias lay still, assessing his body as the smell of biscuits entered his nose. It had been a while since they had biscuits for breakfast. His breathing was better. He poked at his ribcage. *Yep, still sore, but not as bad.* He was about to get up when there was a knock at the door.

Miss Gee-gee cracked the door open a couple of inches. "Good mornin', Mr. Ben."

"Good mornin', Miss Gee-gee. Come to see how Tobias is feelin' this mornin'."

Tobias stretched his neck but was unable to see Ben. He watched as a hand appeared inside, handing Miss Gee-gee something. "Here you go. Boil some of these into a tea. It should help him breathe. It's what his papa used to do."

Tobias waited as the conversation went silent. There were a couple of footsteps, and then the shadow disappeared from the door. Within seconds, it reappeared. "Miss Gee-gee—I ain't never been in no negro house . . . but can I see him?"

Miss Gee-gee took a step back from the door and put her hands on her little stomach. "Why, sure you can."

Ben stepped in and removed his hat. Tobias watched as he scanned the little room, first seeing the babies playing on the floor. Then his eyes found Tobias, whose eyes darted between Ben and Miss Gee-gee. The latter was clearly eyeing Ben.

Ben smiled. Although he was almost as tall as the loft, he climbed a couple of steps so that he was eye level with Tobias. "Boy, you ever comin' back to work?" His face gave way to a silly grin. Being so close, Tobias noticed that Ben had a single mole at the right corner of his upper lip and a dimple in the middle of his chin. Their eyes locked on one another. Staring into Ben's eyes, Tobias was tongue-tied. He had missed Ben.

"We got lots to do, more work pilin' up every day. I brought you some red bark, for tea. See, I listen to you. You remember telling me about it a couple of weeks ago? I found it! You'll be breathin' real good soon, I reckon."

The thought of being outside again, of being with Ben, of doing something, anything, appealed to him more than lying in this bed. Tobias couldn't help but snicker at the silly grin on Ben's face and the look in those sad brown eyes of his. "It's breathing, not breathin'," Tobias murmured.

Ben laughed as he shook his head. "Sick and sassy, I done seen it all now." Climbing back down, he nodded to Miss Gee-gee before putting on his hat. "Thank you, Miss Gee-gee. I'll be out your way now." Miss Gee-gee held her eyes on him as he left.

Over the next couple of days, Miss Gee-gee alternated between the cabbage root and the red bark, bringing about a vast improvement in Tobias's breathing. Listening to him, she added a little sweet milk to the concoctions that she stirred up each morning and night. One night, while Tobias sipped his tea, Miss Gee-gee finally shared with him the secret of the poison: it was actually a reaction to the pollens blowing in the air, and it would probably lessen come winter.

7

When Tobias was well enough to breathe and carry a stick at the same time, he wasted no time in ridding himself of his bed. He joined Ben on what would be an all-day trip to the Jonesboro Estate. Master Lee had negotiated a trade of farm equipment for a new type of corn that Mr. Jonesboro had acquired from Georgia. Hearing that the corn matured twenty days faster than the type they had been planting, Master Lee had conned the old man into taking two old ox plows and an unusable cotton gin.

Ben had the equipment loaded onto a flat wagon before dawn. Because of the weight and distance, they would need to take two mares. Dexter said it would only take one, but Ben wasn't taking any chances. Sitting high on the seat of the wagon, Ben took the reins, which lay between his feet and Tobias's. Taking a negro along for help in the event of a mishap was his father's idea—at least, that's what Ben had made him think.

The two were quiet until they cleared the small bridge that marked the entrance to the farm. Passing the graveyard, Tobias raised his chin up towards the mostly unmarked graves. "Why do you put the dead down in the ground like that?"

"What else are you goin' to do with them? Stink up a shed if you don't." Ben tried not to smile at the idea that he was going to spend all day with Tobias, just the two of them. He had missed Tobias over the last couple of days more than he was willing to admit. He was smitten, alright, there was no denying that. Given his sexual thoughts and how he spent his free time, Ben was surely going to hell for all the seed he had spilled thinking of Tobias.

Tobias remained focused on the dirt graveyard as they passed it. "Just seems odd."

Ben cleared his throat as he thought about the two of them. More and more, he had been worrying about whether others saw that he had taken a liking to Tobias. "Now, boy, I can't be coming down to get you no more. You needs to meet me next to the smokehouse from now on. Ain't got no business comin' after you."

"Why?"

"Just can't."

"Okay . . . Why do you call me 'boy?' Is that not a child? We're the same age."

"I dunno, it's just a sayin'." Ben chuckled at how dumb Tobias could be at times.

"Well, then, if you don't know, you can call me Tobias . . . It's better than boy, I think. Should I not call you boy?"

"You better not!" Ben guffawed. "I'll take a whip to you if you do. Pa hear you talkin' like that, he have Dexter tend to both of us." As soon as the words left his mouth, he knew it was the wrong thing to say. Sure, he was teasing, but he shouldn't have said it. Ben waited for some sort of reaction that never came.

"What is this stuff?" Tobias looked at the equipment.

"It's an old cotton gin, and them there are plows." *Don't he know what a plow is?* Ben had a lot to teach Tobias. He smiled at the thought.

"How far is this place we're going to?" Tobias hadn't been off the farm since he arrived. Even the work they were doing on the fencing and the dam never took them off the farm.

"About three hours. Just yonder from Bender Creek. Mr. Jonesboro's place. Ain't much of nothin' but a hundred-year-old house and a whole lot of dirt. I say he does more dickerin' than anythin' else. What's with all the questions this mornin'?"

Tobias looked at Ben, his eyes narrowing as if confused. "Just curious—I guess."

Ben welcomed the silence, if only for a minute. It gave him an opportunity to think. Thinking was all he had been doing—mostly about being with Tobias. Of course, there was no way that could ever happen. Sure, he knew that his father and Dexter had relations with several of the young slave women on the farm. As much as it was unspoken, having sex with negro women was as common as an apple raisin pie. Some owners even had children by these women. *Light-skinned babies. There are several of those down on the London farm. Old Mr. London and his boys are as fertile as tomcats.* Ben shook his head in disgust as he refocused on the road.

Seeing that the road had been washed out ahead, Ben drew back on the reins, slowing the two mares to a walk. Maneuvering one wagon wheel at a time down and up the hollow, he felt the wagon dip to one side, pushing their knees together. The touch sent an electric jolt through Ben's body. He held his breath as their legs rested on one another. They were touching. Ben planted his foot firmly on the floorboard, ensuring that it wouldn't move. If he never got any more than this, he was good. He had reached heaven.

They rode for miles, their thighs and knees resting on one another, Ben thinking of nothing else until Tobias broke the silence. "Can I ask you something?" Tobias adjusted himself in his seat, moving his leg off Ben's.

The removal of his leg caused Ben to inhale deeply. It was something so trivial, yet it took his breath away.

"Can I?" Tobias repeated.

"Yeah. What is it?" Ben scrambled to bring his thoughts under control.

"The other day, you said that you hated yourself. Why?" Tobias turned his entire upper body towards Ben.

Queasiness overtook Ben. How could he answer that question without telling a lie? He couldn't. "Um," he said, searching for something to say. "What my pa does. The farm. I'm against it." He had never spoken those words to anyone until now. There was a stirring in his belly. "No person should be treated like Dexter treats them. My ma, my pa, they allow it to happen, and it shames me that I am a part of—"

Unaware that he stopped in mid-sentence, Ben reflected on a conversation he had overheard his pa and Dexter having last year. They were talking about negro sympathizers who wanted to send all of the negroes back to Africa: Some owners had emancipated their slaves. Just let them go.

Ben said aloud, "You know there's talk about abolishin' it." Tobias's body went rigid. Ben knew he shouldn't have said that. Why give hope to someone when maybe there was none? "It will probably never happen, though," Ben continued. "It's the law of the land, and some things don't change." Ben knew it was illegal to import slaves into the country too, but this didn't seem to stop people from doing it. He kept these thoughts to himself.

"I get why you hate Dexter and maybe even your pa, but why yourself?" Tobias's voice was soft, his concern coming through clearly.

The passing scenery was a blur to Ben as he gazed out over it. He didn't know how to answer Tobias. "Someday, all this will be mine. Pa is one of the wealthiest men in the state. What do I do, just let all the negroes go? *Go on everybody, y'all's free!*" He said the last sentence in a mocking tone. "We would lose everythin' . . . everythin'." Ben snapped the reins. "Come on, girl. Stop listenin' to our conversation and pick it up!"

"Could you do that? I mean, really let us go. I could go home?" Tobias asked.

Ben was silent. He felt a clenching in his stomach at the thought of his future, should he free his family's slaves. He would have to leave Kentucky. Maybe go to New York where nobody knew him. He would be bankrupt and alone. There would be nothing he could do. He remained silent, and Tobias's question hung in the air with no answer.

A mile down the road, Ben raised his head. "I'm glad you're feelin' better. You scared me when you were sick." He wanted to change the subject. "It reminded me of the day I first saw you."

"Yes. Miss Gee-gee said I was in a bad way. She was even concerned that I would infect the babies with whatever I had." Tobias laughed, "The *poison.*"

Ben thought about that first day. He'd nearly had an out-of-body experience—like he knew who Tobias was. He had seen no color. Even the fact that Tobias was another man meant nothing. It was as if Tobias was a part of him that he hadn't even known was missing. Standing in that corridor in the auction house, Ben must have appeared to be out of his mind that day, but there had been no way he was leaving without Tobias. He released a heavy sigh at the realization that his life was a jumbled mess.

Shunning any more conversation, Ben searched internally for answers, but there were none. An hour and a half later, they rode onto the Jonesboro Estate to make the swap. As planned, they were back on the road and heading home within an hour. Mr. Jonesboro offered Ben lunch, inviting him to come in and rest a spell, but Ben wouldn't have it. He wanted to be alone, and in the wagon, he could at least keep conversation to a minimum.

That evening, after driving the wagon up to Charlie's shop, Tobias watched as Ben reared back, bringing the two horses to a halt. They had said almost nothing to each other during the entire trip home. Tobias sensed something was wrong, and at one point, he even asked if everything was okay. Ben had met his question with a short murmur, and Tobias had retreated into his own head.

Filled with thoughts of home, Tobias recalled the lush green woodland that he spent so much time in as a child. He thought of his family and what each of them were most likely doing right now. His father, mother, and little sister—he saw their faces. He could only hope that, somehow, they had escaped capture. He had looked for them continuously during the march down towards the shore; in the camp, where hundreds of captives waited to be loaded on the slave ship, he had watched for them. On the ship, everyone had whispered the names of their loved ones to the people next to them, in hopes that those names would reach their loved ones and be carried back. His names never returned.

Tobias watched as Ben walked off without saying another word. Again, he wondered if he had upset Ben in some way. After Tobias finished helping Charlie unload the bags of seed, he walked towards his cabin.

When he reached the row of cabins, there was just enough moonlight for him to see Obi and Rudo standing in the middle of the row.

"Greetings Obi, Rudo," Tobias called to them.

They both looked up towards his voice. Tobias could sense that something was wrong. "How's it going?" he asked. "Everything okay?"

"Fine, how are you?" Rudo asked without really asking.

Seeing that Obi was glaring at him, Tobias said, "Fine. Just returned from the Jonesboros' with Ben—Mr. Ben."

"Is that it? That's all you doin' with Mr. Ben?" Obi inched closer to Tobias's face.

Surprised at Obi's aggressiveness, Tobias took a step back and shot a questioning look at Rudo. Since the three of them had arrived together, Tobias thought he shared a connection with them. But tonight, something was off—he could tell by the way they were looking at him, by the short and clipped sound of their words.

"Why ain't you workin' in the field with the rest of us? Or is you too good for that?" Obi asked. "Is you tryin' to be a house slave or his friend? 'Cause that ain't going to happen. So what you doing?"

Tension climbed up through Tobias's back to his neck. "I'm not trying to be anything. I'm trying to stay out the way of Mr. Dexter, that's all."

Rudo held out his hand across Obi's chest. "Hold on, now. He ain't the fight." He looked over at Tobias. "We talkin' 'bout runnin'." He lowered his voice even more. "Obi wants to leave tonight. Hardly any moon. We wait until ain't no more light shinin' from the big house. Everyone sleep. You want to go?"

Tobias swallowed hard, glancing around nervously to see if anyone was watching them. "I—I don't know." He thought about what Ben had said about masters letting their slaves free. Ben had even talked about the possibility of the law changing, the fighting that was going on. "But what if Dexter catches us? He catches everybody. There's talk about setting us free."

Both Obi and Rudo looked at him. "Wha's you talkin' 'bout?" Obi snapped.

"There's some that know this is wrong. They're fighting for us!" Tobias tried to keep his voice low. "One day, we'll all be free. I will get to go home."

Obi sneered, "Boy. You stupid. You think some white man is goin' to fight for you? Just let you walk away after he paid good money for you?" He guffawed and rolled his eyes. "Where you hear that from?"

Tobias knew he couldn't say that Ben had told him. They would never believe him anyway. "I don't know, but I know I heard it."

"If you comin', be down at the river after the lights go out." Obi turned towards Rudo as if dismissing Tobias.

Tobias lowered his head. Every muscle in his body had tightened. The thought of leaving Miss Gee-gee with the babies! She could never manage all of them without him. He couldn't leave her. And Ben— what if he did inherit the farm one day? He would surely follow his heart and let them all go. It could happen. "I'll think on it. If I'm not there, don't wait for me." Tobias took a deep breath at the thought of freedom.

8

Emmett sat at the head of his table, rubbing on his belly as he watched Dolly clear the empty plates from the table. "Well, Dolly, you have managed to fatten me up a little bit more with that roasted chicken tonight."

Ben sat to his father's immediate right, and their guest this evening, Dexter, sat to Emmett's left. Ben had been silent throughout dinner, still deep in his head with his troubles. His silence was mostly unnoticed as it was no different from most nights.

"Mr. Ben, may I take your plate?"

It took Ben a second or two to realize that Dolly was talking to him. Standing off to his side, she waited for the okay.

"Yeah, I'm sorry. I'm done." Ben grabbed his yeast roll from his porcelain plate before pushing it away from his body.

Dolly disappeared with the empty plates and then returned to retrieve the bowls of turnips and sweet potatoes with molasses. She and the other cooks would make their own meal for the evening from the table scraps.

"Dexter, you know Benjamin went out to the Jonesboro estate today for that new corn I told you 'bout. Thinkin' 'bout plantin' about twenty acres next spring."

Dexter had stuffed his tobacco down into the front of his mouth. Waiting a second or two, he spit a large wad of tobacco-filled saliva on top of the remaining food on his plate before answering Emmett.

Ben watched his mother's face tighten as Dexter spit on her china. When Dolly came around to retrieve his plate, Clara stopped her. "Dolly, would you be so kind as to wrap Mr. Dexter's food in cloth so he may carry it home with him?"

"Yes, ma'am." Giving Dexter the eye, Dolly's narrow face cracked a slight smirk.

Dexter's upper lip curled to one side, and his brows dropped between his eyes. Ben couldn't refrain from laughing at his mother's wit as he watched Dolly carry his plate off.

Clara dabbed the side of her mouth with a small cloth napkin that had been in her lap. "Now, Mr. Dexter, should you ever want a place at my table again, you may want to learn some manners and refrain from spitting in the presence of a lady."

"Why, yes, Mrs. Clara. My apologies," Dexter grumbled, his face red as fire.

With the entire table now cleared, they sat waiting for Dolly to return with her sweet potato pie and their evening coffee.

"So how's that boy of yours comin', Benjamin?" Emmett asked. "I see you've been working him. You succeeded in puttin' a little muscle on him, might turn into something yet." Emmett gave Ben a wink of approval.

Ben cleared his throat long enough to concoct his answer. "Yea, Pa. He's young and tough. Not too smart, though."

Dexter interjected, "Have you had to take a whip to him yet? I hear he can be a little sassy. Goin' to have to whip that out of him."

"They all need a whip to remind them of their place," Emmett added. Ben's eyes moved between his father and Dexter as they talked.

Clara said, "Dolly tells me that he's congested more times than not. If Gee-gee can't make him any better, have the cattle doctor take a look at him."

"Yes, Momma. I'll watch him." Ben thought about the red bark he had taken down to the cabin last week. It seemed to have helped. "Not sure what it could be. Some days he's good, and some days he ain't."

Dolly entered the room carrying a large dessert tray. Stepping to the right of Clara, she gently placed a slice of pie in front of her. "Will you be havin' tea this evening, ma'am?"

"Yes, thank you. Can you have Penny come from the kitchen, please?" Clara removed a small satchel from a decorative box on the table and placed it in her teacup.

"Why, yes, ma'am. Is something wrong, Mrs. Clara?" Dolly's petite posture stiffened.

"Now, I wouldn't have asked for Penny if I could speak to you, would I?" Clara tapped her fingers on the table.

"I'm sorry, Mrs. Clara. Don't mean no disrespect."

Moments later, Penny stomped into the room. Wiping her wet hands on the apron that lay over her blue and grey dress, she looked everyone over. She was a big light-skinned woman who had been cooking for the Lees for many years. Penny rarely came into the dining room due to her big mouth, which kept her in trouble. "You call, Ms. Clara?"

"Yes, Penny. The meal was fine, but I believe the turnips aren't good this year. Did you taste them?"

"Sure did, Mrs. Clara. Tasted them myself. Tasted right fine to me." Penny wiped her hands with the dishrag that she had carried out with her.

"Send them down to the quarters."

"Yes, Mrs. Clara." Before leaving, Penny looked directly at Dexter, shooting him the evil eye.

After Ben retired to his room for the night, there was a knock at the door. "Yes, who is it?" This was a silly question—he knew by the lightness of the tap that it was Corinne, coming to check on him. Typically, it was the last thing she did in the evening.

"Mr. Ben, will you be needin' anythin' else this evenin'?" Corinne laid several pieces of folded laundry at the end of his bed. "Here you go, sir. Here's a clean shirt for in the mornin'."

"Thank you, Corinne." Ben ran his hand across the clean shirts. He could smell the relaxing scent of lavender wafting from the fresh laundry.

"Mr. Ben, will you be needin' anythin' else this evenin'? I'm tired, sir." Corinne walked over to the window and opened it about three inches. She was petite like Dolly, but her sweet-tempered voice set her apart from anyone else Ben knew.

"No, Corinne, think I'm just goin' to read until I fall asleep. Goodnight." Ben smiled at her as he reached for his book on his nightstand.

About half an hour went by before he heard footsteps outside his window. Laying his book across his chest, he listened to the voices that accompanied the steps. It was Corinne and Penny, making their way to the servant's quarters just behind the house.

Tired, Ben cupped his hand at the back of his globe-shaped oil lamp. Softly blowing into his hand, he put out the flame, causing the room to go dark. It had been a long day, and he'd rather dream of tomorrow—of spending it with Tobias.

9

The sun had yet to rise when Tobias rounded the corner, heading up towards the smokehouse. The smokehouse and blacksmith's shop had been combined into one building, with an entrance for each on opposite ends. Directly across the yard in front of the stables, Dexter was climbing onto a horse. Master Lee and Charlie were standing on each side of him, holding the horse still. Once on the horse, Dexter held his rifle out as if checking it. He was shouting something about not having all day.

Charlie moved towards the barn and then spun on his heels back towards Dexter. "You goin' to need a sleepin' roll, sir, or wills you be back this evenin'?" He had a feverish look on his face as he tried to assist Dexter. Seeing that something was wrong, Tobias froze.

"If I catch this nigger before sundown then I'll be back," Dexter bellowed.

"Is you sure?" Charlie stumbled backwards a few steps as Dexter's horse jerked and stepped to the side.

"Sure about what?" Dexter barked as he holstered his rifle. "Move! Get the hell out the way!" He spun his horse around and kicked his spurs into its side. The horse whinnied as its hoofs dug into the ground, trying to get traction. Dust flew up where the animal had stood, causing both Emmett and Charlie to wave their hands across their faces. In a full gallop, Dexter rode past Tobias as if he didn't see him.

"Couldn't have been gone but a couple of hours. Are you sure all the horses are accounted for?" Emmett's voice trailed off as he coughed up some dust.

Charlie walked about two steps behind Emmett. "Yes, Massa, I sure. Counted them twice. Ain't none missin'. He must have left out of here on foot."

"Bring everyone in from the fields. I want a full count of everyone!"

"Yes, Massa." Whenever Dexter was away, Charlie, although a slave himself, was in charge of overseeing all the field hands.

Emmett walked passed Tobias without looking at him and headed up towards the house.

Putting together that it was Obi and Rudo who were gone, Tobias walked over to Charlie. "What happened?" Tobias quietly asked.

"That damn Obi, got rabbit in his blood. He's gone again. Lord have mercy on his soul when Mr. Dexter finds him."

"Just Obi?" Tobias asked.

Charlie gave Tobias a strange look. "Whatcha mean, just Obi?" He leaned closer to Tobias. "Boy, whatcha know?"

Tobias crossed his arms across his chest and then dropped them to his side. "Nothing. I don't know—" Tobias stopped at the sound of the bloodhounds barking in the distance.

"So what will happen to Obi when Dexter finds him?" Tobias asked.

"He'll be lucky if he survives the whippin' Dexter will give him." Charlie walked into the barn to retrieve a horse. "Let me get on out to the fields and gather everyone up 'fore they start working."

Tobias looked up at the early morning sky before following Charlie. He couldn't believe that Obi had actually done it. He wondered if they hadn't realized that Rudo was also gone. "Where does one run to when they run?" Tobias asked.

"To the north, I reckon: Ohio, Indiana, Pennsylvania. Might even try for Canada if the mountain lions don't eat you for you gets there."

Charlie tossed a saddle on an old dapple-gray horse that stood patiently for him. "You need to head on back. Ain't no work until everyone is accounted for."

"Should I wait for B—Mr. Ben?" Tobias asked.

"No need. His pa goin' have him tied up all day."

Tobias thought about Obi and Rudo out there. He wondered how far they had gotten. Part of him regretted his decision not to go with them. Could he have actually gotten back home? Across the ocean again? He realized that he didn't even know where home was. It was just a place far off somewhere.

Within a matter of minutes, Charlie had his horse saddled up and was ready to leave. "Head on back. Let everyone know ain't no work today till everyone is accounted for."

Tobias hurried back towards his cabin. The farm was in disarray as other slaves left their work areas to return to their cabins. As Tobias neared the men's cabin, Rudo approached him from the other direction.

Taken aback at the sight of him, Tobias called out, "Rudo!"

Never slowing his stride, Rudo glanced at him and nodded as if to say, "Not now."

When Tobias made it back to his cabin, he found that Miss Geegee had fed the children and now had Stuart and Henry tending to the babies.

"I hear someone run in the night." Miss Gee-gee slowly stacked the breakfast tins and moved them over to the door. She hardly looked at you when she spoke, and because she frequently mumbled, he had to pay close attention to make out her words.

"Yes, it was Obi." Tobias kneeled down to help the twins with the babies.

"Don't know no Obi. Reckon him a youngster. Gets himself hanged being foolish."

"But what if he makes it? Finds freedom?" Tobias used his hand to wipe excess porridge from the face of one of the little ones. "Go slow, Henry. Let her eat what's in her mouth first." He looked over his shoulders towards Miss Gee-gee. "Charlie told me there were other states were we can be free. Is this true? Can you walk there—is it close? Could I get back to my village?"

"No, now you hush that talk! If Massa Lee hear you talk like that, he whip us all. I dunno nothin' 'bout runnin' except they follow that there North Star until they can't go no more. Then I suppose they free."

Tobias took a seat in the rocker. "How long do we have to wait here?"

"Till they say we ain't got to wait no more." Miss Gee-gee grumbled something else, but Tobias couldn't catch it. His mind wandered, thinking about where Obi was as well as his own family. Would he ever see them again? Would he ever be free?

Today was not at all that much different from the day of his capture—he felt as lost today as he had then. He had been with his father that morning and not hunting with the other young men because tribal custom said he couldn't. Six months prior to that, he had failed the ritual of becoming a man.

Several of the spiritual leaders had led Tobias and twelve of his peers deep into the forest. It was a rite of passage that all males in their village had to undergo. They were to remain for two weeks by themselves, finding their own food, water, and shelter from harm. He remembered it as if it was yesterday: staring into the eyes of a wild boar that he was to slay. He had seen a living thing and couldn't make the kill.

Because Tobias couldn't take the boar's life, the village banned him from ever holding a weapon from that point forward. He had failed.

Because he could not provide for a family, he would never marry like he had told Ben he planned to do. He had watched other young boys returning as men and saw the disappointment in his father's eyes. From that day forth, the young men carried their own weapons and hunted with the elders in the village. Some took on wives soon after they came home and moved into their own huts. This was never to be for him.

This had happened one other time that Tobias knew of. Another tribesman now lived in a hut with an older man who had been designated as his protector. The protector had no wife, so the high priest had chosen him to look after the young man. They lived as man and wife, and the young man fulfilled the wifely duties.

Tobias thought about Ben. They shared a connection; at times, Ben even filled in some of the emptiness Tobias felt. Tobias relaxed into the chair. There was a shift in his heart, a pang. What was he to learn from all of this? He missed his father. Oh, what a great teacher he was.

The next morning, Ben sat outside the smokehouse, waiting for Tobias to show up. He hadn't seen him at all yesterday, thanks to Obi. Instructed by his pa, Ben had ridden into a little town called Madison to have reward papers for Obi's capture printed. The small printing press produced a local newspaper called the *Bluegrass* that came out once a month. The paper supported slavery, mostly talking about the financial loss of freeing the slaves and insisting that the Bible sanctioned slave labor. As far as Ben was concerned, it was a rag not fit to wipe his butt with.

Hearing the clop of a horse in the distance, Ben looked up and saw that Dexter had returned. There was a frown on his face. When he came into earshot, Ben asked if he had seen Tobias.

"Ain't seen him this mornin'," Dexter shouted back. Just as he finished, Tobias came around the corner and started towards Ben.

"Here comes your nigger now!" Dexter called.

"Boy, you ought to be runnin'. Where you been?" Ben yelled in Tobias's direction.

"What did I tell you about calling me 'boy?'" Grinning, Tobias picked up his step.

Ben turned to see if Dexter had heard this. He saw his father stepping out of the stables.

"Boy, who you think you talkin' to in that manner?" Emmett pivoted towards Tobias. Ben saw that Dexter had heard as well and had turned his horse around. "Ben, tell that negro that talkin' like that just cost him some lashes."

"No, Pa!" The hair stood up on the back of Ben's neck, and his pulse quickened. "Um, he didn't mean no harm." Ben didn't know what else to say. What could he possibly say that would fix this?

Dexter climbed down off his horse and grabbed his whip. "Here you go."

Ben caught the whip before he even realized what it was that Dexter had tossed to him. Dexter was now on guard, his hand over his pistol holster.

"Go on. Take him around back to that tree and lay down ten lashes. That should drive some of the sass out of that mouth." Both Emmett and Dexter closed in on Tobias.

Ben's heart was in his throat. He couldn't breathe. Though his pa's orders shocked him, there was no refusing them. Ben had never whipped a person. His lip trembled as the pain in his chest increased. Tobias had become his friend. "But Pa, he was joking. He never meant nothin' by that ole sass."

"Son, you don't joke with negroes. When they get like that, you have to stop it. Nip it in the bud. You have to train them. Now take that negro round the other side and fix it!"

Ben had no idea what he was going to do, but he knew he had to get Tobias out of there. "Come on, boy!" he shouted. There was nothing but dead weight when he grabbed Tobias by his arm. Ben stared deep into Tobias's glazed eyes, which were bigger than he had ever seen them, his face panic-stricken. "I'm sorry," Ben pleaded in a whisper.

He could feel Tobias shaking, but he went willingly as Ben led him into the stable. Several seconds passed before Ben's eyes adjusted to the low light inside the building. Looking around, he saw the post to which he needed to tie Tobias and the lead rope that hung from it. He fought to hold back his tears. "Don't look at me," he told Tobias.

Tying the rope to the post, he bound Tobias's wrists together with the other end, making sure there was no slack in between. Ben's heart pounded. "I said, don't look at me!" he cried.

Having Tobias firmly secured to the post, Ben took a couple of steps backwards. His world was spinning. His body floated backwards as if he had no control over it. He stood there with the whip in his hand, staring at the back of Tobias's head. *I can't.* Tobias's back blurred as Ben's eyes filled with tears. *I can't.* Tobias stood motionless, his arms and face pressed to the wood.

As Ben stood there, staring at the back he was to whip, the entire world faded away. He failed to hear Dexter walking up behind him.

"Benjamin, your father asked me to come in. Make sure you don't kill the boy whippin' him. A good whippin' is not punishment but a teachin' moment. This is how these animals learn. You got to teach them."

Dexter gently removed the whip from Ben's hand and then steered him off to the side. Within seconds, Dexter unleashed the first crack of the whip, sending it backwards before it soared forward, slamming into Tobias's back.

Tobias let out a gruesome shriek that drove deep into Ben's ears. Tobias struggled to hold his body up with his feet. *Stop it . . . stop . . . stop it . . .* "Stop!" Ben cried. He grabbed Dexter's arm as he was rearing back for his second strike and then grabbed the handle of the whip. "No! You are not goin' to whip him. Stop it!" he commanded.

Bright red blood seeped through the slash in Tobias's shirt. The whip had cut through the thin fabric right in the center of his back.

"What are you doin'?" Dexter attempted to push him out of the way.

Fighting to control the whip, Ben threw his shoulder into Dexter's rib cage, causing Dexter to take a step back. "He's my slave. He belongs to me, and you will not strike him again or else!" Ben was ready to fight if it came down to it. "Get out of here. Go! Get out!" His voice never wavered.

Dexter lowered his arms to his sides as he raised his chin. Ben saw the fire in his eyes. He was staring down the devil.

Heart pounding, Ben continued, "If you so much as speak of this, you will be charged with illegally whippin' another man's property. I didn't give you any such order! And if you breathe so much as a word of this to my father, you will see no mercy from me as I unleash a fury over your soul." Standing face to face with Dexter, Ben no longer felt any hesitation about taking him on. Crushing Dexter, he thought, would come as easy as sin. As the rage burned inside him, he almost wished Dexter would make a move.

But Dexter backed down, never shifting his gaze from Ben. His eyes were cold as his nostrils flared. Without a word, he exited the stable.

Ben ran to Tobias and worked to free his hands. Ben was shaking so badly that he couldn't undo the knots. They had tightened as they supported Tobias' weight.

As he fought to free his friend, Ben cried, "I'm sorry, Tobias. I am so sorry." Gasping for air, he fought to hold back the tears that were forming in his eyes. He knew he had to keep it together, to regain some control of the situation. Freeing Tobias, he held his body as it slumped to the dirt floor.

There was blood everywhere that Ben touched. He had to stop the bleeding. "I'm sorry, I'm really sorry." He looked around for something to use as a compress. "Oh Lord, can you forgive me? Look what I've done." Ben worked to remove Tobias's shirt. Tears ran down his face, but he didn't care as he daubed the shirt over the twelve-inch cut. Tobias twisted and screamed every time Ben touched him. There was too much blood; he needed help.

Leaping up, Ben tore out of the barn, running across the field towards the summer kitchen, where he found Penny. Seeing the pot of hot water on the fire, he shouted that he needed the water as well as rags. Penny scurried to the pot. "What you need this for?"

"Tobias's been hurt." He looked away from her, trying to hide his tear-filled eyes. The words played again in his head. *Tobias's been hurt.* That was a lie. Tobias had said a simple word and been whipped for it. The rage begun to build within Ben once more as he thought of his pa's ridiculous order. All over a word.

"Where he at?" Penny asked.

"In the stables!" Ben took the rags that Penny had gathered up and plunged them into the boiling water on the fire.

When he returned to the barn with the rags, he knelt before Tobias, carefully applying them to the wound. Tobias said nothing. His shoulders curled over his chest, and his breathing was rapid.

"Can you hear me? I'm so sorry for this. This is all my fault." With the back of his hand, Ben wiped the snot mixed with tears from his face. "I am so sorry. I knew you meant nothin' by what you said." He wept as he pressed his hand lightly over the rags on Tobias's back.

Hearing the stable door open, Ben looked up as Penny and Dolly entered. They had followed him with more rags.

"Oh Lord!" Dolly hollered when she saw Tobias. "What happened?"

"Dexter—he took a whip to him. Tobias sassed me in front of my pa. He meant no harm. He was playin'." There was a pull on his shoulder, and Penny maneuvered her large body between him and Tobias.

"May God have mercy on his soul!" With her right hand, Dolly traced the shape of a cross on her chest. "Nothin' is covered up that will not be revealed, nor hidden that will not be known!"

"Stop all that Scripture hollerin' before Mr. Dexter hears you!" Penny said as she removed the rag to examine the cut.

"I'm sorry, Penny, I'm so sorry!" Ben cried as he stood up and allowed the women to tend to Tobias. "This is all my fault," he said as he once more wiped tears from his cheeks.

"Chile, you ain't got nothin' to do with this. This here is Mr. Dexter's work. How he see fit to whip someone over the littlest thing." Penny shook her head before turning towards Dolly. "And you need to hush your mouth. God don't want nothin' to do with Mr. Dexter's nasty soul."

Looking at all the used up bloodstained rags, Penny tore the sleeve from her dress and used it to slow the bleeding. Ben stared at the gash across Tobias's back. He had seen hundreds of such wounds, never thinking twice about them. The desire to die washed over him. He wanted the pain to stop.

After Penny gained control of the bleeding, she wrapped her arms around Tobias and began humming under her breath. Although Ben didn't know the words to the hymn, he recognized the soothing melody as a lullaby that Corinne had sung when she rocked him to sleep as a small child.

Ben wished he was the one holding Tobias. He would tell him that he loved him. That he would make it right. Standing over the women as they cuddled Tobias, Ben's legs went weak. Seconds later, the room went dark.

10

When Ben came to, he was in his bed. He didn't know how long he had been sleeping, but looking towards the window, he could see that it was dark outside. When he remembered what had happened, he bolted upright in the bed. He had to see Tobias. He fumbled for the box of matches on his nightstand to light his oil lamp. Only then could he see the time on his pocket watch on the dresser. He knew it would be there because it rarely left that spot—he had no need to carry around such extravagance.

Nine-thirty. Where is he? Ben needed to see him. He wanted it to be a dream, but it was too real. As details flooded his brain, he looked at his shirt, expecting Tobias's blood to be on it. It was clean. Ben scanned the room, looking for the bloodstained shirt. The sound of the whip cracked in his ears, causing him to spin. He was alone. Then there was a light knock on his door.

"Mr. Ben." Corinne called to him in a whisper, and then the door eased opened about an inch. "May I come in, Mr. Ben? It's me, Corinne."

Ben tried to say something, but his throat was too dry. It was all coming back to him, flooding him with an overload of emotions.

Corinne made her way towards him. "I washed your shirt. Did the best I could to gets the blood out. Afraid to say, but I couldn't get it all out. I let it soak until mornin'."

"Oh, Corinne, what have I done?" Ben fell into her open arms. Rocking him, she eased the two of them onto the edge of his narrow bed.

"Tell me it isn't so. Tell me Tobias is okay." Ben buried his face into the pit of her arm and breast like when he was a child.

"Afraid I can't say that, neither. It was one lash, but ole Mr. Dexter hit him good. Miss Gee-gee got the boy now. Ain't one lash goin' to kill a man. Do more damage to his soul than anything . . . Hush now." Corinne rocked Ben and hummed "Amazing Grace."

Ben's eyelids were too heavy to hold open. He closed his eyes. Through nausea and a pain in his chest, he listened to her voice. He didn't know if he could ever look Tobias in the eye again. None of it could be undone. Remembering little details, he realized that he must have passed out in the stables.

Corinne stopped humming. "Don't know why Mr. Dexter stopped with just one lash. Ain't none of my business no way, I suppose."

Ben knew the answer to that. Was Corinne asking him, he wondered? He couldn't talk about it, not yet. "I—I need some air." He pulled himself off her.

"Shall I open a window for you?" Corinne lightly brushed a couple of loose curls out of Ben's face. "You have so much hair. I know it drives your mammie crazy."

"No, I think I'm goin' to go for a walk."

"Where you goin' this time of the evenin'?"

"I need some air." Ben stood up and went to straighten out his suspenders. "How did you get my shirt off of me?" He tried to ignore the quiver in his stomach.

"Mr. Charlie helped you back here. Say you passed out. Afraid you hit your head. Tells me to watch you, but I can't say nothin' to Massa Lee or Mrs. Clara. So I tell them you sick and skippin' supper."

"Are they still up?" Ben looked towards the door.

"Mrs. Clara's in the parlor. Massa Lee gone to bed about an hour ago."

"Thank you, Corinne. That will be all for this evenin'." Ben walked over to the door and held it open for her.

He waited as long as he could before stealing down the back stairwell and out the back door. The night air was clammy with not much of a breeze. The sky was clear and filled with stars. How he wished that he, too, could be a million miles away. With that notion, he headed down the mile-long dirt driveway that led up to the farm. The road was lined on each side by fifty-foot tall red oak trees, which shielded him from the moon as he walked. His only thought was of Tobias. No man should be whipped like that. Was the world all mad, crazy as a rabid fox? He looked through the trees in the direction of the slave quarters. The cabins were filled with darkness and ominously quiet at this time of night. Even the squawking blue jays and busy squirrels that dwelt in the woodlands had retired for the evening. He could barely make out the tiny cabins. He could never show his face down there again, surely never look Miss Gee-gee in the eyes.

When Ben came to the end of the long driveway, he thought about how, with another step, he could be gone. Like Obi, he could vanish into thin air. Ben had dreamed of taking that next step long before Obi ever came onto the property. But now, the thought of never seeing Tobias again was too great to bear. Closing his eyes, he thought of Tobias, his delicate dark chocolate skin. It glistened when wet—not like his own skin, which was dull and dry. He was in love with Tobias; there was no question about it. The thought of lying with another man had never been as clear as it was until he met Tobias. He thought of Tobias when he touched himself, and only of him. He was in love with someone whom he could never be with. Why did society get to govern whom he could love and whom he couldn't? He now knew he had as little control of his life as Tobias had of his.

Turning around, Ben headed back towards the house. He knew it was late and hoped the house would be quiet when he reached it.

As he passed by the summer kitchen, Ben's stomach grumbled. He had missed supper, and he wondered if there were any scraps in there. Perhaps one of Penny's fine sweet potato pies, or her bread pudding, which was his favorite dessert. There had been persimmon cookies in the middle of the dining room table. Was that yesterday or today? It had all run together.

Approaching the house slaves' living quarters, Ben heard muffled voices coming from inside the two-room cabin. Quietly, he peeked through the unglazed window frame and saw Penny and Corinne sitting, sewing by candle light. He couldn't hear what they were chattering about, but he watched as their hands moved their needles in and out of the pieces of fabric they held.

Realizing that he was smiling, he swallowed and straightened his shoulders. Relaxation swept through his body—the first calmness he had felt in hours, maybe even days. All it took was the sight of Corinne, the only person who had ever called him special. *You're going to make a difference in this world someday,* she had told him. He snickered. *Boy, was she wrong.* Remembering that she had slept on the floor of his bedroom until he was almost seven years old, Ben replayed the games they played and how she had pretended to shoo the ghosts away.

"Do you love me?" Ben remembered asking Corinne many years ago. He would never forget the look in her deep smoky eyes, he knew the answer before she gave it to him. "As if you my own . . . I loves you likes you my own child." His eyes filled with tears as he recalled her sweet words that day, "*Mr. Ben . . . my papa tells me when I was a little girl that the most important day in your life is the day you know why you were born.*"

Ben glanced through the framed opening over at Penny and tried to be quiet as he chuckled. Everyone was scared of Big Momma Penny when she got to stomping. A big ole stick of dynamite, pa called her. She was the only cook he had ever known. She let few people, including Pa, in her kitchen. Again, Ben acknowledged the warm tingle that washed over his body, a sense of peace. It was a rarity in his life, but he recognized it when it happened, and it was usually in the presence of Corinne and Penny.

When Ben made it back to the house, he headed straight for the plate of persimmon cookies on the table. Quietly grabbing a handful, he left the dining room and entered the hall where the main stair-case was. Taking the steps two at a time, he made the wooden stairs creak louder than he'd intended. Reaching the landing, Ben saw his mother exit the parlor below. His first thought was to hide, but she was staring right at him.

"Ben, do you have a minute?" she asked.

"No, ma'am, I'm tired." Ben replied.

"Ben, I am not asking you. Please come down and talk with me," Clara unapologetically instructed.

Ben knew that, on the rare occasions when his mother took that tone with him, it was never good. He made his way back down to the parlor.

When he got there, he took a seat in his father's chair next to the fireplace. "Yes, ma'am?" he said. The smell of his father's tobacco pipe rose from the leather, causing Ben to twist his nose. Lined with floor-to-ceiling bookcases, the room harbored Clara's prize collection of books from around the world. The place smelled of oak from the fire that burned around the clock all winter.

Clara remained standing as she looked up at the large painting of her father hanging over the fireplace. "Ben, you need to think of your future. I lost the battle with your father to let you continue with your education, and I regret that. But now, the army appears to be waging yet another war on the Indians out west."

She paused, allowing Ben to interject, "Well, ma'am, I ain't much like no education no way, and ain't got no beef with no Indians."

Clara rolled her eyes and took a deep breath. "Ben, listen to me for a minute. God knows I tried to teach you proper English, but much like your father, you don't seem to take to education. I never thought you would take to the army either. I believe you are as unsuit-ed for war as you are for any more schooling." She rested her hands on her hips.

"What are you tryin' to say?" Ben knew he needed to stay calm, but such a conversation was trying this late in the evening.

Clara was silent for a minute as she drew in a long breath. Clearing her throat, she continued. "What I want to know, Benjamin, is whether you see yourself running this plantation when your father no longer can. Is that even what you want?" Her voice softened. "Honey, I wanted so much for you."

"Well, ma'am, I don't know what I want. Ain't much thought of it till recently."

"What about going to New York for a while? I would love for you to get out, experience the world and all that it has to offer." Clara paused for a second. "You might find more young men such as yourself."

"Ain't goin' to no New York, with city folk walkin' around all high and mighty." Ben sat up in his chair. "Ain't nothin' for me to see but buildings and people." The thought of being surrounded by so many people made him nervous, and what did she mean by men such as him?

"Oh, Ben, I so wish you weren't so much like your father."

"You married him . . . Are we done?" Ben stood up. If there was one thing he wasn't doing, it was going to New York.

"Just think about it. Maybe not New York, but somewhere that you would like. There's a whole world out there for you to see."

Ben looked at his mother, puzzled as to the entire conversation. It occurred to him that maybe Dexter had said something. If Dexter told anyone, though, it would have been Pa, and this whole conversation would have gone differently.

When he reached his room, he fell onto his bed. *Did Dexter say something?* He thought about going to New York. It would never happen. He had read about New York and had seen pictures of the big buildings they were building and the people in fancy suits. It wasn't a place that he wanted to visit, but for that matter, neither was anywhere else. Still in his clothes, he drifted off to sleep, his thoughts of Tobias turning into dreams.

Tobias woke to the sounds of Miss Gee-gee's feet scooting along the floor. Raising his head a little, he saw that he was on the lower mattress, lying on his stomach. There was a burning feeling on his back, and then he remembered that Dexter had taken a whip to him yesterday morning. His head fell back onto the mattress as the pain from his back increased.

"Now, you just hold still. Let's me get that dressin'."

The pain increased as Miss Gee-gee lifted the rag, which had attached itself to dried blood from his back. Tobias tried to focus on something else. There was only the burning feeling digging into his back. He lay still with his eyes closed. Yesterday played out in his head, jumbled. His thoughts were everywhere. One thing he knew for sure was that Dexter had taken a whip to him. The pain he was feeling was all Dexter. A monster. Tobias couldn't even recall what exactly he had said to Ben to make Master Lee so angry. He remembered the terrified look on Ben's face, how Ben had tried to stick up for him. There was the sound of the whip and the moment it tore through his flesh. He felt the rip of tissue leaving his body, revealing what lay beneath. His pain over shadowed everything, and he filled in bits of memory between the throbbing. *It was Charlie, he helped me back to the cabin. Dolly was there, and so was Penny. Penny was crying . . . so was Ben. Why was Ben crying? He kept saying he was sorry.*

Tobias gripped the mattress as Miss Gee-gee lightly pressed down on his back, cleaning around the wound. "Ain't as bad as it probably feels. Old Mr. Dexter's aim ain't what it used to be. Shirt took more of it than you."

Tobias disagreed. The pain was proof, the burning sensation never subsiding.

When Miss Gee-gee was finished, she applied several oak leaves to the wound to aid in the healing process and to keep the swelling down. "You be up again by evening."

Tobias listened to see if either Henry or Stuart were still in the bed above him. Miss Gee-gee had told him the other day that they would be going to the fields soon. They were old enough to work a couple of hours in the morning and perform small chores around the farm in the afternoons.

Not knowing what time it was, Tobias was having a hard time getting a grasp on anything. *Ben was arguing with someone . . . He was arguing with Dexter. Ben stopped him.*

He couldn't hold the thought for long before another deep burning sensation rushed over his back. To distract himself, he thought about picking plants with his father, how his father had schooled him on everything: the name of the plants, their uses, how to administer them. He was a good student and pleased his father often. As the sounds of screaming returned to him, he remembered the flames, which were now burned into the back of his eyelids. The entire village was on fire, smoke filling the air. He would never forget the stench from the belly of the ship. The auction house, that tiny dark cell, the weakness and wishing for death. He opened his eyes, trying to rid his thoughts of all that had happened. He now welcomed the pulsating pain that overtook his head. Anything was better than the darkness he had endured. Only through pain did he know he was still alive.

Tobias drifted in and out of sleep for most of the day. It wasn't until midday, when Henry and Stuart came in, that he realized it was Sunday. They had been to church and then over to Charlie's shop. Whenever Henry went missing, he could always be found down at Charlie's shop. He said he wanted to be a blacksmith when he grew up, just like Charlie.

Welcoming the noise of the two little ones, Tobias rubbed his eyes, trying to wake up. He could smell fish cooking. Every Sunday, Miss Gee-gee cooked up a big dinner: fried fish, lentils, and corn meal. The thought of it made his stomach growl. He hadn't eaten since yesterday morning. Looking towards the fireplace, the large cast iron skillet in which the fish crackled caught his eye. His mother used large leaves and would wrap the pond fish and cook it in a pit of ashes. Oh, how he missed her cooking, especially her stews. The food was different here; it left him hungry an hour after eating it. There was never enough.

Miss Gee-gee soon had dinner ready. He ate sitting on the mattress with Henry and Stuart under his feet. The three ate quietly. After dinner, when the boys were in bed, Miss Gee-gee took to her rocker like she did on every other evening. For about an hour, she would sit and nap before starting her evening's sewing. Tobias had taken over Pearl's job of threading the needle for her.

While she and the babies slept, Tobias could hear Henry and Stuart up in their bunk whispering and playing. Tobias needed to get up and move around a little. Miss Gee-gee had stitched up his shirt and had it hanging on the back of the door. He slowly eased his shirt on before grabbing up the dirty pots, tins, and spoons that were still sitting in front of the fire. Washing everything up after dinner had also become his responsibility after Pearl moved to the female quarters.

Stepping onto the porch, he felt refreshed as the evening air hit his face. The sky lit up the tattered cabins and the path towards the outdoor scullery, which Tobias took. The moon and stars were the only things in this new world that looked the same as in his old world.

Tobias passed by the cabin that held the young single men. He could hear them laughing inside. It sounded like a party, as they shouted and stomped their feet against the decaying wood floor.

When he reached the scullery, which was no more than several large metal tubs and buckets for fresh water, he was frightened by two shadows standing in the darkened corner. Within a split second, he recognized one of them as Rudo. The other was a young woman who Tobias didn't know.

"Hey, Tobias," Rudo said, as he wiped his mouth.

Tobias looked at the girl and noticed she was fastening the top buttons on her dress.

"What are you doing out here?" Rudo asked him.

"I was cleaning up the bowls for morning." Tobias's feet shuffled backwards as he tried to leave them alone. His eyes darted between Rudo and the young girl. "I'll come back later."

"Wait, I want you to meet my girl. This is Laura." Rudo smiled as he pushed her towards Tobias. "We's goin' to get married," he said.

Tobias now realized why Rudo hadn't run with Obi. He was shocked to see that Rudo even had a girlfriend. Rudo, Obi, and Tobias were all about the same age—of course, he had a *girlfriend*. Ben had said that he'd once liked a girl. Tobias wondered if Ben still liked her. *Who was she?* Ben had said her name was Mary. Was she one of the girls whom Ben said he had kissed?

After Rudo introduced them, Tobias excused himself, saying he would leave his dishes and come back later.

When he returned to the cabin, Miss Gee-gee was sitting in her chair on the porch. "Chile, can I talk with you? Now, people talk, you knows that. They comes to me about you and Mr. Ben."

Tobias smiled when she said Ben's name.

"They sees the way you two be carryin' on. Just member, you two ain't the same. He's your massa and will always be your massa. You understand what Miss Gee-gee's tellin' you?"

"Yes ma'am, I understand," Tobias responded. She, however, didn't understand. No one did. He and Ben were friends—at least, that's what Tobias had thought until yesterday. Maybe she was right. Maybe Ben was no different from his father or Dexter.

"Next time, he might not be there to save you from Mr. Dexter. You got to learn your place."

My place? Tobias heard what she was saying and knew she was right. The wound on his back proved it. He couldn't take another beating. With all that he had lost, they were close to breaking him. Finding that he couldn't look at her, he lowered his chin. He was only sure of one thing: he didn't understand this country or its people at all.

11

Tobias knew that, in the next couple of minutes, the morning sun would be peeking over the ridge, telling him that he was late. This morning, he was walking faster than usual in order to keep anyone, especially Dexter, from looking for him. Waking up late, he had rushed out of the cabin without breakfast, stuffing his pockets with a handful of walnuts. He figured that he could eat them when, and if, he developed an appetite. The morning humidity was thick, and he struggled to fill his lungs. He was thankful for the distant singing of a cardinal; its sweet chirping took his mind off how sick he was feeling.

He hadn't seen Ben since Saturday, and Miss Gee-gee's talk last night sat in his stomach like a pit. He had not slept much last night, and his heart was in his throat as he wondered how today would go. He was angry. Angry that Ben had pretended to be his friend, angry that his own foolishness had led to his beating. This was a feeling almost unknown to him before his capture: he was angry all the time, at everything and everybody. Was he going crazy? Between his poor breathing and the constant feeling of uncertainty, he wanted to sleep all the time.

Seeing Ben standing exactly where he had been standing on Saturday morning, prior to all hell breaking loose, Tobias relived the events of that day as he approached Ben.

"Mornin'," Ben mumbled. His eyes never made contact with Tobias's.

"Morning," Tobias answered. His stomach was one big knot, He swallowed, trying to remove the lump forming in his throat. The two stood in silence about a foot from each other. Tobias waited for Ben to look at him.

Ben raised his eyes to meet Tobias's. "How you feeling this mornin'?"

"Fine."

Ben scoffed as he rolled his eyes. "You ain't feeling fine. How's your back? I wanted to come see you, but Corinne said I ought not to."

"Miss Gee-gee tended to it. Said it wasn't as bad as it feels. Still pretty sore." Tobias watched as Ben lowered his head and diverted his eyes. Those eyes held sadness, and Tobias got the feeling that Ben wanted to say something. In his peripheral vision, Tobias saw other slaves heading out to the field. There was a lot going on around them, yet none of it mattered. Tobias wondered if Ben was going to say something, anything, or were they going to stand there looking at one another all day.

"I—I have some things I ought to say." Ben stopped and looked around before continuing. "Figure we could do some work down by the river and check on the dam, make sure them beaver's ain't built it back up." He cracked a half-smile as he gazed at Tobias.

"Sure. Whatever you need. I'll put the stuff on the wagon and have Charlie fix up a horse for us." Tobias walked towards the stables.

"I'm sorry, Tobias. I am." Ben's voice was low, low enough that Tobias could pretend he didn't hear him and keep walking. He wanted to be mad. The throbbing pain in his back told him that he should be, and in order to stay mad, he had to keep walking.

The two worked in silence for a couple of hours, clearing a small amount of debris that the large rodents had managed to build up.

The sun was on fire as it hung over their heads, and their reprieve was the coolness of the river.

Tobias moved slower than usual, and he noticed that Ben was working far harder than he usually did. When they finished, Tobias headed up the embankment with his pitchfork.

"Blood." Ben murmured from behind him.

"What?" Only after Tobias replied did he realize what Ben had said.

"The back of your shirt. You're bleedin'." Ben rushed up behind him as he reached the top of the bank. "Take your shirt off. Let me take a look at it."

Tobias focused on the tenderness of his back. He could feel the dampness of his shirt as it pressed against his skin.

"Take your shirt off. Let me see." Ben didn't wait. He worked open the front of Tobias's shirt and let it drop off his shoulders.

"It looks like it opened up a bit." Ben's voice cracked trying to get the words out.

Feeling the light pressing of Ben's fingers around his upper shoulder, Tobias sucked in a big breath.

"Is it bad? It hurts—" Tobias asked before the pain silenced him.

"Give me your shirt." Ben removed Tobias's shirt from his arms. "Let me try to clean it and see where it's bleeding." Tobias thought he heard a sniffle coming from Ben.

Taking the shirt, Ben scurried down the embankment to the edge of the water. He plunged the shirt entirely into the water, then looked at the blood. He dunked it several more times until the blood had washed off. Running up the bank, he lightly patted at the blood on Tobias's back.

"Ouch. Okay, okay, not so hard," Tobias cried as he flinched his shoulder, trying to dodge the cloth.

"We need to bandage this when we get back. Wrap it so the bleeding will stop." Ben slowed his patting. "It's bleeding in one spot. Lie down, let me hold this on your back until it stops."

Tobias took to the ground right where the two were standing. He lay next to the front wheel of the wagon, the body of which shielded them from the burning sun. Silence filled the air as Ben held the wet shirt gently against Tobias's back. It wasn't long before the coolness of the shirt brought Tobias's breathing under control, more so than it had been all morning. Ben's touch was soft, relaxing him into a sleepy state. He wanted to stay mad at Ben, but he couldn't. He knew deep down that it wasn't Ben's fault—Ben had tried to protect him.

Tobias jumped at the sound of Ben's voice. Opening his eyes, he lifted his head and looked around. *Did I fall asleep? How long was I sleeping?*

"Did you say something?" Ben asked.

"No . . . I didn't say anything." Tobias repositioned his head, which lay across his arms. The throbbing in his back had subsided to a tolerable level.

"I thought you said something. Were you sleeping?" Ben asked again.

"I guess so. Is it still bleeding?" Tobias wanted to roll over, as the pressure of lying on his chest limited his breathing.

"No. I don't think so. But it's going to keep opening unless we put a bandage over it."

The two of them were lying silently, out in the middle of nowhere. Tobias's mind drifted back to the many questions he had had before he dozed off. *Why is Ben nice to me? I am a slave. Why am I not with Rudo and Simba, working in the fields like everyone else? Why did Ben stop Dexter? That is twice Ben has come to my rescue. Why?*

Tobias found himself staring at Ben. The other boy's energy captured Tobias's attention, made him crave him even more. Something was drawing constantly at Tobias, making him want to be around Ben. Ben made the world seem as if it wasn't actually ending. When Tobias wasn't thinking about how much he missed his old life, a life that seemed so long ago, he thought about Ben. Ben's touch quieted his soul. Tobias closed his eyes as he released a sigh. There was something familiar about this moment, but he couldn't put his finger on it. It was surreal. "Ben? Can I ask you something?" Tobias lay perfectly still, wondering how to frame his question.

"Yeah, of course you can. What is it?" Ben leaned in closer to him.

"You stopped Dexter." Tobias stopped as he tried again to make sense of what he wanted to say. "I—you—" Pausing long enough to sit up, he looked into Ben's gentle eyes. "Why are you kind to me? Why me? Sometimes, when we talk, I feel like there is something you want to say but don't." Tobias watched as Ben broke eye contact, his attention drawn to something in the dirt.

Tobias innocently moistened his lips. "Ben, sometimes—"

Ben looked up. His next actions caused Tobias to stumble over his words. His hands took Tobias's face and held it there, looking deeply into the other boy's dark brown eyes. Tobias could feel his heart beating in his chest. *Or is it Ben's heart?* In the blink of an eye, Ben pressed his lips against Tobias's, ever so lightly. Without a thought, Tobias fell into the kiss, his head rolling back as Ben's mouth pressed a little harder into his.

It was over as fast as it had started. Ben released Tobias as he pulled away. "I love you, Tobias! I know I shouldn't, but I do!"

Tobias could feel the energy pouring from Ben's soul. As they stared into one another's eyes, Tobias didn't know what to say. *They had just shared a kiss.* No, Ben had kissed him, but he liked it. In Tobias's mind, the pieces were coming into place, and things were making sense. A rush of excitement tingled through his body. Swallowing hard, Tobias thought about when he had seen Rudo and Laura kissing. He had wondered what it would be like with a woman. When that day came, would he have feelings for her? The feelings that he had been missing were there all along, with Ben. Only Ben sparked those feelings within him. Tobias swallowed again and released a deep, satisfied sigh.

In some crazy, twisted way, Ben was to be his protector. Flashes of the young man in his village that had lived with the other man came to Tobias. That couple had always held his fascination, and he never knew why. It was all making sense. He was to love Ben.

Tobias's heart raced with the realization that the Gods had shown him his future. He was to be with Ben. Tears welled up behind his heavy eyelids. He wanted to feel Ben again, the hunger of his kiss, the smell of his breath. He knew nothing about kissing, but he took Ben's hands, as Ben had done with him, and leaned in until their lips met again. He could taste the apple that Ben had eaten earlier on his breath as he inhaled. Feeling the weight of Ben's body, Tobias pushed back, their mouths pressing tighter together. Finding a rhythm, Ben's hand lightly touched his face. Tobias released a moan of ecstasy as his body gave way to Ben.

Hungry, the two kissed for several minutes before they both had to come up for air. Their lips swollen, their chests rose and fell in unison.

Tobias lightly wiped saliva from Ben's lip. "You are to be my protector." His voice was low, barely a whisper.

Ben pulled back and chuckled. "I'm not your protector. You saved me. I know you don't understand, but before you, I thought my life was over. That this was all that life would ever be for me. Until you, I wanted to die. It's all I ever thought about. Whether I actually died, or lived out the life that I thought was planned for me, it didn't matter— it was all the same, until you." Ben kissed him again and again until Tobias stopped him.

"No," Tobias cut in. He tried to explain how he had failed in the ritual walk, coming clean on how he was to never marry and how he, too, was living a life of uncertainty.

Ben replied, "I don't know what the hell you just said, but it doesn't matter. I don't care if you call it voodoo or the Gods, or if spirits and leprechauns spoke to you, or for that matter if the doggone birds were flyin' north instead of south for the winter. Just say you feel the same about me." Ben hovered over Tobias as if he was ready to pounce.

Tobias smiled as a feeling of euphoria washed over him. It was a lightness that hadn't been present in a long time—ever since his failed ritual walk into the woods to become a man. He tried to think of the proper English words to describe his feelings, but he couldn't come up with anything. Instead, he threw his body into Ben's, causing the other boy to fall backwards as they sank into a deep, long kiss.

Tobias could feel his erection as it firmed up the front of his britches. Their arousals, pressing together through the fabric, were sending Tobias over the edge, and he released several incoherent whimpers. Chest to chest, they moved slowly against one another as Ben deepened the kiss. Tobias squirmed as Ben cupped his buttocks and pressed into him. Unaware until it was too late, Ben slid his hand up and across Tobias's back. The pain shot through Tobias like an electric jolt.

Tobias lifted himself up and off Ben's body, screaming and jumping in a circle. His arms and hands flapped as if he was trying to cool himself off or fly. "Oh damn, I'm sorry, I'm sorry!" Ben shrieked. His face had a haunted look as he sat up.

Tobias didn't know if all of his jumping and screaming was going to help matters, but it did send a nest of birds flying from a nearby tree. He gritted his teeth as he stared at Ben, who was sitting up against the wagon wheel. He wanted so badly to return to him, to lie with him, but the pain was too consuming.

"C'mon, let's get you back." Ben stood up and wiped the grass from his britches. "We need to take care of that there back of yours." Looking around, Ben reached down and grabbed his hat, which had fallen off at some point. Tobias's eyes followed him as he approached. He didn't want to go back, but the pain was too great to refuse Ben's offer. Ben stepped close to Tobias and took hold of his hands. "I say I will never hurt you, but somehow that's all I ever do." He smiled into Tobias's alluring eyes as his fingers lightly rubbed Tobias's hands.

The ride back to the farm was quiet. Tobias's thoughts were scattered; he was too excited to think straight. He thought of them lying next to the wagon, kissing. Adrenaline was running rampant through his body, and he wanted to squeal. Approaching the farm's entrance just before sunset, Tobias was overwhelmed with the thought that everyone was staring at them, as if they knew something had happened. Surely not. He was being silly. There had been no one around for miles where they were. *Stop being wary.*

Feeling the pressure of the bandage that Ben had wrapped tightly around his torso, Tobias snickered at the notion that it was keeping his heart from exploding out of his chest. He fought to contain his grin as he reached his cabin. He had to be careful; Miss Gee-gee could see through anything. Walking into the cabin, he noticed there was no fire in the fireplace, no sign of dinner being cooked. Miss Gee-gee was in her rocker, her eyes fixed on him as he stepped into the room. Henry and Stuart must not have come in yet. The babies, Harriett and Niles, were lying on the lower mattress.

Tobias avoided eye contact as he stooped down to peek at the babies. He softly tickled Harriett. She smiled up at him, and he laughed. He could feel Miss Gee-gee's eyes boring into on him. "Do you want me to get a fire started for dinner?" Her piercing stare was making him nervous. He didn't want to look at her, but when no response came, he did. Her eyes were locked in the same position as they had been before. Tobias took a step towards her. Was she asleep with her eyes open? His heart jumped in his throat, and he stumbled backwards when it hit him: she was dead.

Her body sat lifeless in her chair. He had seen her do it a thousand times—"*I just sit a spell, then I get supper started.*" He had heard it every day from a woman who kept busy from sun-up to sundown. Kneeling in front of her rocker, he eased his head down onto her lap and pulled her now-cool hands to his cheeks as he said a prayer aloud in his native tongue. Lightly stroking the blanket she had laid across her lap, he quietly recited the prayer again.

He tried to say it a third time, but his mind would not focus. He had known this day would come, yet when he left the cabin this morning, he had never imagined that it would come today. When he left, she had been getting Henry and Stuart ready for . . . *Oh no, I can't have them come in and see her like this.*

Tobias's pulse quickened as he thought about what he should do. His mind was a jumble. *Think, Tobias, think.*

He had to get help. Coming to his feet, he wanted to close her eyes, but his hand trembled; he didn't have the strength to do it. With a glance at the babies, ensuring that they were alright, he bolted out the door to the men's cabin. Simba was the first to step outside, followed by Rudo.

"Come, come quick, Miss Gee- gee has passed. She's in the cabin." There was nothing else to be said.

"Go get Charlie!" Simba responded before taking off in the direction of Miss Gee-gee's cabin. Tobias stood still as Rudo, too, rushed passed him. A second or two passed before he realized that he had to find Charlie. He sprinted towards the stables. Within minutes, he and Charlie were both running back to the cabin.

Ahead of them were Henry and Stuart. They were playing marbles in the dirt with several other children. Thank goodness they never came straight home like they were supposed to. "I have to get the boys," Tobias shouted to Charlie as he changed his course.

"Take them to Dolly. Have her tend to them," Charlie said, as he hurried ahead.

By the time Tobias reached the cabin, a small group of women was swarming around it and had removed Harriett and Niles from inside. Tobias pushed his way through the crowd to find Pearl in front of the cabin. She was huddled, crying, in the arms of a tall, skinny young man. Tobias paid him no mind as he took Pearl and wrapped his arms around her, bringing her close to his chest.

After a couple of minutes, Charlie stepped out onto the porch and removed his hat. "I'm sorry, but she is gone." He was talking to no one in general; his eyes stared out over all of them. "Simba and I will carry her out. Start in the morning on a proper coffin for her."

The women sang a hymn as Miss Gee-gee's body was removed an hour later. She had been washed and bound in a sheet, her body placed onto a cooling board. She would be placed in the barn until a coffin could be constructed.

Within twenty-four hours, Miss Gee-gee was given her proper homecoming. Master Lee had given the farm the day off, something he had never done before. The most time he had ever allowed was a couple of hours in the late afternoon for a service, after a good day's work had been achieved.

Tobias had never seen slaves come from other farms, but a few were allowed to walk up the road to attend the homecoming. By the crowd that was gathering at the service, it seemed that Miss Gee-gee had been loved by everyone.

They gathered around the coffin, which Charlie and Simba had carved out of old barn wood and lined with donated fabric from the women. The coffin sat in the center of the corridor of the slave quarters. They sung, filling the sky with their beautiful voices. When they were done, the men lifted the coffin and, with a procession of men and women, walked down the main driveway under the massive oaks. They crossed the bridge over the river to the negro cemetery. As they marched, they sang, holding the coffin up high. When the coffin reached the gravesite, they waited for the end of the procession to arrive as their voices rumbled through the valley, echoing off the mountain walls.

Miss Gee-gee's body was placed lying east to west, with her head pointing east, towards Africa. Tobias and Pearl stood with Corinne and Simba on either side of them. Henry and Stuart were behind Pearl's legs, hiding their faces, as Miss Gee-gee's body was lowered into the ground.

When Tobias raised his head, in the distance, he saw Ben and his mother watching from the second floor veranda of their house. His initial thought was to ask himself why they were not here. Surely, Miss Gee-gee had meant something to them. But looking around at the crowd, the deep pain in everyone's faces answered his question. There was no place for them at a negro's burial, not even if they had owned her.

12

"Tobias . . . Tobias!" Ben softly called as he stood in front of the cabin. He hadn't talked to Tobias since the afternoon of Miss Gee-gee's death. When Tobias emerged from the cabin, the sun caused him to squint as he focused on Ben.

"Good mornin'." Ben glanced around, taking note of the other slaves heading out to the fields. "How you doin'?"

"I'm a little tired. Haven't been sleeping well." Tobias stopped short of the step leading off the porch. He was shirtless but still had the bandage tightly wrapped around his torso. Ben chewed on his thumbnail, trying to hide his glances at Tobias's biceps.

Tobias gave him a half-smile before sitting on an old stump on the porch. "The boys are still over at Dolly and Charlie's, and the babies are with Miss Etta. Not sure how long they are going to stay there. How have you been?"

Ben's mind traveled back to the last time he had been with Tobias. It had been the best day of his life. Not being able to talk to him the last couple of days had been torture. "Okay, I guess. Seen you at Miss Gee-gee's service. Momma and I watched from the veranda. Sorry to hear about her. Pa says she was a good . . ." Ben paused, lost as he searched for the proper words. "Are you up to doing some work?" he quietly asked.

"Just sitting won't bring her back." Tobias squeezed his hands into fists as he gave a half shrug.

Ben took a step forward, placing one foot on the porch and then resting his hand on that leg as he leaned in. Work was the last thing on his mind. He wanted to be with Tobias, comfort him, and be close as he grieved. "Was she like your momma?"

Tobias looked puzzled. "Who?"

"Miss Gee-gee," Ben replied. He was surprised it needed clarification.

"Not really. I loved her and all, but she was not like my mother. More like . . . what do you call them . . . a grandmother?"

"Bet you goin' to miss her though. Did you eat somethin' this mornin? I brought you some ham, if you hungry." Ben unfolded a piece of cloth and revealed several thick pieces of smoked ham. Tobias reached out and took Ben's offering.

Unbeknownst to either of them, Dexter stood watching them from across the field.

"I don't want to talk here." Ben's eyes rolled to the left and then the right, quietly signaling his concern about the people around them.

"Let me get my shirt, and we can go." Tobias jumped to his feet and was in and out of the cabin within minutes.

Saying nothing about the other day, they took to rebuilding the hog pens on the back end of the stables. When Ben was sure they were out of anyone's earshot, he cleared his throat loud enough to get Tobias's attention. "I meant what I said the other day. 'Bout how I feel about you. Been doin' some thinkin'."

Tobias's work slowed as he turned his attention to Ben. "Uh-huh."

"We could meet at night, after supper. Continue here what we do during the day. Ain't nobody suspect nothin'." Ben took a deep breath and then exhaled. His heart raced as he plotted his future happiness.

"Okay." Tobias made a slight grin. "I'm alone in the cabin now."

"No, that's too risky. Too many people, someone might see me there. Come to the oaks. You can meet me there. No one can see us down in the trees. When the moon rises high over the house, come to me, I'll be waitin'.'" There was a flutter in Ben's stomach just thinking about it.

"But—" Tobias raised his chin.

"Don't worry. I've been out there at night. No one will see us. It's too dark. The oaks will protect us; they'll make us invisible to all the world." Ben rubbed his bottom lip as he thought about his plan. In the grove, they could lie undetected by anyone. "Dexter's the last one up the road at night. When he leaves, he secures the gate behind him." They could be together.

From over the rail of the pen, Tobias saw Simba out in the field, working behind his plow. Part of the plow was hooked to Simba's body, with its tip burrowing into the dirt as the old ox pulled them along. Tobias watched as Simba dug his feet in the ground, trying to keep the plow steady and upright as the ox pulled it through the field. Simba was covered in sweat as the sun shot its rays of heat down upon them.

"Am I to do that someday?" Tobias murmured.

Ben looked in the direction that Tobias was looking. "What? That? Never! I would never let that happen." Ben recalled their conversation the other day. "I laughed at you the other day when you called me—"

"Protector?" Tobias finished his sentence.

"But I will be. I swear, as long as I'm breathin', I will never allow anythin' to happen to you."

"Because you own me?" Tobias broke eye contact and looked down.

Ben read Tobias's face. "No . . . because I love you!" Taking Tobias's hand, he placed it over his own heart. "This belongs to you." With a quick glance around, he lowered both of their hands as well as his voice. "What happened last week will never happen again. No one will ever lay another hand on you." He had no idea how he could do this. It would mean standing up to his father. Ben's anxiety increased as last week's incident played out in his head. His pa didn't take "no" from anyone, not even his wife, if he was set on something. Out of the corner of his eye, Ben saw movement and released Tobias's hand. Taking a step back, he saw that Dexter was riding towards them. Ben's pulse quickened. What did Dexter want?

But Dexter said nothing. When he rode by them, he gave Ben a slight nod and continued down the path towards the house. Ben turned back towards Tobias. "Let's get some work done. I think he's watchin' us." This thought made Ben nervous. He would have to keep his eye on Dexter and not let his guard down. "We'll talk again later tonight."

In the dead of night, Tobias made his way out into the giant oaks. His heart pounded like that of a cat chasing a mouse as the cool air filled his lungs. Bursting with excitement, he had to slow his steps in the dark, to force his body not to run. They had shared a kiss, and he wanted more. Swiping away at a harassing cicada in front of him, he focused on where he was stepping, listening for Ben as he thought of that kiss.

Tobias smiled when he first heard what sounded like an owl's call being carried to him on the gentle breeze. Immediately, he knew it was Ben—it was the worst impression of an owl he had ever heard.

Tobias must have been five feet in front of Ben before he saw him kneeling beneath the leafy canopy created by the massive oak trees.

"You're right, it's dark out here." Tobias stopped in front of Ben and started to sit.

"No, not here." Ben took Tobias by the hand and led him about thirty feet deeper into the grove of oak trees. "Here." Ben pointed to a quilt spread out over a carpet of dried leaves.

Tobias stood over the small patchwork quilt as he listened for something, anything indicating that they weren't alone. The rattling buzz of the cicadas and the susurration of the branches swaying above them was all he could hear. Being in the dark didn't scare him—he was used to running through the jungle at night by himself. So why was he nervous?

Ben lay on the quilt. "Sit down." A slight smirk brushed his face as he gently patted the quilt beside him. A devilish grin turned the corners of his mouth.

Tobias hesitated before taking a seat. He wondered what was going to happen. Was Ben going to kiss him again? Tobias forced himself to take a breath. *When did I get so nervous? I was fine when I left the cabin.* A light touch on his hand from Ben caused him to jerk his hand back and suck in a breath of cool air.

"Relax, no one's out here."

Tobias sighed deeply. "How long have you been out here?" His eyes had adjusted to the low light of the moon, and he was able to see Ben's beautiful smile.

"About an hour. Beginnin' to think you weren't comin'." Ben moved in closer to him. Their eyes locked onto one another. Leaning in, Ben gently kissed him. The ever-so-light touch of his lips caused Tobias to gasp for air.

The gentleness in the kiss, the sweetness in Ben's innocent eyes as they focused solely on him, sent a warm sensation throughout his body. Meeting Ben's piercing stare, Tobias initiated the next kiss. It was wet and awkward as they struggled to find the place they had been the other day. Feeling a light push across his chest, Tobias realized that Ben was trying to lay him down.

"Wait, wait!" Tobias broke free and sat up. "I've never done this." His heart was pounding as he tried to think of what to say. He could feel his entire body quivering as if he was about to explode.

"Me neither," Ben murmured, as he reached for Tobias again.

Tobias leaned back to keep the distance between them. "But you said you kissed lots of girls."

"No, I didn't." Ben again reached for him.

Tobias stuttered, "Yes, yes you did. You asked me if I had a girl-friend. I said no. I asked you, and you said no but you had kissed—"

"Tobias, why are you talkin' so much? Are you nervous?" Ben placed his hand over Tobias's hand.

"No . . . Yes . . . I guess so." Tobias gulped. Ben laughed, and the sound somehow chipped away at some of Tobias's tension. "It's not funny."

Ben quieted. "I know. It's sweet." He took hold of Tobias's hand. "Take off your shoes." He quickly removed his own shoes, tossing them at the foot of the quilt. Tobias took off his shoes and placed them next to Ben's.

"Now, come here," Ben said as he leaned toward Tobias.

Drawn in close, Tobias closed his eyes just as their lips met. This time, Ben held the kiss for a second or two before pulling away. "Kiss me," he whispered, as he placed his hand behind Tobias's neck and pulled him even closer.

Within moments, their kiss deepened, and Tobias took in Ben's warm breath. He let Ben lay him down and slowly maneuver himself on top of him.

Through the fabric of their britches, Tobias felt Ben's erection between them as their legs became entangled. Ben let out another light moan before moving to Tobias's neck. The feeling of Ben's warm breath against his skin forced an uncontrolled whimper from Tobias. Moving down and then across his neck, Ben softly laid tiny kisses diagonally all along and around his Adam's apple. Tobias ran his hands through Ben's thick mass of hair. When Ben's lips returned to his, Tobias could taste himself on Ben's lips. This fascinated him. As his breaths became rapid and shallow, Tobias felt possessed by an urgency for more. Taking Ben by the shoulders, he abruptly rolled Ben onto his back. Tobias pressed his body into Ben's as his hunger built. He could feel Ben squirm under him as their bodies moved against each other, each kiss harder and more urgent than the previous.

Feeling Ben's fingers run down his spine, Tobias was pulled in closer, more tightly, against his lover's body. The coolness of Ben's skin intoxicated him, driving his euphoria. Everything he was feeling, hearing, and seeing was new to him. Like a baby coming into the world, all senses had been breached. Tobias's body was responsive to every touch, and every breath Ben took deepened the link between them. Time stood still as the two feverishly kissed one another, only an occasional mew or whimper echoing between them.

Lost in his senses, it took Tobias a second to register that Ben's mutters were actually words—he had said something. Their kisses slowed, and Ben pulled back.

"Stand up." Ben quietly repeated as he wedged his arms between their bodies and pushed away. Suddenly pulling Tobias back, he kissed him again. "Stand up."

With the gentle persuasion of another kiss, Tobias complied with Ben's instructions, keeping his eyes on Ben as he did so. Ben quickly rose to his feet as well, standing within inches of Tobias. As their eyes locked onto one another, Ben worked to free Tobias of his tattered shirt. Within the silence of the grove, Tobias could hear Ben's breathing as he undid Tobias's last button and then slowly unsnapped the button on his britches.

"Oh, Tobias, you don't know how long I've waited for this, dreamt about it!" Ben lowered Tobias's britches, allowing him to step out of them.

Tobias stood naked, the light of the moon cast over his body. He had never been so far removed from himself as he was at this moment. He waited for Ben to lead him, his heart racing, his stomach fluttering; he could hardly breathe.

"Your body is so beautiful." Ben ran his hand through his own tousled hair, trying to keep it from obstructing his vision of Tobias.

Ben took half a step back. Dropping his suspenders from his shoulders, he freed himself of his shirt. Under a sky of stars that seemed to be raining on them, Ben stepped in for a kiss. Tobias's eyes closed as Ben's warm lips brushed across his mouth. That single kiss burned through Tobias like lightning striking a tree, yet he yearned for another.

"I love you," Ben whispered as he drew his lips back and rubbed his finger across his bottom lip to dry it. Ridding himself of his britches and underclothes, he took Tobias by the hand and silently steered the other boy down on top of him. A soft cry escaped from Ben as Tobias settled his weight on him. Finding each other's mouths, they kissed again as their naked bodies slid against each other. Protected by a forest of oak trees, the world escaped Tobias as he surrendered his soul to his lover.

Their hands exploring each other's bodies. Ben's skin was cool to the touch. Tobias couldn't get enough; it was all driving him to a point of no return. Within minutes, the two exploded into a wild and fierce state as their bodies moved against each other. With no space left between them, their hearts beat in harmony against each other's chests.

"I'm gonna, I'm gonna—" Ben cried.

With a molten wave of pleasure, everything seemed to explode at once as Tobias spilled between them. Simultaneously, Ben let out a strange cry as his nails clawed Tobias's back. Tobias could feel the contraction and twitch of Ben's member and could feel the arrival of added wetness between their compressed bodies.

Ben's entire body trembled several more times and then went still under him. Surely, Ben was still alive as was evident by the thumping of his heart against Tobias's chest.

Not wanting to move, Tobias hesitated before rolling off Ben. Easing onto his back, Tobias fought to catch his breath. His naked body spread across the quilt, and he ran his hands across it. The quilt was composed of the baby blanket and clothes that had once covered his lover as an infant. In silence, he looked up through the trees at a sea of stars as his breathing gradually returned to normal.

Ben stirred and then opened his eyes. Even in the obscure lighting, Tobias could see that those eyes were wild and dark. Smiling at Ben, Tobias ran his hand across his stomach and then held his fingers to his nose. "What is this?"

"What?" Ben's voice cracked as he cleared his throat.

Tobias held his fingers up to Ben's face. "This?"

"Are you kiddin' me? It's seed. You've never spilled?" Ben took Tobias's fingers and licked them. "How is that possible?"

"I think there is much for me to learn." Tobias watched as Ben gently licked his fingers clean and then smiled at him.

"Holy shit!" Ben rolled onto his side and lay against Tobias. "Have you ever heard the story of the birds and the bees?"

Tobias reached over and ran his hand down the side of Ben's body. He mapped in his mind the curve downward just past Ben's ribcage and the curve up again at his hip. Sliding his hand down and across Ben's butt, he found that he could cup it in one hand. He had no idea what Ben was talking about. Nothing was as important as the moment he was living in.

"Are you listening to me?" Ben smiled as Tobias continued to feel his soft, round ass.

Tobias released a heavy sigh as a smidgen of pain from his back brought him back into reality. He didn't know what had occurred between them; it had been almost animalistic. His mind raced to make some sense in all of this, of his relationship with this man next to him.

Lying still, he listened to Ben's breathing. It had turned into a light snore. For about an hour, Tobias lay there, not wanting to move for fear of waking Ben. His thoughts were everywhere. There was a feeling of joy, yet he was overwhelmed with guilt for feeling so happy. He missed his family. *Are they even alive?* Miss Gee-gee—had she known about him and Ben? Of course not. She had died before this started—or had she? *When did this start? What is this?* Everyone in the village back home knew of the relationship between the young man and the elder. Was this the same?

Hearing a delicate snore, Tobias turned to face his lover. Ben's slender body lay still in the night, shadows from the massive oak branches dancing across his naked body. Tobias's heart began to flutter again as desire surged within him. He knew Ben was asleep, but he couldn't deny himself. Touching Ben's shoulder, he gently ran his fingers down his arm and then back up across his chest. Ben mumbled as his body stirred, and his eyes opened. Without words, Tobias and Ben reunited. Their bodies and souls came together as they lay on their sides, facing each other. Ben pushed his hips up onto Tobias's body as they became alive again. That evening, for a second time, they made love to each other under the majestic oaks.

13

Miss Gee-gee had been gone almost a week when Charlie told Tobias that Harry and Stuart were going to be staying with him and Dolly. Niles and Harriett were too small for Charlie and Dolly to take in, and it looked like Master Lee was going to be selling them off to the Fisher farm by the end of the week.

"Now, Tobias, you know you can't stay up in that ole cabin by yourself. 'Bout time you move on into the cabin with the rest of the young fellas. Massa Lee talkin' 'bout rippin' that ole cabin down. Use the wood for somethin' else," Charlie told him.

Tobias had gone up to Charlie and Dolly's cabin to say good morning to the boys. "Yes, sir," he replied, upon hearing that he would have to move. He fought off a yawn as he thought of Ben. For the last three nights, he and Ben had been meeting under the oaks, making love, talking and sleeping. One morning, they had scurried off minutes before Dexter was scheduled to arrive for the day.

It was Sunday, a day of rest for the entire plantation. Tobias hung around Charlie's cabin until they left for church services. Tobias had attended once and thought the whole thing was foolish. *How could there be one God?* he wondered, as he contemplated what he was hearing. Now, Sundays had become his and Pearl's day to reconnect.

While most everyone was down at the old church a mile from the farm, Tobias and Pearl sat on the edge of the river out behind the cabins, with their feet down in the water. The water was cool as it ran across their feet and through their toes. They got a chance to see each other on Sundays since Pearl had started working the fields. She had about as much interest in church as Tobias did.

"So how you doin' with Momma gone? I must say, I can'ts believe she gone. The only momma I know," Pearl said softly.

Tobias had also struggled with the loss. But so much had changed for him since that day. "Yeah, me too. The cabin is so quiet these days." The truth was, he had spent little time in there, since taking to the oaks with Ben.

He watched as Pearl rubbed something that was sewn on the inside hem of her dress. "What's that?" he asked. Now that he thought about it, he had seen her rubbing it once before when they lived together.

Pearl looked up at him, stopping what she was doing in mid-rub. She flipped the hem back over, accidently letting it fall in the water. "Nothin," she replied.

"Come on, Pearl, I saw you playing with something. What is that in your dress? It's too late, I saw it," Tobias said, now more curious than ever.

Pearl averted eye contact. "You promise not to laugh?"

"Yeah, of course." He watched her.

"No, say it: I promise not to laugh!" Pearl demanded.

"Okay, I promise not to laugh." She reminded him so much of his little sister.

Pearl hiked up her dress and flipped over the hem, exposing the metal button. "Miss Gee-gee says this button came off my papa's jacket. Says it was in my hand the day I arrived here. Miss Gee-gee been sewin' it in my hems since I was a baby."

"Wow," Tobias said quietly. "I wish I had something of my mother's or father's. I'm starting to feel that I will never see them again. Is it hard for you to know that your momma and papa are down the road from you and you haven't never seen them?"

"No . . . I don't know them. Ain't never seen them. Miss Gee-gee's all I know to be my momma," Pearl said matter-of-factly.

"Can I see the button?" Tobias asked.

Pearl moved her dress over so that he could touch the metal button. She watched as he rubbed his fingers across it.

As he continued to rub the button, he released a heavy sigh. "I have to move in with Jonas, Rudo, Simba, and the guys."

"Why you move in there?" Pearl asked.

"Charlie told me that Master Lee is tearing down the old cabin. I have to move." Tobias didn't want to think about moving into the all-male cabin. "What's going on with you and Jonas? I see the way he looks at you." The last couple of weeks, he had noticed Jonas talking to Pearl twice. Both times, Pearl had been smiling at Jonas, and the two would laugh and giggle about whatever was being said. Tobias didn't like Jonas, and he figured that Jonas didn't like him either. On top of that, it didn't sit well with Tobias that Pearl was twelve and Jonas was almost twenty.

"I don't know. He says he likes me, but all he do is kiss me like a rabbit. I marry him if he ax me to." A smile appeared on her face and then vanished.

Tobias's mouth fell open. "You're too young to get married. You're twelve!"

Pearl shot back, "How ole you supposed to be?"

"Well, not twelve. You're too young to have children. And Jonas, he's ugly anyways. Why not Ikenna? He's the same age as you. Do you think Ikenna is handsome?" Tobias couldn't imagine Pearl kissing Jonas.

Pearl picked up a rock and tossed it in the water, "Nay, now he's ugly. He got funny little eyes way up high on his forehead." She laughed and then stopped, raising an eyebrow. "Jonas say you and Mr. Ben be off every day, all day, and you comes back lookin' likes you ain't done no work."

Tobias looked at her. "What does Jonas know? Just because I'm not dirty doesn't mean I'm not working. Sometimes, I'm as dirty as he is!" A flush of adrenaline tingled through his body. Tobias wanted to tell her the truth. It was safe. "He treats me good. Not like Master Lee treats you. I never told anybody . . . but we're friends, real friends, like you and I are."

"He ain't no friend. He your massa," Pearl replied.

Her words stabbed him in the gut. Embarrassed, he instantly regretted saying anything, and he changed the subject. He had been moments from telling her everything, confident she would understand.

That night, Tobias and Ben lay naked under the oaks, listening to the buzzing and clicking hum of the thousands of cicadas that made the trees their home. The sultry air that had been hanging around all day had followed them into the late night. Their bodies were drenched in sweat that worked as a lubricant during their midnight romp. Later, Ben snuggled under his arm, his breathing shallow, and Tobias soon wondered if he was asleep.

As they had not seen each other all day, the sex had been immediate tonight, the two tearing away their clothes as they pawed and kissed each other. It had been a long day for Tobias. In addition to being in a constant state of horniness, with thoughts of Ben at the forefront of his mind, he had also been grieving throughout the day. The loss of Miss Gee-gee had made the absence of his family more pronounced, and this made him feel guilty about wanting to be with Ben. He hadn't seen flames every time he closed his eyes, or heard the sound of his people crying as the village burned. When those images did occupy his thoughts, he felt guilty at his relief that they were not constant.

"You're quiet tonight. Are you okay?" Ben asked, as he nestled himself under Tobias's arm.

"I thought you were asleep." Tobias had been enjoying the feeling of Ben's small frame wrapped in his arm and the sounds he made when he breathed. It brought closeness to him, as if they were one.

"No. Just enjoyin' layin' here." Ben breathed deeply. "What are you thinkin' about?"

Tobias's arm was going numb. "Um, about home, my mother." His voice trailed off as he pulled his arm out from under Ben's body.

Ben sat up and lightly kissed him, twice, on his bottom lip. "You never talk about her. I feared asking about her—I didn't know if I could. The guilt kills me at times. You not bein' with your family, and me wantin' you all to myself. I know that's not fair to you." Ben brushed the long strands of hair out of his face and then ran his hands through the top of his hair several times, trying to comb it into place with his fingers.

Tobias intentionally changed the subject. "I talked to Charlie this morning. He said they're tearing down the cabin."

"Oh?"

"He said I have to move into the men's cabin." Tobias watched as Ben twirled a lock of hair from his bangs down in front of his eyes.

"Who's in there? There's a lot of people in there... right?" Still trying to get comfortable, Ben folded and then unfolded his legs before stretching out on his stomach facing Tobias.

"Yes." Tobias reflected on his conversation with Pearl—what Jonas had said to her about how Tobias was never dirty. Jonas was watching him. He didn't know if he should say anything to Ben about it; it could anger him, change the mood, and he just wanted to lie there and enjoy the moment. Silence filled the air as Tobias softly caressed Ben's shoulders and stared down his back to Ben's ass. He liked Ben's ass. It was small but solid: all muscle. "I saw Dexter staring at us the other day. Do you suppose he knows something?" The question seemed more ominous after he asked it.

"I seen him too. He might. I don't know." Ben reached out and laid his hand on Tobias's thigh. "I forgot to tell you about the other day. The day we were workin' down on the river. When we came back, Dexter asked me if we had run into any trouble."

Tobias went rigid. "What'd you tell him?"

"I didn't tell him nothin'. Told him to stay out my business. He's fixin' to get one from me if he don't. I didn't think about it at the time, but I reckon he may have been fishin'. We have to be careful, that's all." Ben's hand moved further up Tobias's leg, gently stroking his thigh. "If you move into that cabin, they'll know that you're leavin' at night. We have to think of somethin'."

Tobias hadn't thought about that. He couldn't imagine a night without Ben. These past couple of nights had been absolutely the best of his life.

By the end of the week, Tobias had settled into the men's cabin. There was no bed or mattress for him there. He had given the mattresses in his old cabin to Charlie for the boys. This forced him to take to the floor of the men's cabin with just his blanket. He and Ben hadn't had any time alone for the last two days, and he knew that if Ben touched him right, he would explode in his underclothes.

Yesterday, at the end of the day, Ben had told Tobias to meet him at the stables on Sunday after supper, explaining that there wouldn't be anyone there on a Sunday evening.

Counting down the minutes, Tobias sat in the middle of cabin row, surrounded by people who had gathered to celebrate Rudo and Laura jumping the broom earlier that day. Laura was pregnant, and she and Rudo were expecting their first child.

The banjo player kicked up the music, signifying that the party had officially begun. Several people were dancing around the fire pit as others laughed and talked around them. The women were busy with the community meal, which was just about ready. Tobias sat taking it all in. There were so many similarities to a party at home, yet the scene was not familiar at all.

Pearl came over, pulled him into the dance circle, and attempted to show him how to keep rhythm with the banjo. Stomping his feet like he thought the rest were doing, he saw Penny talking to a man under the old oak tree. "Who is that?" he asked Pearl.

"Who is who?' Pearl responded.

"With Penny. Sitting over there, under the tree," Tobias whispered as he tried to watch his feet.

Pearl glanced over her shoulder. "That's her husband, Samuel."

"Penny's married? How come I've never seen him?" Tobias asked, as he lost the timing of the banjo.

"Master Lee sold him to the Sebo Farm after they were married. Say he didn't give them permission to marry. He couldn't sell Penny because he loved her cooking, so he got rid of Samuel. That's why she's so mean to everyone. He visits her a couple times a year. He stay right down the road." Pearl huffed, trying to catch her breath as she danced and gossiped at the same time.

Later that night, Tobias seized his first chance to escape to the stables. Seeing Charlie still at the party made Tobias sure that he wouldn't be anywhere around the stables that evening. Ben was waiting for Tobias inside, and they made their way up a wooden narrow ladder to the hayloft. Ben spread out a blanket that he had taken from the house, pulled off his boots and overalls, and was naked within seconds.

Tobias looked around the tiny crawl space. Neither of them could stand up in there; the rafters every few feet made it look even smaller than it was. "Why are we up here?" Tobias whispered. He knew that if Charlie caught them, not even Ben would be able to save him from what Master Lee might do. As much as he liked Charlie, Tobias didn't trust him. He was too close to Master Lee.

Ben crawled on his knees closer to Tobias. "We can't be out there. There're too many people still up. It's a full moon tonight, plus their fire. Somebody might see us in the oaks." Ben tugged on Tobias's drawstring, trying to undo the knot. "What's wrong?"

Tobias's eyes dropped to Ben's erection, which was standing at attention. "I worry someone will hear us." He wanted nothing more than to make love, but it seemed so risky with so many people still up and outside. They were so close that he could hear the music.

Ben undid the knot and worked to get Tobias out of his britches, slipping them down over his butt. "Stop worryin', I saw Charlie drinkin' up a storm with Simba and Mosses. He ain't comin' in here. Ain't no reason to. The blacksmith shop is all closed up too, so he's done for the night." Ben gave Tobias a kiss. "Come on," he begged, leaning back onto the blanket. "I'm as randy as a drunk rooster in a chicken coop."

Staring into Ben's dark, solemn eyes, Tobias smiled and conceded. Removing his shirt, he lay next to Ben on the blanket. At first, as they kissed, Tobias listened for any unfamiliar sounds around them. But within minutes, the feel of Ben's naked body ignited the hunger that had been building in him all evening.

Later, the two laid entangled in each other's arms as they quietly tried to regain control of their breathing. Limited in his movement, Tobias remained on top of his lover. The wetness between them, a sweet mixture of semen and sweat, allowed their bodies to slide effortlessly against each other. Tobias gently kissed the salt from Ben's slender neck. With the touch of Tobias's lips, Ben rolled his neck and he released a low whimper. Closing his eyes, he fell into a light sleep.

Tobias must have fallen asleep as well. He awakened to Ben maneuvering his body on top of him. Opening his eyes, he knew that Ben's impish smile meant he was ready to go again.

Lightly stroking the back of Ben's head, Tobias ran his fingers through his hair as the rhythmic movements of Ben's hips stirred his senses.

"Do you know how to . . . poke?" Ben whispered into his ear. "I want you to poke me."

The sensation of Ben's mouth as it lightly nibbled on Tobias's ear was maddening. Although Tobias had never done anything like that, the two had skirted and flirted around the possibility a couple of days ago, when Ben took Tobias's finger and inserted it into him as their bodies grinded against one another. Tobias knew this pleasured Ben, most times sending him over the edge immediately.

"Are you sure?" Tobias grew more excited at the thought.

"Yes, I want to feel you inside of me. All of you." Again, Ben nibbled and kissed the lobes of his ear.

In their tiny space, Tobias slid to one side, allowing Ben to move under him and roll onto his stomach. Their bodies meshed, Tobias's erection pressing against Ben's back as he slid into position. Raising his hips, Tobias took hold of himself as he mentally mapped out where he was going. Slowly lowering his body, he was met with resistance. Ben was tight. Pushing with a little more force, he entered him.

Within seconds, Ben let out a squeal as his entire body sprang upward and then to the side, escaping from under Tobias.

"What happened, are you alright?" Frightened, Tobias watched as Ben moaned in pain. "Did I do that?"

Ben didn't answer as he gritted his teeth and blew out air from his mouth. His eyes closed as he puffed, trying to breathe. His body continued to twist as he gasped for air. "That hurt like the dickens!" He moaned. "What did you do?"

"I didn't do anything. I tried to put *it* in your rump, and that's when you screamed. Did it hurt?"

"Hell yea, it did!" Ben shrieked.

"How do people do it if it hurts?" Tobias asked.

"Stop talkin', Tobias, please!" Ben muttered.

After a couple of minutes, Ben was able to breathe normally. When a small grin appeared on his face, Tobias knew he was going to be okay.

Sitting up in the loft, they had about two feet of space above their heads. The music had stopped outside. Tobias peeked through a crack in one of the boards to look for any sign of life. The glow of the fire had vanished. However, he knew better than to discount the possibility that someone might be walking about.

"Can you see anythin'?" Ben asked.

"No, not really, but it looks like the celebration's over." Tobias relaxed by Ben's side. "I'm sorry I hurt you."

"I didn't know it would hurt like that." Ben rubbed his buttocks again.

Tobias laughed as he replayed the scene in his head. "I've never seen you jump like that. You damn near threw me down to the ground. I'm sorry."

"It's not that funny. It hurt." Ben breathed a deep sigh.

"Maybe we can't do it like other people do," Tobias whispered.

"We can try it again . . . but not tonight." Ben flashed a half-smile that looked more like a grimace.

Tobias took a deep breath and slowly released it. "I wish I understood all of this. You, me, what this is." He gently kissed Ben as he drew in his breath.

Ben returned the kiss. "What's there to understand? I love you. Not bein' able to have relations don't change that." Ben pulled back and tilted his head slightly. "What's wrong?"

"Nothing." Tobias lied. His heart was heavy; so much was weighing on his mind. The last thing he wanted was to bring down the mood with his insecurities.

"No. I felt somethin'. In that kiss, you weren't there. What's wrong?" Ben placed his hand on the side of Tobias's face and caressed it lightly. "What is it?"

A thickness grew in Tobias's throat. Cupping his hand over Ben's, he forced a smile. "I love the feeling I have when I'm with you, but I don't know your world. There is still much for me to learn. I'm a slave in this world, and you are my—"

"Hush now! Don't say it!" Ben tried to keep his voice low. "You are more to me than a slave! We can leave! Head up north where no one knows us. Where negroes are free."

There was a churning in Tobias's stomach. There had been times he regretted not running when Obi ran, but he had never thought it was an option to leave with Ben. The thought of going anywhere besides back home took him by surprise. Until now, it was the only thing he had considered. He knew, though, that Ben could not live in Tobias's world either. "Are you saying that we would be together? Live somewhere else? Could you leave? This is your home."

He and Ben had never actually had a conversation about Obi running. However, he had gathered from bits and pieces of conversation that Dexter had only spent a day searching the immediate area before turning the hunt over to professional slave catchers. Could it really be that easy to vanish? Others talked about running and being caught as if it was a death sentence. Was it impossible? Had Obi been successful, or was his body lying dead in the woods somewhere, rotting or being eaten by animals, never to be found?

Ben's eyebrows arched as he shook his head. "This is not my home. Neither of us belong here. I have too much love for you to contain it, to keep it a secret, all bottled up inside. To continue like this, it's . . . it's too much."

Tobias listened and tried to make sense of it. He had spent months out at sea on that ship. Could he escape and not go home? "I guess all I ever thought about was returning home. One day seeing my family again." There was a tug in his stomach.

"What are you sayin'?" Ben's eyes widened.

Tobias couldn't hold back a sigh as he searched for something to say. Ben was ready to give it all up for him. How could Tobias let him do it if he wasn't going to stay here in America once he was free? He saw the nervousness in Ben eyes. Seconds ago, Ben had told him that he loved him, yet all Tobias was thinking about was finding a way home. He turned away from Ben as he spoke. "It's late. We need to talk about all of this in the morning, when our heads are clear."

The sad look on Ben's face as he hastily departed was obvious. The plan was for Ben to leave first; Tobias would wait, ensuring that the coast was clear before he left. He knew Ben was hurt, he had seen it in his eyes. Their conversation was unfinished. How could he deny Ben, his love for Ben, a life that makes sense? He had seen with his own eyes his village burning, his little sister struggling in the arms of a kidnapper. There was no village to go back to. But he had been unwilling to face that thought until now.

The walls were closing in on him as he waited. He tried repeatedly to moisten his throat by swallowing, but his mouth was too dry. He waited as long as he could before he hurried down the ladder, his sudden movement frightening the horses and sending them into a fluster.

"Shhh, easy girl, it's just me. Sorry about that." He froze as the two horses whinnied and thrashed about in their stalls. He approached them and held out his hand for them to smell. "That's it girl, it's just me. See, nothing's going to get you," he whispered, trying to calm them. Once they appeared to have settled, he fled the stable, forgetting the need to be careful. The air choked him; it felt as if someone's hands were around his throat. He had to sit down.

As he sat up against the backside of the stables, the moon cast enough light that he could see the slave quarters. He couldn't go back there tonight. There was no place there for him but a floor. At least out here, he could think. Drawing his knees up into his chest, he made himself smaller. Ben had offered to go somewhere where they could be together. If Ben *was* to be his protector, he should listen to what Ben and the Gods were telling him. He knew better than to question the Gods.

Tobias's hair rose on the back of his neck. He wanted to go to Ben and tell him yes, he would go with him; yes, he loved him; and yes, they belonged together. His heart sank with the knowledge that it would have to wait until morning, a lifetime away.

14

The Lee family and Dexter sat at the breakfast table, waiting for Penny to bring in the morning meal. As usual, Emmett and Dexter discussed politics and the day's events. Ben had hardly slept a wink the past night. He had offered Tobias a life away from here, and he had been rejected. His life was bleaker than ever, his heart broken. He couldn't forget the look on Tobias's face when he suggested that they run. Ben took a sip of his coffee, avoiding eye contact with Dexter. This morning, avoiding interaction with Dexter would be vital to his keeping it together. Just the sound of the man's voice made Ben want to slice his throat right there at the table. He rubbed his thumb over his knife. It could be over in a second, and Dexter would bleed out right there on the floor.

"You know, Dexter," said Emmett, "I thought that the five acres we switched over from corn to hemp this year was going to save us." Master Lee's voice was booming as he and Dexter talked about the farm's latest financial problems. "That corn out there ain't fit to sell to a northerner. Ah, shit, I tell you . . . I was thinkin', we should take that slave Rudo and stud him for some extra cash. How many brood-mares do we have?"

Dexter's eyes turned up as though the answer was on the ceiling. "We have three, but ain't much left of Sarah—maybe two, max three babies from her. How many you thinkin'?"

"The way I look at it, if he does one each from them over the next five years, that's fifteen heads I ain't got to pay for." Emmett tapped his fingers on the table as he eyed Penny, who had just entered the room.

"Sir." Penny politely placed a plate of potatoes, eggs, and ham in front of Emmett.

Emmett never looked at her. "I think I've seen his wife is with child, so that makes sixteen. Let Rudo know that, if he can deliver me twenty heads, he will have earned his freedom. Five more, and Laura can go too." Emmett removed his napkin from the table and laid it in his lap.

Ben glanced over at his mother, who was quietly eating. *How can they sit here and talk about people as if they're animals?* He shot a look at Dexter but turned away when Dexter caught his stare.

After a couple of minutes, Emmett wiped his mouth clean with his napkin and leaned forward in his chair. "But for right now, looks like we should plan on selling off six or seven young males that will fetch a good price. Need to take them to the auction house before winter sets in. See if we can get seven hundred a piece for them. That should help us get through next year. If we have a good year, we can replace them."

"Well, sir, I think that's a good idea. I will look at them this afternoon while they're in the field," Dexter responded.

"Ben, I know you ain't goin' to be happy, but Dexter tells me that one that you purchased still ain't worth a damn." Emmett crossed his arms over his chest and looked directly at Ben. "I need to sell it too, since you ain't been able to do nothin' with it. Sell him while he's lookin' fat and healthy."

Ben's heart leaped into his throat. Had he heard what he thought he'd heard? "But Pa, he's mine, and I ain't selling him!" Ben heard his tone and tried to make it sound less defiant. But selling Tobias was not an option.

"Boy, now you listen here to me. You be lucky to get your money back out of that negro. He has to be sold . . . He ain't a playmate!"

Emmett paused. His face was tight as he stared down Ben. "Frankly, son . . . you're a little old for a playmate. That negro ought to be in the fields by now." He threw his napkin onto the table and leaned back. "Dexter, see that he is taken with the others to sell."

Ben couldn't believe what he was hearing. He wanted to say more, but the severity in his father's tone told him that he dared not continue. *Tobias will not be sold. That can't happen.* Ben looked up to see Dexter's shrewd grin. Feeling the table for his knife, Ben stared back at him and forced himself to stay planted in his seat. His eyes locked on Dexter's throat. He could slice it before anyone knew what was happening. If he was going to be damned to hell, it might as well be for a good reason.

He had to warn Tobias. He was to be sold before winter. That could be anytime. He had to think of a way to change his father's mind, and he needed time to come up with a plan. He couldn't lose Tobias, even if Tobias didn't want him. His appetite was gone. He wanted to excuse himself, but Dexter was watching him. His gut said that, somehow, Dexter was behind this. Ben had to go to Tobias. He had to convince him to run, for them to leave together.

It was an hour before Ben was able to meet Tobias. He found Tobias waiting for him in front of the smokehouse, just like every other morning. But his stomach told him that this was far from any other morning.

"Good morning," Tobias said.

Ben detected elation in Tobias's voice, and this threw him off. After the way they had left things last night, Tobias seemed too excited, his energy bizarre.

"Good mornin'," Ben answered as he walked passed him. "Let's get this wagon loaded. We got some fencin' that needs tendin' to on the south end."

Within minutes, they had the wagon loaded with the needed supplies and had attached an old gray mare to the front of it.

"Are you ridin' or walkin'?" Ben asked as he pulled himself up into the driver's seat.

Tobias chuckled and shook his head. Ben knew he was laughing at him, but he didn't care. He had to get them away so they could talk.

As soon as they were far enough from the house, Ben slowed the mare to a walk. He rolled his jaw muscles, trying to loosen them, as he mentally ran through what he had to say.

Drawing a long breath, he exhaled and cleared his throat. "Pa is plannin' on selling you this winter. He's in trouble with money and lookin' to sell off a couple of slaves plus you. I tried, Tobias, I swear I tried to talk him out of it. We have to run. Now I don't know what you were thinkin' last night, but we got to go up north, where you will be free." Ben brought the wagon to a stop. He knew he had to convince Tobias to listen to him. Last night's conversation had not been at all what he thought it would be. He thought he had offered up the perfect solution for both of them, and it had been rejected. In Tobias's silence, Ben wondered what Tobias was thinking. It occurred to him that Tobias might think he was lying—making a deceitful attempt to convince him to leave.

Ben pushed on. "I hears things from Dexter. How he catches 'em. We know what not to do. We can outsmart them and turn their own game around on them. We ain't got much time. We can head to the Mason-Dixon Line and be free in Pennsylvania." He tried to read Tobias's face. "Damn it, Tobias, tell me what I ought to do. I got one foot in the grave and one foot waitin' on you! You say this ain't never goin' to be your home. I sure in the dickens don't have no attachment to it neither, so say somethin'! " Ben's mind raced as he waited for Tobias's answer. The silence was earthshattering.

"What's the Mason-Dixon Line?" Tobias smiled. "How far is it?"

Ben smiled back as a sense of euphoria washed over him. "Ain't far by wagon, I reckon a couple days." He could hardly contain himself. "We can leave right now. Keep on goin'!"

"Slow down, let me think!" Tobias said.

For Ben, there was no need to wait. "Wait for what?"

"We need a plan." Tobias's voice was a few octaves higher than usual.

Ben repositioned himself and snapped the reins. "Giddy up, girl." Tobias was right; they needed a plan. They worked in silence for most of the day as Ben ran through various scenarios in his head, working out the details.

That evening, Tobias and the guys from his cabin cooked catfish that they had caught in the river. After dinner, other slaves joined them around the fire to tell stories. As long as they kept the noise down, and as long as they were in the field by dawn, Master Lee didn't much mind how long they stayed up.

Pearl walked up next to Tobias, her face gloomy. "Hey, Pearl." He smiled at her in hopes of getting a smile back.

"Hello, Tobias. Have you seen Jonas? I need to talk to him."

"He and Simba walked over to Mr. Charlie's." Tobias pointed towards the blacksmith's shop. "They said they would be right back." He paused long enough to redirect his train of thought. "Can I talk to you about something?"

He stood and brushed off the seat of his britches. Leading Pearl away from the fire, he waited until they were too far away to be overheard. "Me and Ben are thinking about running. Escaping to the north, where I can be free. He said he would take me there. Master Lee is planning on taking me to auction before winter. That could be any day, so we don't have long." The two continued to walk side by side.

"Why he sell you?" Pearl's voice escalated.

"Shhh." Ignoring her question, Tobias used his hands to ask her to lower her voice. "Can I tell you something else?" He paused, not sure he should say what he was about to say. "Ben and I have fondness for each other. We want to be together."

Pearl stopped walking. "What do you mean, together? He your massa."

"No, Pearl, he told me that he loves me. Do you love Jonas? It's the same for us."

Pearl's face frowned. "You both are boys. Ain't never heard of two boys loving each other."

"I know of someone who lives with a man. He is his protector, but they live as man and wife. It is as the Gods wanted." Tobias watched Pearl, trying to gauge whether he should continue talking. Perhaps he had said too much.

"But he beats you." Pearl's voice, again, was too loud.

"No, he didn't. That was Dexter. Ben could never lay a hand on me. We have to leave soon. We're thinking of a plan. What do you know about running?" He studied her eyes once more. "You can't tell anyone, not even Jonas. He's good friends with Charlie, and I don't trust Charlie."

They stood at the end of the row of cabins, two figures in the dark. "What are you goin' to do? You have to follow the North Star. It will take you to freedom, they say."

"What's the North Star?" Tobias asked.

Pearl looked up and pointed. "There! That's the North Star, right there! Summer's almost over, you have to wait. You can't run in the winter, won't be able to see the star but on a clear night. You have to wait until spring, when the snow melts and the sky is clear."

"But I don't have that long," Tobias snapped.

"Then you have to change that. If you real sick right now, likes you about to die, ain't nobody goin' want you. Massa Lee goin' have to wait until spring. I reckon it take you that long tills you well again." Pearl's eyes were wide as she held up a finger in Tobias's face. "You gets what I am saying?"

Tobias got it. He would use his breathing troubles to make him appear much sicker than he was. They would have all winter to plan and work out the details, and they could run first thing in the spring, before the auction house re-opened. A weight had been lifted from him, and he half-listened as Pearl ran down a list of things he should do to get ready.

15

B en and Tobias put their plan into operation the next day. At the dinner table that night, Ben let it be known in casual conversation that Tobias had taken ill again and was losing a lot of weight. He described how Tobias didn't look good, and he was glad to cut his losses and get a new slave before winter.

Emmett nodded his head as he listened to him. "You know Ben, I think you're right. That negro has been nothin' but a waste of good money. You likely to lose all your money if you carry him down to the auction house sick, though. We ain't never sold a sick slave. Negroes comin' out of here is fit, strong, and a good purchase for someone else. He should be startin' to push a plow. I think we should hold off on him until spring. If we wait, we can get a couple hundred dollars more for him, I think."

Ben hid his excitement. He couldn't believe that his pa had taken the bait so easily. Now, Ben would have to keep Tobias out of sight over the winter. It was common knowledge that Ben hated the cold and rarely left the house after the first storm. Between using the cold as an excuse not to go out and Tobias being sick, things could appear mostly normal—like he had gone back to his lazy ways.

As the weeks passed, Ben and Tobias hashed out their plan. They saw less and less of each other as Tobias took ill more frequently. Finding pokeweed, Tobias had collected the small purple berries from the plant and stashed them in a cloth under his bedding. He ate small numbers of the nasty tasting berries, which kept him feeling like he was going to vomit at any moment. Because he was so sick, one of the men in the cabin took pity on him and offered his mattress in exchange for Tobias's tiny floor space next to the door. Being sick, Tobias asked those around him to tell him stories. Specifically, he was interested in hearing about freedom.

Unknowingly, they told him about the North Star and how it led those that escaped to freedom. Those that had been caught and returned shared stories of their journeys, whether they had been on the run for days or weeks. He heard, over and over, that some of the biggest concerns were the hounds' ability to track someone and the harsh punishments inflicted on those who were caught.

Using a numbering system that he and Ben created, every ten days, Tobias knew to stop eating the berries. Within a few days, his nausea would dissipate, and that allowed him to get up, do some work for a couple of days, and check in with Ben.

One morning, Ben sent word down to the cabin that he needed him to return to work.

They met in the stable. "How are you feelin'?" Ben looked around before placing a quick kiss on Tobias's lips. Leaning back, he propped one foot against a stall.

"Awful." Tobias leaned against him for another kiss. This time, it was slow. As their lips mingled, Tobias savored the tangy scent of Ben's breath. He missed Ben's kisses, his touch, being in his presence every day. These last ten days had been especially rough due to a near-overdose of berries. Several days ago, Tobias had realized that he must have eaten a berry that was more toxic than the others had been. Within minutes, the pain in his stomach had increased, along with a burning sensation in his mouth.

"I worry about you. If this is safe, what we're doin'." Ben's erection, still in his britches, bumped against Tobias's thigh.

Tobias reached down and gave him a light squeeze. "I see someone is feeling . . . what is the word you used, *randy?*" Tobias wanted to make love as well, but there was no way his stomach would agree. "Don't worry. I know what I'm doing." He could never tell Ben how sick he had really been these past few days. "I wish we could play, but my stomach is still a little upset. Do you mind? Maybe tomorrow, we can go somewhere." He forced a suggestive grin to validate his words.

Ben kissed him again before responding. "Okay, but I have a surprise for you when we do." His smoldering eyes made Tobias's heart skip a beat. Whatever Ben's surprise was, he was up to no good. Second-guessing his decision not to have sex, Tobias stepped back. He needed separation to restrain himself.

"What have you been up to since we last talked?" he asked, wiping his lips dry.

"I've been able to swipe a few more dollars from Pa's stash. Got us a map and found out pa wants me to ride into Myrtleville with him in two days. Taking four—" Ben stopped.

"It's okay, you don't have to say it." Tobias knew that they must be heading to the auction house. Visions of that cell rushed back: the smell of vomit, sweat, and urine that had taken days to leave his nostrils. He sighed, more to clear his nose than anything else. "Are you going to go?"

"Rather not, but I reckon I ain't got much choice." Ben avoided eye contact.

Tobias attempted to fill the void with conversation. "Tell me again where we're going. What's it like?"

"Pennsylvania. I ain't never been, but I hear we can buy land, a farm. We about to elect a new president. It happens in that there state. Don't know who it's goin' to be, don't much care. Hear folks up there don't think like we do down here. Got what they call Quakers, and they're passin' laws tryin' to end slavery. Be a nice place for us to settle." Ben walked over to the door and peeked out before returning. "Take us a little while to get there. A couple of weeks."

Elections and presidents meant nothing to Tobias. He had really been asking about the landscape and terrain. Thoughts of returning home flitted in and out of his mind as his eyes followed Ben. He even entertained the crazy notion of his family coming to him and Ben. They would all, somehow, live in Pennsylvania. Tobias's stomach rumbled as he watched Ben, who paced the floor as he talked.

"I have to find your papers. Case we're stopped, I can prove that you belong to me. You ain't no runaway. Pa got them in his office . . . somewhere."

"Yes, I belong to you." Tobias repeated.

Ben looked up at Tobias as he chewed on his thumbnail. "You know what I mean." His cheeks were blushed.

They spent the next two hours up in the loft. Tobias lay with his head in Ben's lap and described his life in Africa. Ben's back was propped up against one of the rafters, which gave him a bird's eye view if anyone was to come in, which no one ever did. The two talked in low whispers until suppertime.

As usual, Tobias waited for several minutes after Ben left before he made his departure. As he walked towards the cabins, his stomach moaned. This time, it was asking for food. He hadn't eaten all day. Sure that he could get a meal at Charlie and Dolly's, he walked towards their cabin. It had been awhile since he saw the boys, and it would be nice to visit them.

"Tobias, Tobias!"

Tobias looked over his shoulder and saw that Pearl was walking towards him. "Oh, hey, Pearl. How are you?" He had wanted to talk to her, but he hadn't seen much of her during the past month. He needed to be sure that she hadn't said anything to anybody about what she knew. She was the weak link in their plan.

He waited for her to catch up to him and reached out to give her a hug. Then he saw that she was crying. "Is everything alright?" he asked.

"I'm goin' have a baby." Pearl stopped and wrapped her arms around her middle. "Jonas say it ain't his, but he the only man I been with, and I knows I ain't the Virgin Mary."

"Oh, no." Tobias's heart sank. She was a child herself. "When, when did it happen? When is the baby coming?"

"We do it one time. About two months ago. It hurt so bad, I won't let him do it again."

Tobias looked at her stomach. Now that he knew she was with child, he could tell that her tiny belly was slightly extended. His appetite disappeared. "It's going to be alright." Placing one hand around her shoulder, he brought her body in close to his and wrapped her in his arms.

Despondent, he returned to his cabin. When he arrived, Jonas was sitting on the porch talking to some of the other fellas. Tobias could hardly look at him as he stepped passed them. With his green eyes and light skin, people said that Jonas was mixed, but no one actually knew since they didn't know where he had come from. Tobias thought that he was arrogant and full of himself.

The next day, Tobias met Ben bright and early in front of the smokehouse. A second good night of rest had done his body some good. Other than his hunger, his spirits were good, and he couldn't wait to see the one person that always brightened his mood. As Tobias approached, Ben had his back turned and was looking down towards the field. Tobias eyed the gunmetal-colored britches that Ben was wearing. They were one of Tobias's favorites on him; the way they hugged his buttocks made both cheeks appear nice and round. The fabric clung to his thighs as they tapered down his legs, showing off his solid build. A surge of desire told Tobias that he was definitely feeling better this morning.

Ben turned as Tobias reached him. His eyes were wide, and he tucked his hands in his pockets. "Be careful, Dexter's watchin' us." Ben shifted his eyes to one side.

Tobias glanced over and was met with Dexter's stare. Looking away, Tobias's shoulders tensed. "Why's he watching us?" he whispered—as if Dexter could hear anything at two hundred yards away.

"Dunno. Come on, let's get going." Ben walked towards the flat-bed wagon, which was hitched and ready to go. "We'll head on down by the river before the weather turns and it gets too cold to swim."

The cool water sounded good this morning, though Tobias knew nothing about swimming. He had been in the water enough that, as long as he hung close to the bank, he was okay. "Think he'll follow us?" Tobias allowed Ben to climb up first and take hold of the reins before climbing up next to him.

"No, they got plenty to do today."

"Are you still going to Myrtleville tomorrow?" Tobias asked as he braced for the wagon to move.

"Yep."

Tobias took note of Ben's clipped answer. It was clear that he didn't want to talk. There was so much about Ben that Tobias didn't understand, but one thing he knew was that Ben didn't like to think and talk at the same time.

In under an hour, Ben slowed the wagon. He surveyed the river and the surrounding terrain. "River forks off just up yonder. It should be slow here, not too deep for you. Pulling back on the reins, he brought the wagon to a stop about four feet from the embankment.

"We can head down right here. I packed us some vittles in case we get hungry." Ben dismounted and walked up next to the grey mare. "You want to hang out and eat some grass, ole girl?" He worked to free her from the wagon. "All I ask is you whinny if you see or hear somethin', okay, girl?" He tapped her a couple of times around the base of her neck. The mare took a couple of steps forward and looked around. "Go on, girl, you on your own."

As if in understanding, the horse whinnied a couple of times before moseying along in search of lunch.

Tobias jumped down off the wagon. Straightening his back, he stared at the river. From where he was standing, the water looked to be barely moving, and if he had to guess, the river stretched maybe twenty-five yards across. With the sun directly over them, he could tell that it was going to be a warm day, a good day to spend at the river. Birds sang playfully. Looking up into the trees, he saw several cardinals jumping from branch to branch. This particular type of bird enthralled him: the vibrant red feathers that made up their tiny bodies and their black faces. It was the most beautiful bird in this harsh world. It signaled hope for him—that he too would survive this, that life was beautiful. They had been given wings so that they could spread joy and make others feel good.

"Why are you just standing there smiling? Ready to head down?" Ben asked as he grabbed a sack from the wagon.

Tobias turned his attention from the birds. With a sense of calm— something he hadn't felt in days—he followed Ben as they made their way down the steep, grassy embankment. Reaching the water, Ben stripped completely naked. "Well, are you goin' to stand there, or are you comin' in?"

Tobias couldn't take his eyes off Ben's beautiful figure. His upper body was a golden brown with an abrupt tan line that stopped at his waist. How had Tobias not noticed that distinctive color contrast before? He felt his body responding to the sight of Ben's nakedness.

Ben didn't wait for an answer. He stepped off the shore and into the water. "Brr, it's cold!"

Tobias watched as Ben hunched his shoulders and slowly submerged himself. With his hands out to his sides for balance, Ben kept moving, going far enough out that the water was around his neck. "Tobias, get in here!"

This was the last thing Tobias heard before Ben's head dipped below the water. Tobias's mouth fell open at Ben's disappearance. Before he could react, however, Ben resurfaced, popping up and spitting water from his mouth.

Tobias, still fully clothed, raised an eyebrow. "Do you remember that I can't swim?" The thought had never occurred to him that going to the river meant actually getting into the water.

Ben paddled lightly back to the shore. Arriving at Tobias's feet, he remained on his stomach as his pale buttocks and legs floated behind him. The sight of Ben, with the water lapping up around his ass, was the sexiest thing Tobias had ever seen. Like two biscuits smothered in grease gravy, it made his mouth water.

With a charge of excitement, Tobias began working on the buttons of his shirt. "I can't swim."

"Don't worry, I have you. It's deep in the middle." Ben smiled as he arched his rear out of the water.

Tobias couldn't stop staring at Ben's beauty. Ben's long, curly hair was now completely straight as the weight of the water draped it around his face and neck. His golden tan shimmered as the water dribbled off his exposed skin. Tobias released another heavy sigh as he freed himself of his shirt.

Kicking off his shoes, Tobias paused. "Is it cold?"

"It's nice once you get in," Ben said, keeping his eyes on him.

Tobias drew in a deep breath, released it, and then removed his britches and undergarment. Completely naked, he felt the air brush against him, calming his body.

Ben backed up, giving Tobias room to enter the water. Slowly, Tobias placed one foot in the water, froze, and removed it. "It's cold!"

"Damn it, Tobias, quit being a sissy. Get that big dick in here!" Ben paddled on his back a little further out.

Tobias put his foot back in the water. "Can I just jump in?" he asked. Taking several quick breaths, he threw himself into the river, landing where the water was about four feet deep.

"What the hell are you doin'?" Ben laughed as he moved closer.

Tobias appeared to be hyperventilating as he popped up, his eyes as wide as saucers. Laughing even harder, Ben took him by the hand. "Calm down, you ain't goin' drown. See, you can stand up here."

Tobias got his legs underneath himself, planting his feet firmly in the soil. The water was freezing, sending tremors through his body.

"It ain't cold. Why you shakin'?" Ben moved in under Tobias's arms and pressed their bodies together. Seeing Ben's naked body sent a sexual charge through Tobias, taking his mind off the temperature of the water.

With a naughty smile, Ben gently kissed him. "See, it's not cold," he cooed softly. Wrapping his legs around Tobias's waist, he floated on his back, allowing his fully engorged manhood to come to the surface. He said nothing as his mischievous grin and his erection said it all.

Reaching out, Tobias almost took Ben in his hand. But Ben was too quick, kicking away from him and stopping just out of his reach. "Nope, not so fast, mister." Ben rolled over and swam further away.

Tobias watched, noting that the water was no longer cold. He wanted to follow Ben but was afraid of losing his balance and going under. Ben's body moved about in the water, occasionally dipping completely under, his buttocks sparkling before they disappeared. Oh, the nasty thoughts Tobias was having—if only he could get to Ben.

The two splashed and played in the river for over an hour, occasionally coming together to exchange kisses. In low voices, they talked about their life in the future. It was more than Tobias had ever thought he would have, even back at home. The uncertainty that he had once faced seemed like a lifetime ago.

"Are you hungry? I brought some food." Ben had returned to Tobias's arms, wrapping his legs around his waist to keep him affixed.

"Very." Tobias smiled as he eyed the water cascading around Ben's nipples.

Ben smacked him on his chest. "No, that comes later. I meant for food."

On the shore, they lay on their sides facing one another, eating from the pickles, apples, and the massive turkey drumstick that Ben had stolen from the kitchen. It never occurred to him that the meat might be missed.

After lunch, Tobias must have dozed off as they talked. With the sun blazing down on him, he decided that he hadn't felt this relaxed since their nights under the oaks. He was suddenly awakened by Ben climbing on top of him. He opened his eyes to see Ben straddling his chest. Absorbing his weight, Tobias watched as Ben dipped his fingers into a tin, scooping out two fingers of a yellowy-white paste.

"What is that?" Tobias asked as he watched Ben raise his body and reach behind himself.

"Did you forget the surprise I told you about?" Ben smiled as he returned his fingers to the tin and, again, reached behind himself.

"Are you sure?" Tobias murmured. He watched Ben's face intently.

"I've been practicing all week for you." Ben reached down and gave Tobias a small kiss. Smiling, he reached around, took hold of Tobias, and guided him.

Slowly, Tobias entered. Ben was tight, and he feared hurting him again. Ben let out a gasp and then stopped moving. Tobias realized he was inside Ben, the warmth sliding around his member.

"Stay still." Ben whimpered, his voice failing.

Tobias wanted nothing more than to be still and have this moment last forever.

After a moment, Ben began to stir, moving his hips ever so slightly. Tobias was tormented as the tension built within his own body. Lying still like he was told, he eased his hands up and cupped Ben's ass. He wanted to be careful with Ben, yet his desire threatened to devour him.

Ben's eyes narrowed as he rode Tobias, slowly moving up and down, occasionally releasing an incoherent sound. Every sensation showed on his face. They were experiencing heaven for the first time, together.

Tobias listened as Ben's breathing picked up. A raspy desire escaped Ben's soft, pouty lips as the slick friction brought him closer to the edge. Surrendering all restraint, Ben cried out as he spilled his seed, shooting all over Tobias.

Seeing this sent a surge through Tobias's body—a jolt of electricity that could only come out one way. Tobias shuddered as he emptied into Ben. Somehow, he felt closer to Ben than ever, as if they had shared the same last breath.

Ben collapsed on Tobias's chest, breathless, his body quivering. They both were attempting to catch their breath.

"That was—" Tobias couldn't finish his sentence.

It was several minutes before Ben lifted his head and cleared his throat. "I'm going in the river to clean up. Come on." He rose.

Tobias took a swipe at the goo on his abdomen. "Okay."

They were in and out of the water within minutes. Both were eager to warm up. Tobias thought about getting dressed and decided against it; he was enjoying being completely naked outside. Flopping to the ground, he patted the dirt, signaling for Ben to join him. "What was that stuff you used?" Tobias asked.

Ben brushed his hair out of his face. "Butter."

"Butter?" Tobias laughed as he thought about it. "I guess there is nothing like a little butter on your biscuit!" The two burst into laughter.

"I saw the cattle doctor use lard to check our pregnant cow, and it hit me. But I didn't want no lard in me." Ben lay beside Tobias, nuzzling close to him. He whispered into Tobias's ear. "I love you."

Lightly stroking the hairs that draped the backside of Ben's neck, Tobias's heart was full. He had never been as satisfied as he was at this minute. He tried not to think about the fact that, as he was about to begin another cycle of sickness, they wouldn't see each other again for at least ten days.

16

Ben was cursing the day he had concocted the plot to lay low until they could run. It was killing him, not being able to see Tobias every day. He couldn't believe that it was the first week in October, and they had at least four months left of this charade. He kept telling himself that, if they could make it until the auction house closed for the winter, they would be home free. The bad news was that this might not happen for another couple of weeks; the good news was that he would get to see Tobias today.

This last time around, they had gone almost two weeks without seeing each other. Ben was ready to jump out of his skin if he didn't see Tobias this morning. He paid little mind to his pa and Dexter at the breakfast table. He had learned to tune them out unless there was something he needed to know. Without a doubt, he knew Dexter was watching him. No sooner was the meal over than Ben excused himself, making a dash towards the smokehouse.

His pulse was racing as he imagined being in Tobias's arms again. Soon, he told himself, soon. Coming around the corner, he spotted Tobias. His heart skipped a beat, but for the wrong reason. Tobias stood next to the building, his shoulders rounded and skin green. He had always been lean, but this morning, he appeared skeletal. It took Ben's breath way. "Oh my God, what happened?" Ben couldn't hide the horror on his face as he rushed to Tobias. "Are you *really* sick?"

Tobias shrugged. "I think it's the berries. My body's retaining the poison, I think."

Ben's eyes darted about Tobias's body, and he shook his head violently. "Dear God, Tobias, no more. You're goin' to kill yourself. We have to stop!"

"I stopped four days ago. I haven't eaten since—" Tobias stopped to clear his throat.

"We have to get you to a doctor! We have to do somethin'!" Ben hurried him into the stable for privacy, out of the view of those heading to the fields.

Tobias tried to laugh. "Well, we wanted me sick . . . I'm sick."

"We have to take you to see a doctor," Ben repeated.

"No. No doctors. They'll know. I'll be okay in a couple of days."

"And if not? What if you die in a couple of days? You could be dead by then." Ben took him by the hand. "Dear God, Tobias, what have we done?"

They stood face to face for several minutes, silent. Ben didn't know what to do. He couldn't live with himself if something happened to Tobias. He wanted to press the issue, make him see a doctor. Ben could talk a doctor into coming to them. Everybody knew Tobias was sick—this could add credibility to the plan in case Dexter had any doubts.

Releasing Tobias's hand, Ben ran his fingers through his hair and shook his head. Exhaling deeply, he thought aloud. "I was planning on takin' the wagon out to the south end, fix up some fencing we have out there." He put a hand over his mouth and took a large breath as he looked at Tobias. "For cryin' out loud, I can't believe this. Look at you."

Tobias gave him a half-smile. "No. Let's go. I could use some time away from here. Move around. Not feeling much like working, but I need to move around."

"Okay. Give me a minute to hitch the wagon." Ben gave Tobias a soft kiss on his cheek followed by a deep sigh. Within minutes, Ben had retrieved the horse and had them on their way. Trying not to rock the wagon too much, Ben felt about as sick as Tobias looked.

About thirty minutes later, they arrived at the south end of the property, where Ben had planned to make love to Tobias in the back of the wagon. It was the perfect spot: located on the down end of a rolling slope, it put a small foothill between them and the farm. The fencing must have been down for a while. Dexter had discovered it a couple of days ago as the spot where cattle had been escaping. Ben laughed under his breath. Even the cattle wanted to escape this God-forsaken place.

"Stay in the wagon. I'll fix this fence." Ben grabbed his heavy gloves and wire cutters from the back of the wagon. "Can I get you somethin'?" he asked, before starting.

Tobias shook his head, reaching under his seat for the canteen of fresh water Ben always kept there. "No, I'm fine. I don't mind helping."

"Relax. I'll call you when I need you. Why don't you stretch out back here?" Ben's eyes shifted to the back of the wagon. This was the most they had talked since leaving the farm.

"Yeah, I might do that." Tobias slid from the bench down into the back of the wagon and propped himself up so he could watch Ben work.

Ben began repairing the fence. Keeping an eye on Tobias, he saw that he had pulled a piece of canvas over himself and had dozed off. Over the next couple of hours, Ben worked relentlessly on the fencing as Tobias slept.

Consumed in his work, Ben was startled by a loud yawn. He stopped what he was doing and looked over at the wagon. Seeing that Tobias was awake, Ben couldn't contain his grin. He tossed his pliers to the ground and removed his gloves. "Hey, sleepy head. Have a nice nap?"

Ben made his way to the wagon as Tobias stretched again, this time letting out an even bigger yawn as he pushed his arms out and wiggled his fingers. "I did? How long was I sleeping?"

Ben leaned against the side of the wagon. "A couple of hours."

"Are you done?" Tobias sat up and tossed the canvas off himself.

Ben hopped up on the side of the wagon and leaned in for a kiss. "Just about. Have to tie off a couple of wires, and that should do it."

Tobias looked up. The blue sky had turned grey, and the temperature had dropped several degrees while he was sleeping.

Climbing into the wagon, Ben said, "Wouldn't be surprised if we got rain tonight. We could use it."

Sliding over towards Ben, Tobias nestled in his arms. "I think that nap did me some good. I'm feeling better."

"Good." Ben laid his hand on Tobias's thigh, lightly brushing his pant leg. "So what are we goin' to do?"

"About what?"

Ben chuckled under his breath. "About you. I don't want you eatin' no more of those berries. It's not worth it. From now on, you're goin' to have to fake it, pretend to be sick."

Tobias didn't respond. Instead, he reached for the canteen. After a couple of sips, he moistened his lips and passed the canteen to Ben.

"Thank you." Ben took one long drink, quenching a thirst he'd had for hours. Afraid of waking Tobias, he had stayed away from the wagon.

"Tell me more about the place that we're going." Tobias reached for the heavy canvas and pulled it over his body again.

"Well, let's see." Ben had been researching Pennsylvania since the moment they had decided to run. He had studied it in school, and it was the first place he had thought to go. "Well . . . it has rivers and lakes and mountains, and the weather's a lot like here. There's a little town called Harrisburg where we can get some land. Make our own farm. We'll have horses, mules, pigs, cows, and chickens." Ben slid closer to Tobias and stretched the canvas over his own body. Under the fabric, Tobias reached out and took his hand.

Staring out of the back of the wagon, Ben pretended as if they were surveying their own land. "Over there, we can build our house. Nothin' fancy on the account we ain't got much money. Over there, we can put the stable and some pens for the animals. Keep them close so the mountain lions don't steal 'em." A warm sensation came over him. Talking about it made it real. They were really going to have this, to build a life and future together.

Silence filled the air as they both looked out over the wagon across the plains. It was several minutes before Tobias broke the silence. "Money . . . Where do we get money from?" Tobias asked.

Chewing at his fingernails, Ben spit off to the side. "Pa's got a money chest. Keeps his money in there, hidden in a secret compartment built in his desk. There's enough to get us what we need to get started." Ben really had no idea just how much was in that drawer, but whatever it was, he knew he was taking all of it.

"You're going to steal the money?" Tobias wrinkled his brows as he squared his shoulders. "I don't know—Do we really need it, I—?"

Ben cut him off, "Think of it as just takin' what's mine. I if run, I'm leaving everything behind that would come to me when he died. So I figure why wait, I'll just take my share now, when it can do me some good." Ben guffawed, seeing Tobias wasn't buying his reasoning. "Okay, think of it this way, Tobias: Pa owes you. He's taken everything from you. That's worth somethin', ain't it? Why shouldn't you have the life you were supposed to have? You sure in hell ain't goin' to have it if we can't get nothing goin'. We need money to buy cattle, to build a house, fencing, food—."

"Okay, okay I get it!" Tobias raised his hand signaling for him to stop. After a moment, Tobias released a heavy sigh, "So . . . What are the people like?"

Ben had to think for a moment. "Lots of Quakers."

"Tell me again, what's a Quaker?" Tobias lightly stroked Ben's hand.

"They're religious people. Pa calls them liberals. They are the ones who are tryin' to get rid of slavery." Ben's eyes narrowed. "Ain't never met one."

"Will they be around us, know about us?"

"I don't know. I can't imagine, if they religious folks, they take too kindly to what we're doin'. Guess we'll figure that out when we get there."

"You say religious people as if it's a bad thing."

Ben thought about it for a few seconds. "Well, folks around here that are religious talk about how we all goin' to burn in hell, and how God hates everythin'. Just don't make no sense to me."

Tobias shrugged. "There's a little church down the road that seems okay. I went there with Miss Gee-gee once. They talk as if there is only one God."

Ben nodded, though he wasn't quite sure what Tobias meant about there being more than one God. "I can count the times I been in church on one hand. Ain't never seen any sign that he's even real or knows who I am."

"He—?" Tobias stopped short.

"What? What were you about to say?" Ben held his eyes on Tobias, curious.

"I don't know." Tobias sighed. "You speak about your God as if it's a person, only one. I was taught differently."

"So are you religious? Do you believe in God?" Ben asked as his eyebrows furrowed.

"We—I believe there are many Gods who teach of different things. That we must listen to what is around us. They come in many forms and will enlighten you and guide you in your choices and how you look at things."

Ben nodded as he tried to process this. It was certainly nothing he had ever heard before.

"Okay, so don't laugh, but look at that stick." Tobias pointed to a stick on the ground. "How did it get there? There's no trees around. Why didn't you see it an hour ago?"

"It's a stick! Who cares?" Ben cried.

"But there might be a reason that the stick appeared in your life when it did. Think, think for a minute and ask yourself why. Why is it here for me to see?"

"Good Lord, Tobias, I fell in love with someone who's as crazy as a loon." Ben caught something moving out of the corner of his eye. Looking over, he saw it again, about twenty-five feet in front of them:

a snowflake. "Look there, it's snowin'!" Ben ripped the canvas off himself as he leaned forward to get a better look.

"I don't see anything. What are you looking at?" Tobias asked.

"You don't see it? It's snowin'!" Ben hopped off the wagon and walked towards the newly repaired fence. "Come see!" He whirled. "It's all around us!"

Tobias stood on his knees on the back of the wagon. "I see it!"

In the windless air, tiny flakes floated down past their eyes. More and more, thousands of tiny flakes, shimmering, descending all around them, and sticking to everything. They were mesmerized.

"It's our first snow storm!" Ben turned to look at Tobias and saw that his big brown eyes were crossed as he tried to see the flakes. "What's wrong with you? Ain't you ever seen snow before?" Ben asked.

"What do you call it?" Tobias asked.

"Snow, it's called snow." Ben ran back to the wagon to be near him.

"Where does it come from?"

Ben laughed. "I dunno. You ain't seen snow?" He grabbed Tobias's hand and turned it palm-side-up. "Catch one. It's like ice but soft." He continued to grin as he watched Tobias. "Now stick out your tongue, like this." He hopped back onto the wagon and demonstrated.

They sat side by side, catching the snow with their tongues as it continued to blanket the ground.

"What do you call it again?" Tobias laughed and snorted as he swallowed the snowflakes that he was able to catch.

"It's called snow . . . S-N-O-W!" Ben spelled it out slowly. "If you keep your tongue out there, it will freeze and plum fall right off." He laughed.

Tobias retracted his tongue into his mouth and held his hands out to catch the snow.

By the time they made their way back to the farm, the snow was falling rapidly, dusting all of the buildings with glittering white powder.

Charlie came out to meet them in front of the stables, and he took control of the mare.

"Charlie, I reckon this is goin' to be some storm," Ben stated as he hopped down from the wagon.

"I reckon so, sir. First one of the season. Massa Lee was hopin' for a few more weeks to finish up the harvest, but I say the good Lord felt fit to bring it today."

Ben removed his riding gloves and stuffed them in his back pockets. "Charlie, do you have any boots in the barn that might fit Tobias? He's goin' to need some proper shoes for the winter."

"I reckon I do." Charlie signaled for Tobias to follow him inside the barn. "Let me see your feet." He looked at the tattered shoe that Tobias was holding up. "Good Lord, you got the biggest feet I've seen on a young man!"

Ben watched as the two disappeared inside the stables. They had said their good-byes to each other prior to coming through the front gates, but this moment always hurt. Ben was about to walk off but hesitated. He thought about what Tobias had said earlier about the stick. Looking around at the snow falling, he smiled. *It's the start of winter, and soon the auction house will close.*

Multiple storms hit the farm that week, and everything was soon blanketed in layers of snow. Tobias noted a sense of urgency as everyone rushed to prepare for the winter. He had heard that the work would now focus on land improvements, repairing machinery and outbuildings, and keeping the bridges, dirt roads, and smokehouse open.

Soon after the first couple of storms, Ben got word that the auction house had officially closed for the winter. He and Tobias couldn't have been happier at the news. Although Tobias had stopped taking the berries at Ben's request, he still needed to keep a low profile.

Tobias's daily work now consisted of moving firewood from the main woodpile to the big house, the back kitchen, and the smokehouse. Since moving wood was thought of as a daily task for a slave,

Ben didn't assist Tobias. Coupled with the harsh weather that often kept the entire Lee family inside more, Ben and Tobias's time together, sadly, dwindled even more.

17

At noon on Christmas Eve, everyone gathered at the foot of the big house's front steps, awaiting the appearance of Master Lee and Mrs. Clara. Tobias pushed to the front of the crowd in hopes of seeing Ben. He had heard that, on Christmas Eve of last year, the slaves had received two days off. There had been other gifts as well: the men had received a pound of pork and a fifth of rum from Master Lee. For the women, Mrs. Clara passed out a pound of sugar and six yards of cotton. Those gathered in front of the house gossiped about what they might be given this year. More than the gift, however, Tobias was hoping to see Ben, to look into his eyes. He and Ben hadn't been with each other in weeks, and Tobias longed to lay eyes on him again.

When the front door opened, Tobias held his breath. Master Lee and his wife appeared first, wearing their finest clothes. They were followed by Ben and then by Charlie and Dolly. Although Mrs. Clara was stunning in her red velvet evening gown and sausage curls, Ben held all of Tobias's attention.

Ben stood at the top of the stairs, wearing light brown striped britches, a cream vest and a dark brown coat. Tobias smiled, seeing that the start of a beard and mustache shielded Ben's pale skin and that Ben's hair had been washed and trimmed.

"Merry Christmas, everyone!" Master Lee announced in a booming voice. On one side of him stood Mrs. Clara, and on the other stood Ben. Tobias couldn't suppress his smile. The very sight of Ben caused his heartbeat to race as adrenaline pumped through his body, rejuvenating him. Seeing Ben made him feel alive again, stirring something deep within. It was more than arousal. It was as if his heart started beating for the first time. Ben's presence produced a grin that he couldn't contain, not that he cared to.

After Ben appeared, Tobias missed everything Master Lee said. Drinking in as much of Ben as he could, Tobias was in awe. He knew the Lees would not be out long in this weather, and he was right.

"Thank you all, and may God bless you!" Master Lee's voice trailed off. The Lees were moving, retreating into the house as they waved and said Merry Christmas to the crowd before them. Ben checked the time on his pocket watch before following his parents inside. *Did Ben see me?* Tobias wondered. *Does he know I came to see him?*

Charlie and Dolly remained on the porch and passed out the holiday gifts. The crowd pushed and pulled around Tobias as they fought to get to the front for their gifts. But those gifts weren't important to him. He had gotten what he came for, and it would carry him farther than any pork or sugar could. Those two minutes of seeing Ben were everything—he needed nothing more.

The snow on the ground did little to deter the Christmas Eve celebration in the slave quarters. Tobias watched as women packed their pork in wooden crates and had the men fill the crates with snow. They would take it out behind the cabins and cover it with more snow so the animals couldn't get to it. Food was plentiful now, with all the fresh butchering, but come February, the frozen pork would be welcomed.

This year, for Christmas dinner, the women roasted a wild hog, several salt herrings, and a couple of rabbits. It was the largest meal they had all year, and they took great pride in being able to come together. Tobias watched as rickety old tables and chairs were brought out from several cabins and placed together to make one long, continuous table. Smells of pork, collard greens, and sweet potatoes filled the frigid air, and everyone contributed to the feast in some way, no matter how small. Two old men started the music, one playing the banjo and the other the harmonica. The children were everywhere, playing and singing.

Later that night, Tobias had his first taste of warm peach cobbler and bread pudding. He ate so much that his belly became distended and rumbled as if he was going to be sick.

"What's wrong with you?"

Tobias looked up to see Pearl with both hands on her hips and a belly matching his. "Oww," he moaned, "I ate too much. I think I want to go lie down for a while, but I don't want to miss anything."

"You can't go yet! Doc is telling some stories." Pearl rubbed her little bump.

The moon cast light on them as they walked over to the giant oak tree, where ole Doc sat telling his stories to anyone who would listen. Tobias listened from the back of the crowd and, although he didn't fully understand what ole Doc was talking about, he knew it was a tale. He smiled as he watched Pearl's and little Stuart's faces as they sat, listening to every word. He wondered where Stuart's little brother Henry was, as they were always together. He hadn't seen Henry in hours.

As voices picked up, Tobias was sure some of the men were finishing off their rum already. They were getting rowdy. Their booming voices made him nervous. He wanted to go find Henry, to tell him "Merry Christmas" and see how he was doing. He missed him.

First, Tobias looked around the immediate area. There was no sign of the little guy. Continuing around to the other row of cabins, he called out for Henry. When he came to the end of the row, he looked over and saw light shining through the open doors of the blacksmith shop.

As Tobias got closer to the shop, he saw Charlie inside, pounding on a glowing red horseshoe over a barrel of fire. When he reached the opening of the shop, there was little Henry, sitting on a stump, watching Charlie's every move. Looking more closely, Tobias saw that Henry was wearing one of Charlie's leather aprons. He smiled at the fact the apron was so big, it covered Henry's entire body.

Tobias watched at the doorway for several minutes as he dreamed of the times that he and his father had once shared. He knew this was probably the closest Henry would ever come to having a father. Not wanting to interrupt their moment, Tobias prepared to head back towards the gathering.

The snow crunched behind him. Footsteps were approaching. Tobias turned around as Dolly reached him. "You scared me," he said, taking a breath.

"Stupid is never scared. Why are you standin' here in the cold?" Dolly paused as her eyes shifted over to what he had been looking at. Her voice lowered. "He's a good boy."

Tobias glanced back at Henry. "Yeah, I miss him and Stuart."

"Well, you need to come by more. Come for supper sometime. I seen how skinny you been lookin' lately." She poked him in his ribs.

"Thank you, I will."

Dolly shifted her weight onto her other leg. "Well, I ain't spyin' on you. Come lookin' for you, actually. Got word Mr. Ben is lookin' for you. Say he needs you to bring wood to the house."

"But I stacked it good earlier. There's no way they used all that wood." Tobias knew they should have had enough for at least another day.

"Well, I don't know what you did, but Penny's been cookin' all day."

"Okay, I'll take care of it." Tobias didn't mind. It was too early to go to his cabin; the guys were surely still up playing craps.

With an arm full of cut wood, he made his way across the farm towards the back of the big house. He would first stop and see if Penny needed some for the inside kitchen. Without the use of the wagon, he would have to make many trips, he thought as he approached the boarded-up summer kitchen.

Tobias thought he heard someone whisper his name.

"Tobias."

There it was again. He stopped and looked at the summer kitchen. It was dark inside, but the snow had been removed from in front of the door. "Who's in there?" he asked.

"Get in here!"

It was Ben's voice. Ben was inside. Tobias dropped the wood and pushed the door open.

"Shut the door."

Tobias smiled as butterflies fluttered in his stomach. "What are you doing in—?" Before he could finish his sentence, Ben kissed him. It was a hard kiss, and the roughness of his beard caught Tobias off guard. Drawing back, Tobias gasped.

"I had to see you. I was missin' you so much."

"Then Penny doesn't need any wood?" Tobias was confused.

"She don't need no wood. You stacked enough out back to last till spring!" Ben kissed him again.

Tobias's mouth fell open. "You planned this?" As his eyes adjusted to the dark, he saw the scruffy beard coming down from Ben's ears. This explained the roughness. Ben was wrapped in a blanket that he held tightly around his neck.

"What are you doing out here? It's freezing," Tobias asked, still not believing what he was seeing.

Ben smiled as he opened up the blanket, exposing his slender, naked body. "It's not cold *in here*," he said with a big grin.

Tobias's grin widened as he stared at Ben's naked body. It was the most beautiful thing he had ever seen. "In here?" Tobias looked around the tiny kitchen, still trying to process what was going on.

Ben dropped the blanket and moved into his arms. "Stop talkin'." Ben's lips softly touched Tobias's neck, his throat, and then his lips.

As they kissed, Ben pushed Tobias backwards until they reached a large cutting table. "Lie down." Ben's voice was throaty.

There were several blankets laid out across the table, with two pillows at one end. Starting with the lowest button on Tobias's shirt, Ben slowly moved from one button to the next. The touch of his hands as they brushed against his skin caused Tobias to gasp, his abdomen retracting inward.

Ben gave him a devilish smile. "Merry Christmas," he whispered into Tobias's ear, followed by a delicate bite.

When they finished, the two lay breathless on their makeshift bed. The blankets had been long ago cast to the floor. Tobias's chest pounded as Ben lay under him, his limp legs fallen to each side of the table. Their ragged breaths soon changed to gentle snoring.

Some time later, Tobias opened his eyes. He had no idea how long they been sleeping. Reaching down, he grabbed a blanket and brought it up over them. Ben stirred, changing positions, and then burrowed his nose into Tobias's arm.

Tobias lay there, feeling each breath Ben took, the warmth of the exhales against his skin. A clean, woodsy smell permeated Tobias's nose. Inhaling, Tobias identified Ben's hair as its source. The scent reminded him of the forest after a rainstorm. Tobias inhaled another whiff as he closed his eyes and envisioned a woodland he had known a long time ago.

After a couple of minutes, it occurred to him that someone might come looking for either of them. If the door opened, there would be no time to do anything.

"Ben? Ben, are you awake?" Tobias whispered.

"Yeah," Ben shifted slightly. "Why?"

"We have to go. We can't stay in here all night."

"Why not? Go to sleep, baby," Ben murmured.

"What if we're asleep, and someone walks in?"

"Tobias, no one is comin' in here in the middle of the night. Now, go to sleep." Ben pressed his head into Tobias's chest and brought the blanket up to his neck.

Uneasy, Tobias listened, sensitive to any noise or movement around them. Ben's naked skin was cool against his. The fancy clothes that

Ben had worn hours ago weren't really him. In Tobias's arms, just the two of them, Ben was quiet and vulnerable, the sweetness emanating from his soul. With all that Tobias didn't understand about this place, this world, he knew that Ben made him feel safe.

Tobias stroked Ben's back, feeling the muscles in Ben's shoulder blade as it tapered down to his ribcage. Slowly, his finger followed the same path back up again. He knew they were alike in so many more ways than they were different. The color of one's skin was more than a detail in this country; it's what separated them from one another. Thinking of the various tribes his father had taken him to visit, Tobias could recall many differences from one to the next—their dress, their huts, their beliefs—but skin color had not been among them.

Tobias broke the silence. "What do you think of my skin?" His voice was unsteady.

Ben pulled his head out from under Tobias's chest and arms. "What do you mean?"

"My skin color, what do you think of it?" There was a rise in Tobias's pitch.

Ben looked into his eyes, his face showing that he was baffled by the question. "I like it." Now his voice sounded unsteady.

Tobias rolled onto his back and let out a sigh.

Ben propped himself up on his side. "Your skin is soft, like a fine piece of cloth. It's always soft."

Rolling back to face Ben, Tobias ran his fingers up and down Ben's chest. "No, I mean the color of it." His fingers made their way gently across Bens face, tracing first his eyebrows, then the slight bump on his nose, and finally across his chapped lips. "My skin—the color is the difference between me and you. Dexter treats us, the slaves, no better than his dog. I see how your father looks at us." Pausing long enough to sit up, Tobias looked into Ben's eyes. "What do you think of the color my skin?" he asked again.

Ben's eyes fell to Tobias's stomach. He touched Tobias's chest lightly before laying his entire hand across his right nipple. "I never saw the color of your skin. It's like it doesn't exist. Tobias, I just see you. I look into your eyes, and I see your thoughts." Ben held Tobias's gaze, staring into his dark brown eyes. "I listen to your words, I look into your beautiful eyes, and they tell me everythin' about you that I want to know. Your color . . . I'm blind to it, I don't see it."

Tobias thought for a minute about what Ben had said. Hesitantly, he cocked his head to one side. "If you don't see my skin color, you don't see me. Is it just mine that you don't see? Do you not see Penny's, Corinne's, or Pearl's? If I weren't this color, this color that you don't see, I would not have been stolen from my home. I wouldn't have lost my family. I wouldn't have watched hundreds die in filth. If I didn't have dark skin, I wouldn't be a slave or have a need to run. My color, it has brought me such pain and suffering, but it also brings me great pride. I want you to see my color, see that I am from the Ashanti tribe, from West Africa." Tobias wasn't sure where all of this had come from, but it was how he felt. Staring at Ben, he could see the confused look in his eyes. "What?"

Ben let out a harsh breath. "I guess I said it wrong. Of course I see that you're a negro, but—" He paused. "I didn't mean to upset you. I just mean that I don't care that you're a negro. I love you. That's all I meant by it."

Tobias thought about this. Had he overreacted, or did it really bother him that Ben didn't see his skin color? His answer was that it did, slightly. It was his identity, where he came from. It told a story. "I want you to love me, all of me."

18

S pring had arrived. The warmer days melted away the snow that had blanketed the farm for several months. Tobias and Ben had made their way into the loft above the stables long before the sun rose. It had become their sanctuary over the winter months. With blankets, a pillow, and a small bottle of oil that Ben had seized from his mother's vanity table, they had made this tiny space theirs, a place they could call their own.

Ben stirred. His body was tender but satisfied from their early morning tryst. The sunlight creeping through the boards told him it was time to get up. The sound of the rooster crowing nearby confirmed it.

"You awake?" He lightly nudged Tobias's shoulder.

"Hmm."

Ben nudged him again. "Come on, get up. We got to get dressed."

Tobias made a couple of inaudible noises as he rolled his back to Ben and pulled his body into a tight ball.

"Come on, get up." Ben had just pulled the blanket off Tobias when the sound of voices grew near. Frozen, Ben listened for a second. The door creaked open. Ben bolted upright, his finger on his lip signaling for Tobias to be quiet. Someone was coming into the stable. It sounded like a scuffle.

"Oh, right, nigger. You haven't delivered yet."

Ben took in a sharp breath when he recognized Dexter's gruff voice coming from below. Frozen, he knew even the slightest movement could cause a sound.

"You better not be fucking for fun!" Dexter bellowed.

Tobias pointed to a crack in the floor. Dexter and Rudo were directly below them. They watched through the tiny crack as Dexter held Rudo by his shirt.

"C'mon here!" Dexter demanded. Into their limited view stepped a young negro woman named Sally. She was crying. "Pull that skirt up. Let him have it!"

They watched as the petite woman hiked up her dress and lay on her back across a hay bale. Dexter reached down and began undoing Rudo's britches. Rudo wrestled loose just as his britches gave way. With a shove from Dexter, Rudo took a step forward and lay across the woman.

Tobias's eyes narrowed, his brows pressed together across his forehead. Ben didn't know what Tobias would do; he didn't know what he should do himself. He knew they were breeding—Rudo had to deliver fifteen babies. Neither he nor Tobias could stop it. Tobias would meet a far worse fate if they were discovered naked and together. *Please, Tobias, don't move.* Ben tried to communicate this with his eyes.

Rudo remained inside of the woman for several minutes before giving an unmistakable grunt. He thrusted once or twice more before stopping. Dexter stepped into view. He had his britches undone. Grabbing Rudo by the back of his shirt, he flung him off the woman.

"Get up! It's my turn!"

Dexter lay on top of the woman as Ben watched in horror. When he was done, he crawled off her and zipped up his britches. Spitting his tobacco within inches of Sally's head, he laughed. "That's how you do it, boy. You got to deliver, or you're going to the auction house."

Once the three of them had exited the stable, Tobias sat up, finally able to move. Ben was sickened by what he had witnessed, even more so because his father was behind it. His face burned with anger.

The lack of air was choking him. "Get dressed," was the only thing he could say. He couldn't even look at Tobias.

Tobias said nothing. Reaching for his britches, he slid them on and then reached for his shirt. The two were dressed within minutes and climbed down out of the loft while it was clear. Tobias kneeled to tie his shoe. On one knee, he looked up at Ben. "Dexter's an animal!"

"I'm sorry you had to see that." Ben knew better than to try to explain what Rudo had been tasked to do. This had been going on long before he was born. With fewer and fewer slave ships coming to deliver new slaves, slave owners were left to breeding their own. But there was no explanation that could excuse what they had seen.

"He should die for that!" Tobias wiped a tear from his eye.

Ben hadn't realized Tobias was crying. Of course he was; they had just witnessed something terribly vile done to another human. Seeing the pain in Tobias's face sent a lump to Ben's throat, one that wouldn't go away with a swallow. "We have to go soon," Ben said, his voice flat.

"Okay. You walk out first and check to see if it's clear." Tobias adjusted his suspenders. There was still no eye contact between them.

Ben stood in front of him. "No . . . I mean we have to *leave*. We can't wait any longer. In the mornin'."

Tomorrow morning seemed a lifetime away. Somehow, they would have to get through this day.

"He's not like your father. Why does Master Lee keep him? Does he know what kind of man Dexter is?"

Ben looked down. He still couldn't look Tobias in the eye. He knew the man that his father was, and he was cut from the same cloth as Dexter. His heartache was eating at his soul, tearing its way through his chest. It threatened to devour him and leave nothing but scraps. "That's why pa hired him. To do the jobs that Pa can't do. Dexter is an animal matched by no man."

"But why? How does someone get like that? Does he think we are not human?" Tobias asked.

Ben leaned back against the wall and took a couple of breaths. "Well . . . this is what Pa said. When Dexter was a baby, maybe around three or four years old, a slave woman slit his parents' throats. She gutted them right there in their own kitchen. When they found them dead four days later, Dexter was beside them, covered in dried blood, crying as if he had gone mad. There was an all-out manhunt for her, as well as for the other two male slaves that the family owned, who were missin'. They tracked all three of them over into Allen County and hung them on the spot. Dexter was raised by his aunt and uncle. The uncle was an overseer on a small farm over in Allen County. He would carry Dexter to work with him, and if you think Dexter is mean, I heard the uncle was twice as mean and bitter. They say he had red eyes, like the devil, and taught Dexter everythin' he knew, beatin' every slave he came across, seekin' revenge. He died a few years back. Pa says Dexter ain't so much as whispered anythin' about his parents, so we ain't sure if he even knows, or if he just keeps it inside."

Tobias closed his eyes and crossed his arms. Shaking his head, he spoke several words in his native tongue.

That night during dinner, Ben set his plan into action. As quietly as he could, he cleared his throat. His mouth had gone dry. Interrupting the conversation between his pa and Dexter, he announced that he was heading into town in the morning for spring supplies. "I plan on takin' Tobias to help. Need him to load the wagon in Myrtleville." He could feel his right leg bouncing under the table. He had to pull it together, or their entire plan could unravel right here. "It's a long day of travelin', so we'll leave before sunrise. I told Charlie to get two horses hitched on a covered wagon." Ben took a breath. He was talking too fast. "We got lots to pick up. The list grew this last winter. Reckon we'll be gone all day."

Dexter leaned forward, dropping his left elbow on the table. "Why don't you take Charlie with you? Help with the loading?"

"Don't need his help." Ben looked directly at Dexter. "Don't need the extra weight in an already-heavy load neither." *Mind your business and stay out of mine before I gut you like your ma and pa.*

With the two horses, he and Tobias could dump the wagon and cover a lot of ground on horseback. It would be nightfall before anyone realized something was wrong. Too late for a proper search. That would give them an entire day's head start.

Penny entered the dining room and placed a large platter of food in the center of the table. Ben eyed the food on the platter, sizing up what he would be able to take. Later, he would go to the kitchen, fill a gunnysack with anything he could find. This is when he would grab the money his father had hidden in that desk of his. He was rethinking their escape route, wondering if Pennsylvania was too far. Ohio was closer, and it was a free state. But they weren't any kinder to negroes than Kentuckians were. Flicking his thumbnail between his teeth, Ben weighed his options, completely unaware that he was being watched.

19

The next morning, Charlie had the hitched wagon parked in front of the stables as Ben had instructed. Tobias waited until Ben had Charlie's attention before throwing two sleeping rolls into the bed of the wagon. The gunnysack Ben had told him to grab from out back was filled to the top. He wondered what all Ben had tucked in there. There was no time to look—he had to hide it under the tarp.

When Tobias pulled back the thick leather tarp, he was surprised at what he saw: it was Pearl, hiding and looking straight at him. His heart nearly leaped up through his throat, and he stumbled backwards just as he heard Charlie's and Ben's voices.

"Now, I don't mine ridin' along with y'all," Charlie said, as he and Ben walked out of the stable.

Tobias threw the tarp back over Pearl's head. He didn't know what to do but knew she couldn't come with them. He had to get her out of the wagon without blowing the plan. Trying to get Ben's attention without looking obvious, Tobias stood still next to the wagon.

She was too pregnant and could never make the trip, he told himself. The plan was to ditch the wagon and ride the horses, which she couldn't do. Tobias watched as Ben climbed up onto the front of the wagon.

"Tobias are you climbin' up, or are you planning on walking to town?" Ben asked.

Tobias tapped on the tarp as he warily shifted his eyes towards it. *Come on, Ben. Look at me!*

Ben did look at him, his head slightly cocked as he narrowed his eyes. "Get on the wagon," he mumbled, without moving his lips.

Tobias glanced over at Charlie, who was standing in front of the wagon. Clearly, he was going to see them off. Tobias dragged his feet as long as he could before climbing on.

The jerk of the wagon caused by Tobias's hard mount caught the attention of one of the mares, who released a loud whinny. When Charlie went to calm her, Ben kicked Tobias as hard as he could in an attempt to signal him to relax.

With a snap of the reins, Ben steered the horses away from the stable and towards the front driveway. Once they were out of earshot, Ben snapped at Tobias, "What the hell is wrong with you? Why you acting so nervous? Charlie don't suspect nothin'."

"We've got a problem." Tobias shifted his eyes towards the back. "It's Pearl. She's in the back of the wagon."

"Ah, shit!" Ben hollered. "What do you mean she's in the back? We can't take her. She's a child."

"Well, what do you suggest we do? Stop the wagon and let her out? Let everyone see her get out, right here in the road? You have to keep going. We'll figure it out." Tobias rubbed the back of his neck. The tension there was so tight that he could barely move it.

They rode for about an hour before Pearl popped her little oval face through the canvas behind their backsides. "I have to pee," she announced.

The two men looked at each other but said nothing. Ben's bottom lip quivered as he snapped the reins, informing the horses to pick up their speed.

After about half an hour, Tobias spoke up. "How long are we going to ride without you talking to me? You have to let her pee."

Without saying a word, Ben pulled back on the reins with all his strength, bringing the horses to an abrupt stop under the vibrant hues of the morning sky. "Tell her to get out and go in the woods. Be careful no one sees her!" Ben held his eyes straight ahead.

Tobias knew Pearl heard the order but turned around and mockingly repeated what Ben had just said.

Pearl jumped out and ran into the bright green willow field at the edge of the woods. Tobias added up the months and decided that she must have been at least seven months pregnant.

Ben laid the reins down. "We should have never left! What are we goin' to do with her? She ain't ridin' no horseback that pregnant."

"Well, I'm glad you noticed she was pregnant." Tobias adjusted his butt on the wooden seat.

"What's your plan? Do you have a plan? We have to stay with the wagon now. Which, in case you're wonderin', is goin' to slow us down. Take us forever to get to Pennsylvania now." The entire wagon rocked as Ben bounced in his seat, looking for Pearl.

Tobias took a breath as he held on, trying not to get bounced out of the wagon. "I understand. I didn't know that she was there until it was too late. We have to make the best of it now. It will work out, I promise." Tobias saw the anger in Ben's eyes, and that his lips were stretched thin. "Now, come on, stop being mad. I don't like this side of you."

The wagon lurched again as Pearl jumped back into it. "I'm hungry."

Ben rolled his eyes as he shook his head. "Look in that sack. There's a little food in there." A smile formed at the edge of his mouth as he looked at Tobias. "And hand us some of that bread in there. We're hungry too," Ben barked.

Pearl grabbed the sack. "Can I eat the pears?"

"We ain't got no pears!" Ben told her.

"Yeah, we do. Here, see!" Pearl pulled a jar of canned pears out of the sack.

Ben looked down and, sure as his britches were split, Pearl was holding a jar of pears. "Where'd you get them?" Ben snatched the jar from her hand to get a closer look.

"In the sack. They were in the sack." Pearl was out of breath from her little jaunt into the woods.

Ben grabbed the sack and peeped down inside it. "What in tarnation?"

"What? What's wrong?" Tobias had no idea what was going on.

Ben ran his hand down through the bag. "There's onions and peppers, and jars of pears, apples, and pickles." Ben looked up. "Did you put all this food in the sack, Tobias?"

"No. I didn't put anything in there." Tobias was still confused.

"Well, I sure in the heck—" Ben stopped midsentence as he stared at the sack. "Who put all this food—?" Ben was thinking aloud. "Corinne . . . Penny?"

That night, when Ben couldn't drive the horses any farther, he told the others that they needed to stop for the night. They found an old abandoned barn that was clearly defying gravity after decades of rain, sleet, and baking summers. The single building was far enough off the road that, if he could hide the wagon inside, they would be well hidden. The temperature was dropping fast, but at least the barn would protect them from the wind.

After tucking the wagon away, Ben stopped long enough for the sweet, musty odor of old straw to penetrate his senses. Pearl had taken the horses around to the back so that they could cool down and graze for a bit. With Pearl gone, Tobias grabbed Ben by the arm and swung him into his chest.

Face to face, Ben knew what Tobias wanted. The two kissed for the first time since leaving this morning. "I've wanted that kiss all day," Tobias said. "I'm glad you're not still mad. I was hoping to make

love to you under the moon tonight, like we use to do in the oaks."
He kissed Ben softly.

As their bodies pressed together, Ben felt Tobias's erection
through his britches. "Well, one, it's too cold, and two, we have company." Ben wiggled out of Tobias's arms. "We have to be careful." He
walked over to the giant door and peered out, ensuring that they
were still alone. "Help me shut these doors so we can get around back
to help her."

Tobias tried to grab him again, but Ben was too quick. "C-mon,
I'm not playin'. We need to get them horses some water and get them
settled for the night."

Tobias laughed. "You know what's funny? I've been pretending
to be sick for so long that, a couple of times today, I had to remind
myself that I wasn't sick anymore."

"Yeah, I can tell you're not sick." Ben yanked on the bulge that
had formed in Tobias's britches. "I wish we could have made love tonight, but it ain't so." He glanced once more at Tobias's crotch.

They each took one of the massive barn doors and walked towards
each other, closing the doors and sealing the wagon away. Walking
around towards the back, they found Pearl holding one of the horses'
reins while the other grazed about ten feet away.

"You're holding the wrong horse. She ain't goin' nowhere. It's *that
one* you need to be holdin'. Scared of her own shadow." Ben walked
over to the free horse and gathered up her reins.

"Do you want me to take her?" Tobias asked Pearl.

"Yeah, I have to pee, and I'm thirsty." She handed Tobias the reins
and then hesitated. "Mr. Ben, is it alright if I step into the woods?"

Ben felt as if he had been punched in the gut. The fear in her
eyes when she looked at him was the same as when she looked at his
father. "Pearl, please don't call me Mr. Ben. Ben will do. And you
don't have to ask permission from me for anything that you wouldn't
ask Tobias for."

Pearl's shoulders relaxed a little. "He say you friends. That's why
you takin' him to freedom."

Ben couldn't help but crack a smile as he watched her eyes dart between him and Tobias. "Yeah, that's right," he said. "We're friends."

Pearl gave Ben a twisted smile and then headed towards the woods.

Ben shook his head as he smiled at Tobias. "Are you hungry, or is it just me who could eat the legs off this horse if we didn't need her in the mornin'?" The horse Ben was holding whinnied and shook her head fiercely.

Tobias laughed. "Yeah, I am too, but I don't think she's willing to give up her legs."

Ben patted the horse at the base of her neck. "Don't worry, girl, ain't goin' to happen. You just get us to Pennsylvania." Ben's mind wandered as he thought about what Pearl's presence meant to their plans. It hadn't struck him until now that she was theirs to look after, and the baby, too, when it was born. His vision of his and Tobias's life together looked a little different now. *How will she react when we tell her about us? She'll have to be told at some point.*

"There's water back here!" Pearl called out to them.

"Don't drink it!" Ben responded.

Pearl walked out from the woods. "No, not for me. For the horses. There's a little creek back there." Right away, Tobias and Ben began walking with the horses in that direction.

The sun had fallen completely by the time they put the horses away and sat down for their dinner of canned pears and a hard-crusted loaf of bread.

Sitting on the tailgate of the wagon, Ben looked over at Pearl, who was resting comfortably on the dirt floor. "Pearl, how did you know that we were leavin' this mornin'?" Ben glanced at Tobias.

"I didn't tell her!" Tobias shouted.

Pearl said, "Ain't nobody tells me nothin'. I watched you and Tobias and knows you 'bout to run. Tobias, Jonas say you ain't slept the last two nights. Say you been leavin' out early in the mornin'. Then last night, I see Charlie fixin' up that wagon, so I ax him what he doin'. He tells me you and Tobias goin' into town in the mornin', so I know it's time. I sneaked into the wagon after Charlie goes to sleep." She squeezed her hand down into the jar for another pear.

Then it hit Ben. Dexter would discover Pearl missing long before they realized that he and Tobias weren't coming back. "Ah, gee-whiz!" he shrieked. "Dexter's goin' to be on our trail sooner. They know you were missin', probably since mornin'. They'll put the dogs on your scent, and the dogs are goin' to take him straight to the stable. He'll figure it out, he'll know!"

Pearl had changed everything, but turning back now wasn't an option. Initially, Ben had been thinking of the loss of privacy, of not having Tobias all to himself. But now he realized Dexter could be just hours behind them. Dexter counted his field hands a hundred times a day. He kept track of them like sheep. Ben's pulse quickened as his mind flooded with scenarios of how they would be caught. Hopping off the wagon, he walked over to the door and tried to peek through a rotted wooden plank. He listened for movement as he peered out into the dark.

"What are you doing?" Tobias asked as he followed Ben to the door.

"Nothin'. Just listenin', makin' sure no one's out there. One of us has to stay up. On guard." Ben walked away from the door, leaving Tobias standing there.

"Okay, you've been driving the horses all day. Get some rest. If I feel that I'm going to fall asleep, I'll wake you." Tobias scratched his head as he watched Ben.

"Is you mad?" Pearl straightened out her dress across her lap but kept her eyes fixed on Ben.

Ben knew she was talking to him. "No. I have to figure this out. I need some time to think." He knew she could see that he was mad. She was all of five feet tall, pregnant, and just a kid herself. Why wouldn't she want freedom as badly as they did? He realized that he knew little about her—about as much as any other slave on the property—with the exception that she and Tobias had once lived together with Miss Gee-gee.

"Pearl, let me set a bedroll up for you. It's getting late. Do you want it in the wagon or down there?" He was thinking it might be a little hard for her to climb in and out of the wagon.

"Where you want me to sleep?" Pearl asked.

"Take the wagon. I'll help you up," Tobias interjected.

Ben joined Tobias on his watch as Pearl slept. It was the first time Ben had Tobias to himself. He knew that he was too wired up to sleep anyhow. The two of them huddled by the door. It was a tight fit in the barn with the wagon, two horses, and the three of them. Ben whispered, "Sorry I've been a jackass all day. Your first day of freedom and this is what you get."

Tobias smiled, "Yeah, I guess you're right. It is my first day of freedom." Tobias reached down and took Ben's hands. "It's funny, I didn't think of it that way. I've been free most of my life. It feels like I escaped out of a box that I was being held in. Like I can breathe again."

Ben stroked Tobias's hand. "I knows it ain't the same, but I guess it was me who has never been free, free to live my life, to love—" Ben stopped for fear that Pearl would hear him.

"What?" Tobias asked.

Ben pointed up towards the wagon. "Pearl," he whispered.

Tobias laughed. "She knows."

Ben's mouth fell open. "What do you mean she knows?"

"I told her about us. A long time ago. She knows we're together."

Ben couldn't believe what he was hearing. Never in a million years would he have guessed that she knew. "Well, butter my butt and call me a biscuit." Ben shook his head at Tobias's bombshell.

"Are you mad?" Tobias asked.

"Mad, no. Why should I be mad?" *Should I be mad?*

"That I didn't tell you?"

"No I ain't mad." Ben smiled. "Can I kiss you then?"

"Hold on, there's more." Tobias's face turned serious. "I did tell her that we were running." His tone escalated. "I didn't tell her that we were leaving this morning, I swear. She figured that out all by herself."

Ben was silent for a minute. What Tobias was saying made him nervous. "What if she told someone? Who else knows? For crying out loud, why didn't you tell me this?"

"We can trust her. I know we can. She hasn't told anyone—she wouldn't cross me," Tobias pleaded. "I know her. She wouldn't say a word to anyone."

A voice boomed from the wagon. "I ain't told no one 'bout you two!"

Tobias and Ben both jumped at the sound. Then they started to laugh. Tobias stood up. "Really? You've been listening this whole time?"

"I ain't listening. I'm just lying here, and I can hear you." Pearl sat up in the wagon. "Anyway, I got to pee."

Ben rose and brushed his britches off. She was funny. He liked her. "I'll take her."

For the first three days and nights, they continued at the harsh pace of thirty to forty miles a day. Other than the unrelenting pee breaks that Pearl required, Ben rarely stopped the wagon until it was time to bed down for the night. Not wanting to draw any unnecessary attention to them, Tobias took to riding in the back with Pearl. The few people they crossed paid no mind to a single white man driving a wagon. With a tip of his hat, he politely acknowledged them, as any stranger would do.

They continued to look for abandoned buildings to hide in at night. When they couldn't find one, Ben would find a spot where he could park the wagon in the woods, hoping darkness would shield them. On those nights, he took to sleeping in the wagon, staying with the horses. Tobias and Pearl could be found within earshot, bedded down in the thick brush. In the event that someone did discover Ben and the wagon, this at least gave them a chance to steal away, deeper into the woods.

By their fourth night, Ben had relaxed somewhat. The fear of hearing the dogs any minute was no longer constant. Parking the wagon next to a small stream, he signaled for the others to come out from under the canvas. "Looks like a grand spot for the night."

Tobias helped Pearl down, and the two took a few seconds to study their surroundings. "I hear water," Tobias announced, as he took a couple of steps into the woods.

"Yeah, I got a glimpse of a stream too. May snatch a fish or two out of it and have a hot meal tonight."

Pearl walked passed them and into the woods. "I'll pee first, then gather us up some wood. Need a fire to eat fish."

Ben raised an eyebrow at the thought of a fire. He hadn't thought that part through. "Yeah, I guess a small fire will be okay."

Once the sun had set, the three sat by the fire, trying to stay warm as they cooked a swamp rabbit. Ben had killed the creature with one shot to the head using his slingshot. They also caught several small fish in the stream, and these went nicely with their apples. If he laid his head down, he would be asleep in seconds. His entire body ached from sitting in the same position for four days. He listened as Tobias and Pearl talked. More times than not, his mind wandered, trying to piece their future together.

Tobias heard the sound first. "Shhh, did you hear that?"

Ben moved his ear in the direction of the dirt road. Other than the light from the fire, it was pitch dark. Ben didn't hear anything. He shook his head as he continued to listen; he wasn't convinced there was anything to hear.

But Tobias raised a finger, and then Ben heard it. It was the sound of clattering hooves. Ben nodded, acknowledging the sound.

"Pearl, get up," Tobias whispered as he went to help her.

"Quick, into the woods," Ben whispered. It was more than one horse approaching. He cursed the fire because he knew they would see him long before he saw them. "Get in the woods!"

Both Tobias and Pearl scurried quietly into the bushes. They had talked about this and knew to stay put until Ben's signal that the coast was clear. Just as they disappeared out of the shadow of the fire, three drifters on horseback came into Ben's sight.

Coming out of the dark, they were upon him in seconds. His heart pounded, unsure that they hadn't seen Tobias and Pearl go into the woods. Ben pretended to be startled as he addressed them. "Good evening, fellas."

"Good evening," the closest to him responded.

Ben could see he was a big man, hefty but also tall, judging by where his stirrups draped on the horse. He couldn't get a good look at the other two as they hung back out of the light.

"What's got you out in these parts at this time of night?" the man asked. His face was shadowed until he turned into the light. Ben studied his face—it was no one he knew. The man wore his hat low across his eyes, and the collar on his jacket rode high over his neck and ears.

"I'm travelin' to Pennsylvania," Ben replied, trying to sound as relaxed as possible.

One of the others, a dark-haired man with a shaggy beard and a rifle in his hand, climbed off his horse and moved into the light. "You look like you got quite the meal you fixin'."

"Ain't much, sir. A swamp rabbit I killed and a couple of small fish. This here is all I got." Ben eyed the sack of food, which was about five feet from him.

As the heavyset man climbed down, the third drifter, a short, mousy man who couldn't have been more than five-five, joined him.

"This boy here's got more food then we've seen in two days," the short man said.

The heavyset man chuckled. "I reckon he won't mind if we have a little."

Ben's eyes followed the dark-haired drifter with the rifle, who spoke next. "You say you out here by yourself?" Ben watched as he stared off into the woods in the direction of Tobias and Pearl. The man took two steps closer to the woods and then stopped as if something had caught his attention.

Ben knew that if Tobias and Pearl were discovered, there would be no talking his way out of it. Jumping to his feet, he moved around to the other side of the fire, hoping to get the man's attention. "You're welcome to take some of this if you're hungry. Reckon you do the same for me, if the shoe was on the other foot!"

The drifter paused before moving back closer to the fire. "Won't mind if I do."

The other two also moved in as the first removed the spear that held the rabbit over the fire. With his bare hands, he tore it from the spear and divided it among him and his two partners.

Ben entertained the three drifters for about an hour as they rested next to the fire. He tried to keep them talking as he couldn't chance them hearing any sounds from the woods. He was relieved when the hefty man stood and announced that it was time for them to move on. Ben did nothing to slow them down.

Once they were gone, he cautiously made his way to where he thought Tobias and Pearl were. "Tobias . . . Tobias," he quietly called into the woods.

It was several seconds before he heard movement and Tobias appeared. "Are we clear?"

"Not sure. You and Pearl better stay put for tonight. Not too sure they don't intend on doubling back and ambushin' me." Tobias's eyes were fearful. "I'll be okay. Here, take the pistol." Ben knew that, if they attacked him while he was sleeping, they would kill him before he ever opened his eyes. The pistol wouldn't do him any good. "Use it if you have to save yourself. Don't try to protect me. You wouldn't stand a chance with the three of them."

"But—" Tobias started to say something, but Ben cut him off.

"Damn it, don't argue with me." He shoved the pistol at Tobias but stopped. "You've fired a gun, ain't you?" By the look on Tobias's face, he knew the answer. He turned the gun on its side. "Put your finger here, point the darn thing, and pull your finger back." Handing over the pistol, he prayed that Tobias would have the stomach to use it if it came to that.

For the rest of the night, Ben lay awake in the wagon, waiting for his death.

The next morning, Ben was still shaken up over his run-in with the drifters and was ready to get an early start. Exhausted, he gathered everything up and was driving the horses before the sun was done rising.

A couple of hours into the morning, he was ready to talk. With Tobias tucked in the back, Ben spoke over his right shoulder as he focused on the road. "I bet you didn't know that today is my birthday." He listened, wondering if they were asleep. He had gotten them up and moving early this morning. "Are you awake?" he called.

"Yeah. Did you say today was your birthday?" Tobias poked his head out through the canvas that separated them.

"Yep," Ben said, taking a glance at Tobias.

"So, tell me again why this day is important to your people," said Tobias.

"What do you mean? It's the day I was born. This is a big deal to us," Ben replied.

"But why?"

"Gosh dang it, I don't know why! Why you always have to ask why? It just is!" Ben had never been around someone who asked so many questions. "Why, why, why, is all you ever say! Just say, 'Happy birthday, Benjamin Lee!' Gem-a-nees."

"Happy birthday, Benjamin Lee, Gem-a-nees," Tobias repeated.

"No, no . . . forget it!" Ben shook his head. "Is Pearl asleep?"

"No. She's lying here . . . but she's not listening." Tobias snickered.

Ben thought about his birthday last year. It was just before he had seen Tobias for the first time. Later, Tobias had told him that his people celebrated their births by the season of year and not the actual date. "Since you don't have a birthday, we can share my birth date. It could be your birthday too. We can pretend we were born on the same day. What do you think?"

"I guess. How old am I then, and what do we do on our birthday? Anything special?" Tobias asked.

Before Ben could answer, Pearl poked her head out below Tobias's. "We can have a birthday party! I can make us a cake for tonight!"

"Pearl, shut up and get back in there before someone sees you. We ain't got nothin' to make no cake with," Ben told her.

"Uh huh, I know how to make a cake," Pearl shot back. "Do you want one or not?"

"Pearl, please make us a cake," Tobias answered. "Please!"

"We're twenty, Tobias," Ben answered as he drove the horses around a curve on the dirt road.

As they got closer to a little town called Lexington, the conversation died down, and Ben figured they were asleep. A quick peek under the canvas confirmed his suspicion. Tobias and Pearl were cuddled up, sound asleep, right behind him. She was a beautiful girl—pretty complexion and thick black hair the color of coal. So beautiful, yet so young to become a mother, he thought to himself. He thought of his own mother and wondered what kind of mother Pearl would be.

Upon entering the town, Ben slowed the horses to a walk until they reached the other side. Once they were a safe distance away from town, Tobias poked his head out from under the canvas and looked up at Ben. "What did I miss?" he asked.

"Not much. Looked like any other old town," Ben announced. "Must be Sunday, though. Lots of pretty ladies all dolled up walkin' in town. I thought you were asleep. Is Pearl up?"

"She's sleeping," Tobias replied, as he reached out and laid a hand on Ben's thigh. The light touch of Tobias's hand sent a wave of sensation through Ben's body.

That night, when they had driven the horses as far as they could for another day, they found a spot to camp. Ben built a fire for them as Tobias headed down to the river to see about catching dinner.

Tobias made short work of his fishing trip and was back with two catfish and a tiny bluegill before Ben had the fire ready. How could he catch a fish with just a hook and string? Ben was beyond amazed.

After dinner, Pearl disappeared for about thirty minutes in the back of the wagon. Ben and Tobias sat next to the fire covertly flirting with each other. "Are you *randy?*" Tobias grinned, carefully pronouncing the last word.

"No. I'm tired and dirty, that's what I am. Are you?" Ben smiled back at him.

"No, but I miss you. Holding you and feeling close to you," Tobias replied.

"Me too." Ben leaned in and gave Tobias a light kiss, gently tugging on his bottom lip.

Tobias pulled back. "Um, um," pausing for a minute, he lowered his eyes. "That gun? Your gun, I know I've never said anything, but I never thought I would have to hold it either. Will you teach me someday to fire it? I don't want to be afraid of it, but I know it can kill people and that scares me."

"Ain't no need to be afraid of a gun. Been shooting all my life. Reckon I can teach you too." Ben smiled and was about to give Tobias another kiss but pulled back at the sound of Pearl's footsteps.

"Happy birthday to you, happy birthday to you, happy birthday to you," she sang. She had something in her hand. As she got closer and lowered her hands, Ben and Tobias could see that it was a dirty white mound of something on a piece of board.

"What is it?" Ben asked as he frowned, curling his nose up at it.

"It's your cake! I made it," Pearl answered.

"You ain't made no cake!" Ben shouted, his voice louder than intended.

"Yeah, I did. Taste it," Pearl said as she smiled and sat it on the ground.

Ben and Tobias both reached in with their hands and grabbed a hand full of whatever Pearl had.

"Wow, what the hell is this?" Ben howled.

"Pearl, this is good!" Tobias added. "What is it? I taste apples, am I right?"

Pearl stood smiling at the two of them. "Happy birthday. See, I told you I could make you a cake."

"How did you do it?" Ben again asked.

"I ripped up that old crusty bread we had and mixed it with Penny's canned apples. Mush it all together like dough till the bread gets all soft again, and then let it sit for a minute or two." Pearl dipped her hands into the mixture and grabbed a handful.

After dinner, Tobias and Pearl made their bedrolls inside the woods. After their scare last night, Ben slept out by the fire in case someone came up on them again after dark.

It was early morning when Ben was jostled awake out of a deep sleep. "Ben! Ben!" When he opened his eyes, Tobias was on his knees next to him, violently shaking him. "What is it?" Ben said, struggling to wake up.

"It's dogs. I hear dogs barking." Tobias's voice was tense.

Right away, Ben heard a bark. He kept still as he focused on the sound.

"Do you think they are coming after us?" Tobias asked.

"No, it can't be." Ben shook his head, listening. "We're too far out, and you guys have been in the wagon. The dogs can't pick up a scent if you ain't on the ground. Maybe huntin' dogs. But we best get goin', though, just in case."

Half asleep, Ben gathered his bedroll and went to retrieve the horses. Tobias got Pearl situated in the wagon and then came over to assist Ben. Within minutes, Ben maneuvered the old wooden wagon back onto the road, which was just wide enough for it. A thick wall of forest closed in on both sides, leaving them with nothing to look at but the road ahead. He didn't remember the trees being so dense last night when he called it quits. Damn had he been sleeping well until Tobias scared the crow out of him.

Ben released a huge yawn, as thoughts of a hot cup of coffee wouldn't leave him alone. Boy, what he wouldn't do for one cup of coffee. The sun had not yet come up much over the trees, making the blind corners of the road, which seemed to come one right after another, all that much darker.

"Do you think those were hunting dogs?" Tobias's head poked out from the canvas.

"Yeah, I'm pretty sure, but even huntin' dogs had people on the other end of them." Ben's brain was still in a fog, and he wasn't ready to talk.

Just as Ben wheeled the two mares around yet another blind corner, he was forced to pull back on the reins as hard as he could and yell, "Whoa!"

Unable to stop, the two men on horseback directly in front of him split, one to the right and the other to the left, barely avoiding a crash. All four horses whinnied and stomped. Ben quickly saw that the men were bandits. He took in a deep breath as he snapped his whip, trying to move his horses forward and regain control of them. He prayed that Tobias and Pearl wouldn't show their faces or make any noise. It was too late to give them any kind of a warning; the men were two feet from him on either side.

"You driving those horses pretty fast!" the man on the left stated as he, too, attempted to get control of his horse.

"Where you heading?" the other asked.

"Good morning." Ben was stalling, fussing with the reins as he collected his thoughts. "Train depot."

"What you got in that there wagon?" one of them asked.

"Nothin' yet. Heading over to the train depot to pick up some rifles to fight them injuns. Those featherheads ain't never seen nothin' like what I got comin'. But I got to keep on movin'. Got to be back home by nightfall." The two men looked at each other.

"So you goin' up and back in a day's trip, is you?" the other asked.

"Yeah, got to have Pa's wagon back to him tonight 'for he discovers its missin'.'"

"Alright, boy, wouldn't want to hold you up. Kill one of them injuns for me, will you?" said the one on the left. They parted and allowed Ben to drive his horses and wagon between them. Ben knew that they would be waiting for him when he returned with those rifles—that is, if he returned. Laughing, he snapped the reins and started the slow climb towards a small canyon that lay ahead.

The days began to run into one another as they traveled through the heart of Kentucky. Ben drove the wagon every day for as long as he could. He had never been so tired in his life. Their food supply all but gone, he passed on the meager breakfast of nuts one morning to ensure that Pearl and her unborn child were getting enough to eat. He cracked a tiny smile as he thought about Penny's flapjacks and her amazing biscuits and gravy. He could picture the gravy, the way it hid the biscuit underneath. He was the only one in the house that liked to put orange marmalade in the middle of his biscuit before drowning it in gravy. "Ewe-wee, those were some good biscuits," he mumbled to himself as he licked his lips.

"Pearl's got to pee!" Tobias called out through the canvas.

"Okay, hold on. There are some trees comin' up. I'll stop up there." Ben was ready for a break as well. He would get down and stretch his legs a little.

Stopping the wagon under the hanging boughs of the trees, Ben positioned the wagon so that, if someone came along, they wouldn't be able to see anything between it and the forest. "Okay, it's clear," he said.

Stretching his legs out, he reclined into the back of the wagon. He was caught completely unprepared as Tobias grabbed his head and their lips met. Tobias's lips were warm as he pushed them into Ben, taking Ben's breath away. Ben opened his mouth, giving Tobias full access to him as their lips intermingled. Ben arched up and released a moan as Tobias continued his assault. The sweetness of Tobias's breath invaded his senses, and Tobias's touch so commanding as he took control of the three minutes they had alone. Ben missed their intimacy, their talks, and their lazy days pretending to be working. It seemed a lifetime ago. Ben felt the rise in his britches just as Pearl let out a scream.

Jerking apart, they were both out of the wagon in seconds, running towards the noise. Just inside the trees, Pearl had her back to them. She was working to get her undergarment straightened out under her dress.

"What is it?" Ben asked. His mind was still on the kiss and the feel of Tobias's lips on him. He had to adjust the front of his britches.

"Look, a spirit!" Pearl pointed straight ahead.

Ben's eyes followed her finger, and he was taken aback when he saw it. It was a negro woman, holding a sack and crouching in the tall weeds about twenty feet from them. She looked like a ghost as her piercing eyes bore into them.

Reacting to the sight of the mysterious, motionless figure, Ben extended his arm in front of Pearl and guided her behind him. "Who are you?" he asked as he glanced around, ensuring that she was alone.

"Is you the freedom train? I supposed to be waitin' for you?" The woman's eyes moved between Ben and Tobias.

"What are you talking about?" Tobias asked. "Who are you? Why are you hiding in the woods?"

The woman rose to her feet. "I told to wait here. The freedom train come gets me. They takes me to the River of Jordan, where I be free."

"You a runaway?" Tobias took a step towards the woman.

"Yes. I run three days ago. Been waitin' here in these woods for two days. Ain't nobody come gets me."

Ben studied the woman. She wasn't much taller than Pearl. Clothed in a tattered indigo dress, she looked exhausted. Stepping forward, Ben reached out to her. "Who was takin' you to freedom . . .

to the River of Jordan?" he asked, thinking the woman was possibly touched.

I don't know who. Preacher told me to stay in the woods till the freedom train comes by. I see your wagon and that there girl and thinks it was my freedom train."

Ben had no idea what the woman was talking about and was positive that she was as crazy as a fox. "Ain't no train around here. That's a wagon." He glanced at Tobias and rolled his eyes.

"You say freedom train. What is that?" Tobias asked.

"Don't know. Was told to wait here, and someone would come fetch me. Runnin' to Illinois, where my people is. Mr. Levi drops me off here. Do you know Mr. Levi?"

"So you're runnin'? You a slave?" Ben asked. "Who's Mr. Levi?" He realized that she was a runaway and that someone was helping her. "Who is Mr. Levi?" he asked again, this time with more of a bark in his voice.

"He—he the preacher man."

Ben took a step closer to the stranger. "What preacher man? Was he helpin' you to run?"

The woman's eyes shifted back and forth between Ben, Tobias, and Pearl, as if she was unsure if she should answer. Finally, her eyes settled on Ben. She lowered the gunnysack, which she held by means of a long stick to which it was tied. "He the preacher man who say he was goin' to help me be free."

Whoever this Mr. Levi was, he was on their side, and he might give them a place to bed down for the night. "Let me take you back to Mr. Levi, so he can make the arrangements to ensure you get to Illinois. Can you take us there?"

"Sure can, he up the road." The woman looked at Tobias and Pearl but didn't move.

"Wha's your name?" Pearl asked.

"Bessie, Bessie Davis."

Tobias got Pearl and their new guest settled in the back of the wagon as Ben turned it around and headed back towards the town they had just left. He wanted to meet this Mr. Levi in hopes of a proper meal and a place to lay their heads.

Bessie guided Ben to a little church on the outskirts of the town. The church had a large white house next to it. As they neared the building, a tall, slender young man exited the chapel. He was dressed in a crisp white shirt, black suspenders, and a large black hat. Ben knew that he was a Quaker.

"Good evenin', sir." Ben brought the horses to a halt.

"Good evening." The preacher leaned against the doorframe. "What can I do for you?"

Ben reached behind him and pulled the canvas back. Tobias, Pearl, and Bessie peeked out. "My friends and I seem to have lost our way. Don't suppose you can help a fellow, maybe spare a little food, and point me in the right direction in the mornin'?"

The preacher looked into the wagon, and the sapphire in his eyes sparkled as he stroked the dark brown hairs on his sizeable beard. "Well, not sure what you need—" Coming off the doorframe, he stood straight. "Why don't you pull up next to the barn. Unload over there. Wife just about has supper on the table."

Ben's intuition told him the preacher was a just man. Snapping the reins, he maneuvered the horses and wagon into a tight spot between the barn and a large windmill. Pulling up as close as he could, he ensured the back end of the wagon was even with the barn door. In a whisper, he told Tobias to take the girls into the barn and wait for him. Unhitching the horses, Ben got the mares settled in an adjacent corral.

There the preacher met him again. "I'm Levi. Let's get you cleaned up and put a little food in that belly." He placed a hand on Ben's shoulders and directed him towards the old two-story stone house, which was shaped like a box. Its front door was dead center with two small windows on each side.

Ben washed up using the water bowl and rag that Levi had placed on a table next to the wood stove. There was a small, mousy woman cooking in the kitchen. Levi introduced her as Elizabeth, his wife.

Ben's eyes took in the long, drab dress that concealed the woman from head to toe and then the odd-looking white bonnet that covered her hair. She scarcely acknowledged him with a nod as she immediately brought the food to the table. He followed her there, and wondered where he should sit. Since there was one place setting set at the end of the table, he gathered that he was safe taking one of the chairs on either side of that setting. Levi gestured for him to sit as he took his own place at the table. "So where did you say you're from, Brother Ben?"

"Well, sir, we—I mean me, is from Warren, just below Butler County. My pa has a farm, been in the family for years. Can't say I want any part of it, so me and my friend decided it was time to head up north." Ben leaned a little to the right as the woman sat another place setting in front of him.

Acknowledging her hospitality with a nod, Ben hesitated before reaching for a piece of bread. He hadn't had bread in days, and he couldn't resist any longer. "Wasn't plannin' on Pearl comin' with us, but she saw fit to stow away. Don't say I blame her none, that life was swallowin' us all up whole." Tearing the bread in two, Ben dipped it into his bowl of catfish stew. The first bite stopped him in his tracks. He savored the warm stew hitting his stomach.

"Elizabeth, why don't you take some of this stew and a few pieces of bread out to our visitors? Probably been awhile since they had a good meal." Levi leaned back in his chair as he watched his wife.

After Elizabeth left the room, Levi looked at Ben. "That young lady you got was supposed to be picked up a couple of days ago. She was heading to Chicago. I put her in the woods myself."

"Well, sir, we stopped to relieve ourselves, and that's when we discovered her. Just was sittin' there. 'Bout scared us all the way back home. She said somethin' about a train. Thought she might have been touched."

Levi chuckled as he started eating again.

Ben's eye caught how Levi was watching him. Had he lost his manners there for few seconds, attacking the bowl of stew like a hog at feeding time? Leaning back in his chair, Ben created some distance between him and his supper.

"Where about north are you heading?" Levi wiped his beard, cleaning the stew off of it.

"Pennsylvania, sir. Tobias and Pearl are brother and sister. I'm the legal owner of Tobias. Pa owns Pearl, so she is the only real runaway I have. Believe they can be free in Pennsylvania. Looking for a normal life."

"Do you have their papers?"

"Got papers for Tobias, sir, but ain't got none for Pearl," Ben said.

Levi nodded. "Even in a free state, they aren't free if a slave tracker can prove they're runaways. The only place that is truly free is Canada." He sighed. "Take them on up through Ohio, and cross the lake on into Canada." Levi leaned in as if someone else was in the room who he didn't want listening. "Do you know anything about the Underground Railroad?"

"The train?" Ben repeated back as he tried to connect what Levi was saying to what Bessie had said back there in the woods.

"Yes, the Underground Railroad. Safest way for your friends to travel. Ain't much I can tell you other than that. I'm what we call a Train Station. I'll arrange for someone to pick you up where you found Bessie, and they will carry you to the next stop. I don't know anything about where you're going other than it's your next station." Levi's eyes shifted over to the back door as the knob turned. Both Ben and Levi watched Elizabeth as she removed her shawl and resumed her work at the stove.

Ben wondered if he was going to continue in front of his wife. Did she know what he was doing?

Levi took a sip of coffee. "Now, Bessie was dead set that she was going to Chicago. Don't know what happened there. I'll make arrangements for her again when I take care of you."

Ben raised his head, a sudden realization hitting him. "How much is this goin' to cost me?" All the money he had was to go to their future property. He knew nothing about Canada other than it was a different country.

Levi laughed. "Won't cost you nothing. Doing it because it's the right thing to do. The Lord places no value on the color of your skin."

"So this won't cost me nothin'. Y'all doin' it out the goodness of your heart is what you're tellin' me?" He had read plenty about how Quakers were involved in the movement to abolish slavery, but he had figured it was all through the passing of laws. This was news to him.

"We Quakers believe in the equality of all people. In spite of our small numbers, we are making a difference in this world doing God's work."

"Well, I have to admit, I don't know nothin' about God's work, but I'm grateful for the help." Pausing for a moment, Ben thought about everything he was hearing. He had many questions, but he didn't want to seem like he doubted this man, who sounded like he wanted to help. "So, what happens with my wagon and my horses? Don't suppose you could use two horses or a wagon. It's the least I could do for what you're doin' for me."

"No, I can't say that I can use two more mouths to feed. But when you get to where you're going, send me a note to say you found your church, and I'll send you whatever I get for them."

Levi was silent as he ate the rest of his stew. After several minutes, he spoke again. "It will take a day or so to set up your transportation. We can move your friends into the chapel, where it will be warm. Elizabeth can make a bed for you here in the house. Oh, another thing: you'll travel at night, so be ready to go when I tell you it's time. We usually don't get much warning."

Ben slopped his bread down in the bottom of his bowl, soaking up the last of his stew. He hadn't been this full since leaving home. He considered asking if it would be okay to take his bed with his friends. After just this short time in the house, he was already missing them. Still, sleeping with them might raise suspicions about his true feelings towards Tobias. He decided to sleep in the house.

After dinner, Ben followed Levi upstairs, where Elizabeth had prepared a bed for him and laid out a clean nightshirt.

As Levi started to shut the door, he poked his head back into the room. "See you in the morning. After breakfast, I got to head on over and pay a visit to Mrs. Williams, but I should be back around dinnertime. You and your friends probably need the day to rest up. You have a long journey ahead of you."

Ben realized he had forgotten to ask how long this trip to Canada would take. How stupid of him. "Sir, how long will it take us?" He couldn't hide his distress.

Levi smiled as he shook his head. "Not sure. Couple of weeks, a month, maybe two. Can't say."

Ben's heart sank. None of this was as he planned. His fists pressed together, he walked over to the window. It was dark, but he could make out the church. He wondered what they were doing in there. Were they asleep? Was Tobias still up, maybe peering up at him out of one of those windows? Ben pressed his palm to the glass. *Canada.* He couldn't wait two months for freedom. He couldn't do it.

20

The next morning, before breakfast, when Ben came downstairs, Elizabeth was in the kitchen, her back to him as she tended to something on the stove. Levi was seated at the head of the table, reading his Bible as he sipped on his coffee. Ben saw that two plates were set this morning.

"Morning, Mr. Lee." Elizabeth maneuvered around him with a plate of flapjacks and sausage and sat it in front of her husband's plate. "Have a seat . . . Coffee?" She sounded as if she was trying to be polite.

"Um—yes, yes, ma'am." Ben pulled the chair out and took his place at the table.

"Go on, get started. There's more where those came from." Elizabeth returned to the stove and continued cooking. Ben counted the flapjacks on the plate. There were six, three a piece, and a whole mess of sausage patties. Minding his manners, he took two flapjacks and two sausages and then waited for Levi.

"Sleep well?" Levi asked as he took the remaining four flapjacks.

"Yes, sir." Ben was about to start eating when he realized that Levi was staring at him.

"Let us pray," Levi said.

Ben put his fork on the table. Elizabeth stopped whatever she was doing at the stove and bowed her head. Levi's prayer was short—he got right to the point, thanking God for the food in front of them.

"Amen." Elizabeth mumbled as she resumed her cooking.

"I checked on your friends this morning. The girls were sleeping, but Tobias—" Levi stopped and looked at Ben.

Ben held his breath, waiting. *What? What is it?*

"He was up. Pacing the floor. He asked for you. Told him you'll be out after breakfast." Levi's voice was flat.

"Thank you for checkin' on them for me." Ben's heart thumped, and his breath quickened. He had to push his butt down in the chair to keep from leaping up and going to Tobias. He'd rather be in that chapel, cold and hungry but with Tobias, than in here warm and full.

Ben took a sip of coffee. Not even the earthy, robust flavor was enough to distract him from his thoughts. Elizabeth added four fresh flapjacks to the plate of sausage and then topped off their coffee.

After breakfast, Ben and his two hosts left the house at the same time: Levi going to his morning visitation, and Elizabeth and Ben walking to the little chapel. The air was thick between them, and Ben sensed something was amiss. "Mrs. Elizabeth, I sure am thankful for you and your husband comin' to our rescue like this." Elizabeth stopped in her tracks. Her blue eyes narrowed as she frowned. Pushing up at the bridge of her wire frame glasses, she heaved a large sigh, and her shoulders dropped.

"Let me set the record straight for you. I was forced to choose. I love my husband, and I know it's the Godly thing to do. But my life was much simpler once upon a time—before I was harboring runaways, looking over my shoulder to see if anyone is watching me, and cooking at all hours of the night. Had people just left things alone . . ." She paused. "Anti-slavery societies are popping up everywhere, and I imagine it's what the Lord wants. Blood will be spilled, negroes' and whites'. Far more blood than if we had done nothing." Holding her hand to her chest, she exhaled slowly. "Whatever this . . .this thing between you and that negro is, it is between you and the Lord. There is a Judgment Day for all of us. Believers can only escape damnation by salvation. You will answer to him when the time comes—I want no part of it."

Elizabeth rolled her eyes and shook her head. "Come." She was off again towards the chapel.

Ben wanted to believe she was referring to Pearl, that she assumed she was carrying his child. But there was a pit lying in his belly that told him she knew, she knew the truth. Following behind her, his entire body felt broken as a queasiness began to take over. She had just damned his soul to hell for what they were doing.

Removing a key from her bodice, she unlocked the chapel door and ushered him in. Ben noticed she relocked the door from the inside before moving ahead of him down the center aisle of the church.

Inside, Ben saw no sign of Tobias or Pearl. The building was cold, lit only by the sun coming through the windows. It was much smaller than he had envisioned. Approaching the altar, Elizabeth stopped and looked back at the door. Ben watched her as she slid the preacher's podium two feet to the left. She bent over and, with her finger, lifted part of the floor up. Ben's mouth fell open when he realized she was opening a hidden door designed to match the floor. Peering down the hole, he looked at six steps that led down beneath the altar. It was dark, and he couldn't see how big a space it was.

He followed her down the steps. The space was no bigger than eight by eight and about five feet in height. As his eyes adjusted to the low light, he saw Tobias and the girls lying on bedrolls. Tobias looked asleep. When he opened his eyes, they quickly widened as if he couldn't believe what he was seeing. Springing up, he grabbed Ben and wrapped him in his arms. They held each other tightly, paying no mind to the others in their midst.

As Pearl and Bessie sat up, Tobias and Ben separated. Ben wondered what that hug must have looked like to Elizabeth and Bessie— two men embracing such as they had.

"Are you guys alright?" Ben asked. A tear formed in his eye. One night apart, and he was crying. He knew he couldn't cry in front of the women after what just occurred outside. He exhaled, trying to steady his breathing. Looking around the room, he focused his eyes on the bedrolls on the floor, trying to divert his mind from the emotions building within him. Just then, Elizabeth lit a candle, causing the entire room to light up. The room was lined with long, narrow benches along three walls and smelled of dirt. In the corner, where two benches came together, was a bowl of apples, bread, and a pitcher of water.

Finally answering Ben's question, Tobias said, "Yes, we're fine. Ms. Elizabeth took nice care of us. Fed us supper last night. Mr. Levi was out this morning. Brought us some fruit."

Ben stepped aside as Elizabeth moved around him and retrieved a chamber pot from under one of the benches. Ben and Pearl smiled at each other as Elizabeth climbed the steps with the pot.

"Are we leaving?" Tobias asked.

Ben watched as Pearl lifted her upper body into a sitting position against the bench. He said, "No, not yet." He wondered how Tobias was going to react to the news about Canada. Ben wasn't even convinced it was the right move; how could he sell it to Tobias?

"Oh?" Tobias's eyebrows narrowed.

Ben hesitated as he collected his thoughts, trying to remember what Mr. Levi had told him. "We're goin' to get help. These nice folks are goin' to help us, but were not goin' to Pennsylvania anymore. We're goin' to Canada."

Elizabeth returned with the empty chamber pot. "It's safe if you all want to come upstairs to talk. Maybe get a little more air?"

"Yeah, that might be good . . . Pearl, can you give us a minute?" Ben asked.

Pearl nodded and laid herself back down on the floor, covering herself with her blanket.

Ben followed Elizabeth and Tobias up the stairs. The fresh air hit him as if he had been choking to death and hadn't even known it.

"So, what do you mean, there's a new plan? Canada—what's Canada?" Tobias asked.

"It's another country."

"Another country?" Tobias looked over at Elizabeth and then back at Ben.

"Now, it's not that much farther. I looked at it on a map. Mr. Levi showed it to me." Ben rubbed the back of his neck as he tried to think of something positive to say.

"How long will this take? How would we get there?" Tobias's voice rose slightly.

"I don't know exactly. It's complicated. Sit down, and I'll explain it all to you." Ben paced the floor. He had messed up. It was foolishness, thinking he had it all worked out, that it was as simple as getting away from the farm.

"Can Pearl even make it that far?" Tobias continued. "Why Canada?"

Elizabeth interjected. "She can make it. I looked at her last night. I would say she's seven months. The baby's small for seven months. I have concerns about her age and her ability to deliver this child, but you can cross that bridge when it comes. I know God has his hand on her and will protect her and give her the strength she'll need."

"Oh?" Ben asked, as he thought about what Elizabeth said to him earlier.

"I'm sorry to interrupt." Elizabeth looked away. "I'll let you two alone, but I'll be right outside the door. If someone comes, I'll warn you. Ben, make sure you move that podium over the door, and then you can exit out the back if need be." She walked up the aisle towards the door without waiting for a response.

Ben waited until she was gone before taking a seat in the first row of pews. Tobias took a seat next to him and held his hand. Ben started from the beginning, reciting everything that Levi had told him. In the end, Tobias was receptive to the idea, expressing how pleased he was that someone was actually looking out for them. Not long after, Pearl and Bessie also came up from the tiny room. The four of them stayed in the chapel the entire day, until Levi called Ben for supper.

"I'll be back after supper, and we can talk some more." Ben wanted to kiss Tobias. A thickness formed in his throat as he thought about Elizabeth. Was he really going to hell for simply loving someone? Looking up, he saw that Levi was waiting, ready to ensure the three were secured in the room.

On the second day, Ben learned that Bessie had left in the middle of the night, on her way to Illinois. Levi explained that their train was still being worked out, but he hoped to hear something soon.

That evening during supper, Ben noticed that Levi was missing. When Ben inquired about him, Elizabeth was vague as to his whereabouts. This made Ben a bit nervous.

After supper, Ben went out to visit Tobias in the chapel. Elizabeth unlocked the door and then handed the key to him. "Lock yourself in and don't unlock it for anyone."

Ben did as instructed and watched her go into the house before he opened the hatch. Hearing that Pearl was tired and wasn't coming up, he was happy to realize that it would be just him and Tobias. Levi's absence had actually worked out in their favor.

Sitting in the pew, Tobias wrapped his arms around Ben's shoulders, drawing him in.

"I missed you." Ben gave Tobias a soft kiss. The moment their lips touched, a surge of desire exploded within Ben. Breathless, his lips lingered until Tobias kissed him again. He couldn't imagine a time before Tobias.

When Tobias kissed him next, his hand lightly brushed under Ben's chin and down his neck. He was washed in a sea of pleasure; he loved how fast he responded to Tobias's touch. As their kisses deepened, Tobias tried to lay him down in the pew.

"Um, no, Tobias, no, not here . . . I can't. Not in a church. It's not right." Ben wrangled his way from under Tobias and sat up.

"What's wrong? Is it Pearl? She won't come up." Tobias's eyes were like liquid as they stared into Ben's.

"I can't do nothin' in a church. Don't seem right." Ben could feel his erection pressing into the front of his undergarment. He didn't dare try to fix it in front of Tobias—he would most surely lose this fight if Tobias saw that he was erect.

"What do you mean? Why not in here?"

"'Cause this is where God is and stuff. Don't seem respectful." Without thinking, Ben adjusted himself, relieving his discomfort. He was about to expound on his reasons for not messing around in the church when he heard the front door open. Looking back, he saw that Levi was already in the chapel. *Damn, that was close. We almost got caught. I would have died.*

With a big smile on his face, Levi shoved a set of keys in his pocket. He was undoubtedly in a good mood. "Good news. You're leaving tonight," he announced, as he came down the aisle.

Ben and Tobias both stood at the same time. Certain his erection had subsided enough not to be visible, Ben glanced down at his crotch anyways.

"Got word the Conductor is on his way. Gather your things."

"What can you tell us?" Ben asked. Not knowing the details of their situation—who, what, when, and why—made him uneasy.

"Can't tell you anything. He has no name, so don't ask him. He'll meet you in the woods where you found Bessie. You'll wait there, in the woods off the road. He will stop in front of you, and you'll hear a bird call.

Ben smiled, remembering calling out to Tobias in the oaks, trying to sound like an owl.

"I don't know what he looks like, but you will know that it is him. Listen for the bird call, followed by him calling out 'Friend of a friend.'"

"Friend of a friend?" Tobias repeated.

Levi's eyes shifted between Tobias and Ben "It's your signal. Get to the wagon as fast as possible, and no talking. You understand?"

Both of them nodded their heads. Ben couldn't believe they were moving again. As it sank in, his excitement built. He wasn't trying to do it alone anymore. The responsibility of getting them all to freedom had been more stressful then he ever expected. He had never shared his doubts with Tobias or Pearl, but it would have killed him if they hadn't made it because of him.

"You guys need to get some rest. It may be a long night for you. Ben, Elizabeth said that you have her keys. I'll take those now."

Ben handed over the keys, realizing that Levi was leaving him in the chapel with the others.

☙

At about eleven that evening, Levi was at the door, telling them it was time to go. They piled into the back of the church's wagon and were taken to the spot where they had found Bessie. The wagon slowed to a crawl, but never stopped moving, as the three of them jumped from it and ran into the woods.

Ben wasn't sure if it was the nighttime air, or the thrill of being on the move again, but he was excited, full of energy.

They waited in the dark for hours, with Pearl dozing while Tobias and Ben watched for any movement coming down the road.

Finally, they heard a voice singing accompanied by the grunting of a horse. "This train is bound for glory, this train . . ."

"Shhh, someone's coming," Tobias said.

The voice grew closer. "This train is bound for glory this train, this train. This train don't carry no gamblers, this train." The sound of a horse and cart coming down the road was as plain as day. Ben knew this had to be it. It was time to move. "Pearl. Pearl, wake up."

They watched as the little man stopped his cart along the dirt road in front of them. He climbed down and walked around towards the back. There was a sound of a birdcall, and the voice called out, "Friend of a friend."

Staring up at the stars and moon, the stranger resumed his singing as the three friends popped up and ran towards the cart. The man guided them into the back of his apple cart, which had a false bottom. He moved as casually as if he was doing anything else. He then walked towards the front, climbed back into the driver's seat, and snapped his reins. "This train don't carry no liars, this train, this train don't carry no liars, this train," he sang as he rode into the dark of night with his passengers.

21

After six nights of traveling, covering less than twenty miles each night, Ben and Tobias knew it was going to take much longer to get to Canada than Mr. Levi had said. Their journey was at the complete discretion of this Underground Railroad system.

Although no one would tell them much, Ben was slowly piecing the operation together. They traveled at night and moved from station to station when it was safe to move. Most nights, they were led either by wagon or on foot to the next station by a series of people, different each time. Everyone referred to them as *Conductors*.

The elderly couple at their last stop had fed them well and had hidden them for three days before they were told it was time to move. Ben had grown accustomed to people successfully helping them, but tonight, he was concerned right from the start. They were told there would be no conductor with them. The passage was said to be too risky, so the travelers would have go on alone.

"We need to leave in a couple of hours. How's Pearl?" Ben asked. He had been quiet most of the night after they learned it would be just them going it alone. Pacing out behind the tiny shed where they had been confined for the last three days, he wasn't feeling good about this evening at all.

"She's fine. She's resting." Tobias had come outside looking for Ben, his face conveying the same nervous look. Tobias's eyes followed Ben's stooped posture as Ben paced back in forth in front of him. "What's wrong? Are you worried about tonight?" Tobias asked.

Ben stopped in his tracks but didn't look at him. Biting his nails, he didn't know how to voice his uneasiness without exposing his own fears. "Just thinking about tonight is all."

"What about it? Is it that we'll be on our own again? That's what got you upset isn't it?"

Turning to face Tobias, Ben didn't want to lie to him. It was actually a relief that Tobias knew already.

"Yeah, it's got me a little nervous is all. Kind of got used to someone with us. Travelin' at night, on foot . . .. With Pearl. Maybe we should leave her here."

No, we're not leaving her!" Tobias's tone left no room for rebuttal.

"Okay, okay." Ben nodded in agreement.

"The instruction for tonight, it didn't sound that hard. Look, let me help. I can get us there I'm sure of it. I'm used to the woods; they look the same to me whether it's day or night. It's only a couple of miles. The nights clear." Tobias stopped and looked up at the sky. "See, the North Star is already shining bright. We'll have no problems finding this house she was talking about."

He knew Tobias was right. He heard the conviction in his voice and felt his confidence. Perhaps this was one of the reasons he loved Tobias as much as he did. Somehow, Tobias was the light in all of this darkness. One would have thought it was the other way around, but Ben knew that simply wasn't true. The truth was that he drew his own strength from Tobias, like the sun shining onto a flower. Each day with Tobias left him a better man, a stronger person rising from the shell he once was. Taking a deep breath, Ben felt his chest expand with the rush of oxygen flowing into his lungs. Exhaling, he let his shoulders drop as he took another breath. He had all the faith in the world that Tobias could do this.

Later that night, led by Tobias, the three silhouettes moved cautiously under the moonlight, along the river and through the trees. As he had promised, Tobias would be the one to get them to the next station.

Hours into their walk, they came upon an old cabin in the woods. The dog on the porch sounded the alarm at their presence, and they hunkered down between two trees. Releasing howl after howl, the dog continued until an old man wobbled out onto the porch. "What is it, Rufus? What's out there, ole boy?"

Tobias pointed at the silver moon hanging above them and said, "There's too much moon. Don't move."

He was right. The cabin was less than one hundred feet away. With the full moon, they could easily be spotted. The thought occurred to Ben that, if that hound wasn't tied, it could be on them in seconds. With Pearl, there would be no way of escaping.

"Ain't nothin' out here, boy. Now, you shut up! You hear me now!" the old man shouted, before stepping back inside.

"Let's go," Tobias said.

When Pearl went to stand, she let out a cry and collapsed to her knees. Holding her stomach, she moaned again. Old Rufus started up again.

"Pearl!" Ben went to his knees alongside her. "What's wrong?"

Tobias joined them. Pearl's breathing came in sharp, shallow rasps. Clutching her belly, she let out another cry as she rolled into Tobias's arms.

Ben spotted the old man back on his porch, this time carrying his shotgun. "Who's there? Who's out there?" he hollered.

Pearl continued to moan as Tobias tried to cover her mouth with his hands, but this only muffled her cry.

Ben stood up. "Don't shoot, don't shoot, it's only me!"

"Who's me?" the old man yelled from the porch. "On the count of three, I'm goin' to shoot!"

Ben took a step forward, but Tobias grabbed him by his wrist. "What are you doing?"

Ben didn't answer as he shook Tobias loose. He had to go to the man before the man, or the dog, came to them.

"One!" the old man yelled.

Ben moved towards the tiny cabin. He could feel the weight of his legs with each step. Dry leaves crunched beneath his feet.

"Two!"

Ben realized the old man couldn't see him yet. "Sir, don't shoot, I'm right here. Right here, sir." He waited for the sound of gunfire as he approached the porch and stopped at its edge. He saw that the dog was tied to a post, but this brought him little comfort.

"Joseph, is that you?" the old man asked. "What you doin' out here this time of night?" He peered down the barrel of his gun, with his finger on the trigger.

"No, I'm not Joseph, sir. My name is Jake," Ben lied. He was less than five feet in front of the old man when he saw that the barrel was pointing directly at one of the porch's posts. Seeing this, Ben knew the man must be blind. "Sir, my name is Jake. I ain't got no gun, buts I'm hungry. Been travelin' all night. Can you spare some food?"

"Ain't got no spare food, boy." The old man pumped the shotgun. "Get on out of here 'for I shoot you."

Ben wasn't worried any more of being shot—it would take more than luck for the old man to actually hit him. "Please don't shoot, sir. I mean no harm," he pleaded, as he looked back to where he had left Tobias and Pearl. He could still faintly hear Pearl's muffled cries. He hoped that the old man was losing his hearing as well.

The man lifted his eye from the gun. "I reckon I gives you a little food. You like mincemeat? That's all I got!"

"I'll take anything, sir. I'm real hungry."

Ben watched as the old man lowered his shotgun and felt around until he found Rufus' rope. With two jerks of the rope, he told Rufus to quiet down. "Come on in, boy, out the cold. Ain't goin' to feed you out here."

Ben followed the old man through the dark cabin and was told to sit down at a little table in the kitchen. As the old man fumbled around in the dark kitchen, Ben could hear Rufus continuing to bark outside. He listened to see if he could hear Pearl, but he couldn't hear anything over ole Rufus. He hated to leave his friends, but he'd had to do something before they were all discovered. *Pearl—what is happening with Pearl?* His heart was racing as he tried to collect himself.

"Here you go, boy. Eat up." The old man slid a plate under Ben's chin. "Mincemeat, made it yesterday."

Hungry, Ben took a heaping spoonful and shoveled it into his mouth. That was as far as it went, stopping on his tongue. The taste of molasses and dirt came to mind as he rolled it around in his mouth. *Just swallow.* He didn't know how he was going to swallow it, but he did, one bite after another, until the plate was gone.

"Want some more?" the man asked.

"No, sir, but that sure was good. Taste like my momma's." Ben listened for any sign of Pearl. The only thing he could hear was Rufus's barking and the old man talking about how he could still get around without his sight. Ben had to go. Standing up, he shifted his weight as he prepared to leave.

"Can I get you a cup of coffee?" the man asked.

"No, sir, I need to be gettin' goin'." Ben knew the old fella was lonely out here in the woods by himself. That old hound surely didn't look like much company. But listening for Pearl and hearing nothing worried him.

"What's your hurry, boy? It's the middle of the night. Stay until mornin', will you?"

That was out of the question. Ben shifted his weight to take a step and stopped. "Well, sir, thank you. I think I will if it ain't much troublin' you. I need to go back to the road and get my sack. Got my money and all." Ben took another step towards the door. It wasn't as if the old man could chase him. He needed to get to Tobias and Pearl.

"Well, what are you sittin' there for? It ain't goin' to come on its own," the man barked.

Ben reached out and rustled the chair as if he was getting up. "Be right quick."

Keeping his eye on the man, Ben moved towards the front door. With one step, he was over Rufus and off the porch, running towards were he left Tobias and Pearl. He reached the tree to find them gone. He was sure this was the right tree. He looked down at the ground for any sign that he was in the right spot.

"Tobias . . . Tobias . . . Pearl . . ." he whispered into the dark woods. Moving from tree to tree, he kept glancing at the house.

They were gone. Breathless, in the midst of the dark woods, he didn't know what to do. Surely, they were still here and just couldn't hear him. "Tobias . . . Tobias . . . Pearl . . ." The woods were quiet.

Ben's eyes scanned the old man's cabin and the surrounding woods. He had to find them. Pearl must have been in a bad condition for them to just leave. For a split second, he entertained the idea that they left him—gone on their own. No. Tobias wouldn't do that. Maybe they had continued on to the next station. Yes, that had to be it.

Ben looked around and then up to find the North Star. He had to get his bearings. Damn it, why hadn't he paid more attention to where they were. Ben heard the old man come out onto the porch. With a quickness in his step, Ben turned on his heels and headed in what he believed was the direction of the next station.

Wandering all night, he became sure that he was lost. As sunlight appeared, he felt exhausted and could barely hold his head up. He had to keep going. He had kicked himself in the butt all night for not paying closer attention to the old couple when they gave Tobias the directions to the next station.

Ben walked until he came to a road. It was too narrow for an actual road; it had to be a driveway. Looking one direction, he saw a large house. His heart skipped a beat at the thought that he had found the station. With a surge of energy, he ran the quarter mile down the driveway to the house.

He at least remembered the description of the station, and this matched it—an old farmhouse with a long, narrow driveway and two big barns, one on each side of it. He read the sign that hung on the porch: *Praise the Lord.* He smiled as he exhaled a large breath.

He looked for the lantern, which was to be lit that night and left hanging if it was safe to approach. There was a lantern, but it wasn't lit. Ben examined the house. He was sure this was it.

He could knock. If it was the wrong house, he could make something up, say he was lost. As he stepped onto the porch, the floorboard creaked. Stopping in his tracks, he tried to look in the windows, but there were sheers draped inside. He listened, but the house was quiet. *Perhaps they're not up.*

Reaching out, he knocked gently on the large wooden door. He continued to listen for any noise inside the house. Then he heard footsteps coming to the door, which creaked open.

"Hello," a little girl said, as she stood behind the door.

Ben looked over the child's head for any sign of Tobias or Pearl before lowering himself to one knee to address the girl. "Is your momma or papa—?"

"What can we do for you?" A tall, slender woman appeared behind the child. She was dressed as if she was ready to be escorted to a social. Her golden hair and pastel-white skin made her strikingly beautiful.

Ben couldn't just come out and ask if Tobias and Pearl were there. She wouldn't know who he was. Standing up, he removed his hat and placed it in front of his chest. He knew he was looking ragged.

"Well, ma'am, I was travelin' with my two good friends, and we seem to have gotten separated last night. I was hopin' they may have found their way here." He knew that he had to be careful. It was against the law to harbor a runaway, so he didn't mention that his friends were negroes.

The woman looked him over, her eyes moving slowly as she studied him. "So what did you say your friend's names were?"

"They is Tobias and Pearl, ma'am. We're *friends of a friend.*"

The woman's jaw dropped as she let out a small gasp. "Sir, why on earth would you suspect that they're here?" she asked.

Ben cleared his throat as he searched for the right answer. "Ma'am, my friend Pearl is with child, and she was in some real pain last night. Suspect she was ready to have that baby."

The woman opened the door wider as she took a step backwards. "Come in."

They stood on a white marbled floor. "So you say that you and your friends been traveling awhile. Where might you have slept two nights ago?"

Ben knew she was quizzing him. "I know you don't trust that I am who I say I am, but we don't sleep at night, we travel. However, two days ago, we did stay at old Doctor Miller's place. He and his wife fixed us a real nice bed in his smokehouse. Fed us real good."

The woman's shoulders relaxed, and she smiled at him. "Pearl is alright." She paused. "She overworked herself. She's traveling too fast for someone in her condition. They are in the barn."

She started to walk away, her strides covering a considerable distance. "Come. Follow me. I was just preparing a little breakfast for them."

Ben followed her down the hall, eyeing the various sculptures and paintings along the wall. When she stopped in a tiny kitchen, he hesitated before stepping in, unsure if he would be in the way. "You have a right nice home, ma'am."

"Thank you. Let me grab this basket, and I'll take you to them . . . I must say, Mr. Tobias was worried sick about you and will be glad to see you . . . He wanted to go back out and find you, but I warned against it."

Ben's heart jumped when she mentioned Tobias. Watching the woman, who was slightly taller than his own mother, he tried to determine by her tone if she too somehow knew about the two of them. Her long, slender arms reached out for a loaf of bread and added it to the basket. "Follow me, Mr. Ben."

She led him out the back door and over to a big two-story barn. Inside, it was dark, the only light beaming through the cracks in the wood. The ceiling was high, with wooden rafters running the length of the barn. There was a stack of hay forty feet high along the back wall. They walked up to the wall of hay and stopped. "Hold this." The woman gave Ben the basket.

She opened a hidden door that was fitted cleverly to look like the rest of the hay. Staring at the door, Ben shook his head, amazed at the brilliance of whoever had created it. Stepping into a hidden room behind the giant stack of hay, he saw Tobias and Pearl both sound asleep. Ben put the basket on a table and walked over to Tobias. Stroking his arm, he said his name.

Tobias's eyes opened slowly. Staring up, he looked up at Ben and smiled. "You found us." He sat up and rubbed his eyes. "I wanted to look for you, I did."

Ben looked over and saw Pearl stirring. Looking back at Tobias, he fought the urge to kiss him. The woman's back was to them as she quietly set up their morning meal. She was unmistakably a proper woman. Ben's longing to kiss Tobias forced him to step back. He had to be careful. Releasing a heavy sigh, he brushed his palms together. "I'm so glad I found y'all. I was so scared I had lost you two. What happened to you guys?"

The woman stepped forward and motioned that the table was ready. "I will let you catch up. I will come back for the dishes later."

Ben waited for her to leave and the sound of the latch sealing the door before he gave in to his desire. He knew Pearl was watching, but he didn't care.

After exchanging light kisses, Ben asked, "What happened to you guys last night? When I came out, you were gone. I looked for you all night."

Tobias shrugged as he sat up and observed the table. "I didn't know what to do." Standing up, he took a second to stretch, expanding his reach almost the width of the room. He released a tempered moan. "We waited and waited. I didn't know what to do." He made his way over to the table, tore a piece of the bread from the loaf, and stuck it in his mouth. "We waited as long as we could for you. I thought Pearl was having her baby, and she couldn't have it in the woods. I picked her up and ran with her all the way here. Miss Welch examined her last night and said she needed to rest. It was labor pains, but it's not time. She gave her some tea to calm her down. Been in here all night. What happened to you?"

"Like I say, when I came out I couldn't find y'all. Didn't know if you were gone or not. Ole man was blind. Would have never seen us, no way." Ben chuckled. "Anyways, he fed me some mincemeat pie that would knock your taste buds right out your head."

Tobias turned with a puzzled look on his face. "Well, if he was blind, what did you eat it for? He was blind. He'd never have known the difference."

"See, that's why I need you, Tobias. You're smarter than I am, and you keep me from being dumb." Ben raised his chin at Tobias and then smiled over at Pearl. She was staring, smiling back at him. "You okay?" he asked her.

Pearl nodded as she laid back against the wall.

Ben took a couple of steps closer to Tobias. "I really thought I lost you. There was a part of me that thought that maybe . . . you escaped from me too. That perhaps you were escapin' back to Africa." Ben wasn't sure why he confessed this to Tobias, but he stopped short of telling him about the harsh conversation he had with Elizabeth, and that this was a thought that had plagued him more than once. He was ashamed to say it, but it's what drove him to walk all night. He had to find Tobias, to know that what they had was real.

Pressing his hand over his lips, Ben fought back tears. His heart was heavy and suddenly he felt so alone. His life was filled with self-doubt, isolation, and uncertainty. Having Tobias in his life surely helped, but it didn't erase the years of self-loathing that was all too familiar to him. Taking another step, he was in Tobias's arms and being pulled up into his chest. Placing a gentle kiss on the side of Tobias's neck, he rested his head against the other man's shoulder and released a slow, quiet breath.

Because of Pearl, Ms. Welch insisted that they rest a day or two before she made arrangements for the next leg of their trip. As a widow, she made no bones about Ben sleeping in the barn with the other two. Ben suspected that this had more to do with her valuables than her virtue. He hadn't been in that house but a minute or two, and although it was nowhere the size of his home, the heavy red damask drapery and the furnishings indicated that she was a woman of wealth. Since arriving, he had seen neither hide nor hair of a companion, except for the towheaded little girl, who was an exact miniature of her.

Ms. Welch announced that she would be making two appearances a day, once in the morning when she dropped off their breakfast and emptied their chamber pot and again when she returned with supper. She added that under no circumstances were they to leave the barn, but during the day, they could leave the hidden room and roam about the barn's interior.

On the second night, after supper, while Tobias, Ben, and Pearl were playing jacks, Pearl looked up at Tobias and Ben.

"Why are you smiling like that?" Ben had come to know her many facial expressions and realized that something was up.

"Oh, nothin'." Pearl's grin grew wider.

"What? What is it?" Tobias said.

"Do you want me to say it?" Pearl hunched over and scooped up two more jacks.

"Spit it out!" Ben squawked. Although he was mostly joking, he really did want to know what it was that she wasn't saying. Though pregnant, she was very much a child herself, and he had come to enjoy her little games and foolishness. They hadn't talked about what life would be like once the baby came—it was all Ben could do to manage what was being thrown at him today. Tomorrow was a lifetime away.

Pearl paused for a minute as another tiny smile emerged at the corners of her mouth. "Tobias told me he loves you."

Ben glanced twice between her and Tobias. Though he was embarrassed, her words sent his heart fluttering. His mouth hung open.

"Pearl!" Tobias said in a hushed tone.

"You said it!" she giggled. "The other night when you told that woman you were going back out to look for him."

Ben, still unable to speak, held his eyes on Tobias.

"Well . . ." Tobias stammered. "I . . . do." He lowered his eye, avoiding eye contact with both of them.

Pearl bounced her ball and snatched up several jacks in a row. When she missed, she peeked up at the both of them, and then quickly bounced the little ball again as if it was still her turn.

Ben's mouth was dry as he spoke. "Um, you never told me that you loved me. How come you would tell Pearl but not me?"

"I don't know. I—I come from a place where we don't talk like that. We don't express emotions with words. You're a person who talks everything out. You say things, all the time." Tobias smiled, but Ben knew he wasn't trying to be funny.

"So, you told Pearl that you loved me, but for some reason, you can't say it directly to me?" Ben was speaking mostly to himself as he scratched his jaw and thought about it.

"It's hard to explain. It's our actions, the way we treat each other that reflects our deep commitment to one another. It's *a word*. But I listened every time you said it to me. At first, it meant little, but then, whatever we were doing or talking about when you said it, it started to have feelings associated with it. You would say I love you, and I would feel it."

Ben had waited for so long to hear this. He yearned to kiss Tobias. He wanted it so badly that his heart was hammering away in his chest. But he was embarrassed at the thought of kissing him right in front of Pearl.

"I do. I love you." Tobias's voice cracked as he spoke. His eyes were locked on Ben's.

Ben felt the heat from Tobias's body as Tobias leaned in and kissed him. Ben melted into Tobias's lips, losing any sense that they weren't alone. Tobias deepened the kiss, his mouth warm to the touch, the caress of his lips softer than Ben remembered as he let out a low moan.

"Tobias," Ben whispered slowly, prolonging each syllable in his name.

Pearl cleared her throat as she got up. Quietly, she went out into the barn.

Ben lay on his back, and Tobias followed. Their kisses gradually subsided into soft tugs and bites of each other's lips. They had obliterated all of the uncertainties and harshness of their voyage, if only for a minute.

"I want to make love to you right now." Tobias delicately stroked the side of Ben's face.

Ben wasn't going to deny him; he wanted it as well. He moistened his lips as he prepared for a kiss.

"But we can't. Pearl is out there," Tobias whispered.

"Then tell me again what you said."

"I love you." Tobias followed his affirmation with another kiss as his finger gently ran up and down Ben's neck.

"I love you too." Ben was breathless as he uttered the words. After that, they lay in silence, but Tobias's stare told him everything.

⌇

The three runaways waited in the little room for three more days before Ms. Welch delivered the news that the next station was ready. She told them that the conductor would be there that evening to pick them up. "It may not be my place, but—" She focused her eyes towards Ben. Whatever she was about to say, she was directing it at him.

"What? What is it?" Ben had no idea what she was so reluctant to say.

"I don't think Pearl is well enough to travel. The baby may be near.

"You mean she's ready to have the baby?" Tobias jumped into the conversation.

Ms. Welch looked at him and then at Ben. "I can't say for certain. But her contractions are increasing slightly. I'm afraid the stress of traveling may be too much for her."

Ben looked at Tobias. He knew there was no chance they were leaving here without her. "How far are we from Ohio?"

"You're close. This next station is in Ripley . . . Ohio." Ms. Welch paced the floor.

"I can make it." Pearl stood up. "I wants my baby to be born in a free state. I don't want my child to ever know what it be like in chains, to be sold like a cow. Ain't havin' my baby here," she told them calmly. "We keep moving."

22

"Okay, it is time!" Ms. Welch announced as she stormed into the room. "We have to move now, while it's safe to do so."

Tobias and Ben helped Pearl up and gathered their belongings. As they walked outside, the heavy and humid night air caught Tobias by surprise. He knew that the trip tonight was going to be unbearable. He caught a glimpse of an old man sitting at the front of the wagon, and then they were ushered up underneath it. First Pearl, then Tobias, and then Ben made their way up into a tiny dark compartment. From the top of the carriage, it looked like any other hay wagon, but beneath, the three escapees laid inches apart from each other.

As Ms. Welch closed the hatch and the compartment went completely dark, Tobias heard horses approaching. "Do you hear that?"

As the horses drew closer, Tobias heard a male voice greet Ms. Welch. "Good evening, ma'am. Might I trouble you for a little bit of water? We've been riding for a while, and my canteen is plum dry."

Tobias's heart nearly stopped. He recognized Dexter's voice. Feeling two quick taps on his shoulder, he knew that Ben was attempting to get his attention. Afraid a whisper was even too loud, the only thing he could think to do was tap him back in that hope that he would understand.

"Why, yes. Of course. What brings you men out this way at this time of the evening?" Ms. Welch asked.

"We're tracking two of our slaves. Runaways from Warren County." Tobias felt two more taps.

"Left about a month ago. First believed they might have done some harm to the master's son as he went missing the day they ran. Then we got word they're traveling together."

He said "we," so there's at least two of them, Tobias quickly assessed, just as Pearl took ahold of his arm. Her nails dug into his skin as Dexter continued to talk. Seconds ago, his only worry had been the humid air, and now it was all about to end. Dexter was the devil, and nothing got past him. The tiny compartment was boiling, the heat rising to a level that he knew would quickly overcome Pearl. One sound from them, and it was over. Dexter missed nothing.

Dexter was inches from them; Tobias could feel him. His voice attacked Tobias's soul, as the sound of the whip striking his back echoed in his ears. He could feel his entire body trembling at what was to come.

"Found their wagon and horses back in Fayette County. Preacher said he traded the wagon and horses for some train tickets for them. Said the massa's son was the owner of them. Preacher said he just dropped them off at the station. I lost a whole day trying to catch that train, only to find ain't nobody seen no boy traveling with two niggers."

Tobias could hear Pearl's breathing as the air continued to close in on them. Sweat dripped from her hands and down his arm.

Dexter's voice boomed. "This here is Ronald, the best slave tracker in the state. We believe we is real close to them. Using Ronald here because the dogs ain't picked up no scent. Lazy dogs ran straight to the barn and never left."

"Seems mighty late to be moving hay. Where you heading with it?" Ronald asked, as he looked the old man and wagon up and down.

Tobias didn't know the other voice. It had to be the slave tracker. From the front of the wagon, Tobias heard the old man speak up. "Too hot to travel by day. Heading up to Lewis County."

Ms. Welch spoke. "Well, let me get you that water you've been asking for, and we'll let my father get on his way. Come on inside. Believe the peach pie might even still be warm. Sit nicely with a cup of coffee, don't you think?" There was a flirtation in her voice.

"I reckon it would," Dexter said.

Tobias could hear Dexter and the slave tracker climb off of their horses. Within seconds, the wagon jolted forward. "Giddy up, boys!" the old man hollered as he spun the wagon around and headed down the dirt driveway.

Tobias wasn't sure what came as more of a relief—escaping Dexter or the penetrating breeze that found it's way through the planks and into his lungs.

Pearl moaned with each bump in the road. Tobias began to second-guess their decision to let her continue. The sound of her breathing was hollow. The only thing he could do was pray this journey would be shorter than some of the others had been. Surely, if Pearl was in that much danger, Ms. Welch wouldn't have let her go, right? Tobias could only hope that he was right.

Question after question came to him. Should he somehow try to get the driver's attention? Maybe they could stop soon so she could get some air. Then he could see her and make sure she was okay. He had no way of knowing if anyone else was outside the wagon at any given time. They had been told not to talk and not to open the hatch for any reason. By doing so, they would risk being caught.

Tobias did nothing. He knew there was nothing he could do. When they reached Ohio, he would talk some sense into Ben. They would stay there until Pearl had the baby. Maybe Ohio would turn out to be a place where they could build their life. Maybe they didn't need to go to Canada. Ohio was a free state; why continue farther? Ben had told him that there were lots of free negroes there.

They had been traveling for about an hour when the wagon came to a sudden stop. Tobias heard several voices. It sounded like someone was talking to the driver, but he was unable to make out the conversation. Tobias felt two taps from Ben, and he tapped Pearl in turn. They were wedged in so tight that Tobias wasn't even sure what part of her body he was tapping, but he prayed that she understood. Maybe they were there—in Ohio. Surely, someone would open the hatch any minute. He felt Ben shifting against him. *Are we getting out?* he thought.

The shot rang out so loud that it took a second for Tobias to realize what it was. Pearl let out a muffled scream. Her body jumped. It had been a gunshot, and after it, the wagon rocked. Was it Pearl who had rocked the wagon? Had her scream been heard? Who had been shot? They were trapped in here. Was this to be their coffin? Tobias tried to breathe, but air wouldn't enter his lungs.

He heard raised voices and individuals rushing about as the wagon sat still. Pearl was breathing, Ben was breathing, and he was breathing, although barely. None of them could tell who had been shot.

The muffled voices went silent, and the sound of hooves echoed as the horses distanced themselves from the wagon. The wagon was still. The sounds of Pearl losing her bladder and the urine hitting the ground below them emphasized just how quiet it was.

Tobias wasn't sure how long they lay still, no words spoken, before light peeked in through the planks. It was sunrise. Ben stirred first and broke the silence. "Pearl, are you okay?"

It took several seconds for her to respond. "Yeah, I'm okay." She shifted, rocking the wagon.

Tobias cleared his throat and swallowed heavily. They were alive. He could feel Ben moving next to him, his hand feeling about. "What are you doing?"

"We need to get out of here. Something's not right." Ben's voice was shaky.

Seconds later, the hatch fell open under Tobias. If he had not been tightly wedged in, he would have fallen to the ground. Maneuvering his body, he wiggled out and positioned himself to help Pearl out.

Pearl twisted out slowly with Ben right behind her. The three of them came out from under the wagon at the same time.

"Where the hell are we?" Ben looked around as he stretched his back out.

Tobias looked around. The wagon was parked in the middle of the road, with heavy brush and trees all around them. The morning sun was barely over the tops of the trees, lighting the sky orange and deep red. They had been in the compartment all night, too afraid to move.

"The horse?" Ben said.

Tobias didn't see the old man or the horse. He and Ben both walked to the front of the wagon.

"Holy shit!" Ben stopped in his tracks.

Tobias looked at the old man sitting up in the driver's bench. He was leaning back against the stack of hay, with a stream of dry blood coming from a hole right between his eyes. He was as dead as dead came, there was no question, and the horse was gone.

"Horse thieves!" Ben said.

"They took his boots." Tobias stared at the old man. This was the first real good look he had gotten of him. "He lost his life trying to help us."

Ben looked up and down the road in both directions. In each direction, there was a bend in the road no more than a hundred yards away. This was a perfect spot to ambush someone. "Pearl, don't come over here. Go on. Get in the bushes before someone comes along. Tobias, we have to figure this out." Ben shook his head as he looked back at the wagon.

"Figure what out? He's dead." Tobias watched as Pearl wobbled over to the brush and sat on a downed tree.

"I can see that." Ben moved to the other side of the wagon. "We need to hide the ole man and burn this wagon. If the sheriff finds it, they'll find the hidden compartment. Maybe trace it back to Ms. Welch. Can't have that. Can't leave no clues to what's goin' on." Ben reached up, grabbed on the driver's jacket, and yanked. With one pull, the old man's body tumbled over and onto the ground. "Sorry, sir."

Tobias jumped back as the man fell about a foot in front of him. "Come on, Tobias, help me here." Ben had the man by his feet and was struggling to get control of the lifeless body.

Tobias took the man by his hands. They dragged the lifeless body towards where Pearl was sitting and continued past her another ten feet into the woods. "I hear water." Tobias released the man's hands and looked over at Pearl to ensure that she was all right. A thud, almost camouflaged by moist layers of dead leaves, echoed through the forest as the body hit the ground.

"It's coming from over here." Tobias took a couple of steps towards the soothing murmur of the water. Ben trailed behind him until they came to an embankment. "Down there, there's water. Fresh water."

Running back to the wagon, Tobias retrieved the canteen and took it to Pearl. "Here, you take the canteen. We'll go down and check it out. Drink what's in here, and I'll be back to fill it up."

Ben started down the embankment first, sliding mostly on his buttocks down the ten-foot drop. "It's slippery, be careful," he said. He brushed the dirt off of the seat of his pants as he waited for Tobias to come down.

The two crouched down and drank from the cool stream, the water soothing their dry throats. Tobias was the first to release a deep, gratified sigh. Then he washed his face and neck. "Ahh, this feels so good."

"Mmm-hmm, what I wouldn't do for a bath." Ben followed suit and scrubbed the dirt from his face. "I'll go get the canteen and fill 'er up. Pearl's probably drunk it all by now."

"I'm ready." Tobias stood up. Glancing around first, he leaned in and gave Ben a light kiss. He couldn't help notice the dark circles under Ben's eyes, how sunken they appeared against his thin face. It pained Tobias to know that he was the cause of that. Ben had given up everything to be with him. "I can't wait for this to be over," Tobias said. "To be wherever it is that we're going. To have our life back, to have you, to make love to you, like we used to under the oaks."

"Really?" Ben mustered a halfhearted smile, his eyes just a little brighter than they had been a moment ago. "You're not mad at me for havin' you out here in the middle of nowhere, with a pregnant girl and man with a bullet hole between his eyes?"

"I probably could've lived without the dead guy." Tobias regretted saying this as the words came out. The man had died trying to help them. They shouldn't be having this conversation; it was disrespectful. Tobias placed another soft kiss on Ben's cool lips. "I wanted you to know that I know you're doing all of this for me."

"For us." Ben sharply replied.

"Okay, for *us*." Tobias smiled. "Let's go before Pearl comes sliding down this hill."

Walking back, Tobias saw Pearl stand up when she saw them. Then she suddenly grabbed her stomach before doubling over onto the ground. With a loud gasp, she cried out, "Oh Lord! Something's happening!"

"Pearl!" Ben bolted towards her and, within seconds, was kneeling next to her. "What's wrong?"

"I don't know. It hurts!"

"I think she's about to have the baby," Ben said. "We have to move her deeper into the woods. She's too close to the road!"

"It's not time!" Tobias placed a hand over her belly. "It's too early!"

Pearl screamed again as she clutched her belly.

"Come on. We have to get her into the woods!" Ben said.

"Pearl, we have to get you up." Tobias gently lifted under her arms and pulled her to her feet.

Pearl screamed as the pain hit her again. "Is I goin' to have my baby now? Out here in the woods?" Her dress was soaked.

Tobias, having helped his father deliver babies, knew that her water had broken. The baby was indeed coming.

Pearl lay in the woods for several hours, as her contractions kept coming stronger and stronger by the minute. With each passing hour, she grew wearier. Tobias knew that she wasn't dilating like he had seen in other deliveries. He became afraid that he wouldn't know how to handle this birth. But he knew that both Ben and Pearl were watching him, so he had to focus on staying calm. Meanwhile, he needed Ben to be just as calm and focused.

The baby crowned in the middle of the afternoon. With each push, Pearl's vagina tore, giving way to more of the head. Tobias knew this was it, the baby was here, and he had to do as his father did. He reached in, placed his hands around the baby's head, and gently turned it to the right, angling the head with the shoulders. With another contraction, Pearl bore down as she screamed. If someone had passed by on the road, there would be no mistaking that there was someone in the woods.

When she pushed, Tobias felt the umbilical cord. It was around the child's neck. He knew that he had only seconds to free the baby from it. Pearl pushed again, but the baby was no longer progressing out. The umbilical cord was too short.

Tobias worked and worked until the child was free of the cord. He again rolled the baby sideways as Pearl pushed one last time. This time, the baby slid out into Tobias's waiting hands. It was small and bluish-grey in color.

Tobias held up the baby as he aggressively rubbed it, trying to get it to take its first breath. Nothing was happening. Tobias reached into the little girl's mouth and swept it clean, trying to open up her airway. Then he noticed the color of the baby. The child was dead.

He looked at Ben who was watching, motionless. He had recognized that the child was dead too. Pearl lay trying to catch her breath, her breathing rapid as she slipped in and out of consciousness.

She was in a pool of her own blood. The blood was running outward from her, bright red and expanding by the second. Tobias screamed for Ben, realizing that Pearl was bleeding to death right before his eyes. Handing the child off to Ben, he tore off his shirt and used it to apply pressure to Pearl's torn body.

"Where's my baby, where's my baby?" Pearl mumbled.

"She's right here. Ben is cleaning her up for you. Lie still. You're bleeding," Tobias told her.

"You says I have a baby girl. Is we in free land? Is she free?" Pearl asked.

Tobias paused. "Yes, Pearl. She will never know what it is to be in chains and treated like an animal. She will never know this." As he told her this, he worked to stop the bleeding.

He didn't know what to do. The bleeding wouldn't stop, and he had never seen anything like it. As Pearl lay hemorrhaging, Tobias panicked. Working in a frenzy, he attempted to stop the bleeding with his soaked shirt.

"Can I hold my little girl?" she asked, as the light slowly left her eyes.

Ben squelched a low cry as he watched Pearl's body go limp, her legs falling to the ground. "Is she dead?" he cried, as he took one step back from her lifeless body.

Avoiding the reality of the situation, Tobias kept working, pressing the bloodstained shirt against her torn body. "I don't know what happened. I couldn't stop the bleeding!" he muttered. "Help me. Help me get her out of this blood!"

Ben laid the grey baby girl down in the weeds and helped Tobias to move Pearl's body a couple of feet over. They sat next to Pearl for a couple of minutes, in shock. Then Tobias took the child over to her, resting her on Pearls chest and wrapping Pearl's arms around her baby girl.

They knew they had to do something with the bodies. "They should have a proper burial," Ben muttered. Standing up, he walked past Tobias, who was sitting on the ground, stained in blood.

Paralyzed with grief, Tobias never looked up as Ben retrieved the ax and a shovel that hung on the side of the wagon. Ben was silent as he walked deep into the woods, where he dug two gravesites: one for Pearl and her baby and the other for the old man who had tried to get them to freedom.

23

Crouching down at the edge of the stream, Tobias pounded his shirt against a rock below the water. He executed each strike just as the one before. He could see traces of blood; the stain was still there. He was numb to the presence of Ben, who was sitting behind him, watching. Tobias played the delivery over and over in his head. He had seen his father do it countless times without a hitch. He should have noticed that the umbilical cord was around the baby's neck sooner. He had thought it was going to be so simple. He knew nothing, and it had killed her.

"I should have never done this." Ben's words were barely audible as they drifted passed Tobias's ear.

Tobias stopped but didn't turn around. "What? Done what?"

"Ask you to run. Let Pearl come with us. I should have turned that wagon right around, right then, and said no!"

Tobias pounded the shirt against the rock once more. "Okay, and how would that of ended? I was going to the auction, and Pearl—" Saying her name ripped at him. His throat swelling, Tobias was forced to swallow several times to stop himself from crying. His vision was blurred by a tear that wouldn't drop.

"We could have done somethin' different, gone back. I don't know."

"No, you don't!" Tobias knew the truth. He had killed Pearl. Slamming his shirt against the rock, he crushed his thumb, fracturing the bone. He welcomed the pain. It was something other than his own accountability to focus on.

"Okay . . ." Ben murmured.

Tobias heard the rejection in Ben's voice. He shouldn't have snapped at Ben. He wanted to say something, perhaps that he was sorry, but everything he thought of just seemed like words, and they didn't change anything. The fact was that he had killed Pearl. Bile made its way up into his throat, where it stayed. Tobias looked at his thumb, focusing on the pain emanating from it. He didn't hear Ben walk up behind him.

"I'm sorry." Ben kneeled down behind Tobias and leaned into him. "I love you." Resting his head against Tobias's bare back, Ben lightly stroked his eight-inch scar, the mark of Dexter.

Tobias wiped the tear that had yet to fall, and then he stood up. "There is nothing for you to be sorry about. It was me. I should have insisted that she stay back at the house. I should have listened to Ms. Welch. I thought I knew more than she did, and it turned out that I was wrong. There is nothing for you to feel sorry for." He began to walk up the embankment. "Come on, it's late. We have to take care of that wagon before someone comes along."

"I'll take care of it." Ben stood up and grabbed Tobias's hand. He swung Tobias around and brought him into his arms. "I love you."

Tobias's legs gave way underneath him. He fell into Ben's chest in a ball of tears. He couldn't hold it back; it overtook him, and he erupted into an uncontrollable, primal wail against Ben's chest. Ben held on tightly as Tobias shook violently, clawing into Ben's back, trying to stay on his feet. The raw pain was so deep that one thought unleashed another, and another. It was not just about Pearl; he was grieving the loss of everybody he'd ever known. His entire world had vanished, burned to the ground, and it wasn't as simple as going home. There was no home. His grief surged with every expelled breath.

After several minutes, like a switch had been flipped, Tobias stopped. He had to pull it together, regain his composure, be a man. Wiping his eyes, he tried to shake it off, to tell himself it was that easy. He couldn't look at Ben. He was too embarrassed that he had cried like that. He looked around for his shirt, which he had dropped at some point. Finding it in the dirt at his feet, he picked it up and shook the dirt from it. "Come on. Let's take care of the wagon."

Flames from the hay wagon billowed over the trees, filling the narrow road with thick smoke. It went up quick and fast. They had to hope that an evening rain shower wouldn't put it out before it had burned completely; they knew that they couldn't stick around to make sure. They took to the riverbank and followed it in the direction in which they had been heading.

Then they realized that they had no idea where the man had been taking them. Ms. Welch had never said a thing about the people they would stay with or even how far they would be traveling. They were lost and on their own again.

They traveled in silence, Tobias leading the way along the river-bank. He knew they had a couple of hours of daylight left, but once the sun dropped behind the trees, it was going to get dark fast. He wasn't ready to talk. He thought about what had happened back there—not just Pearl's death, but his own. The tears that had poured from him had left him empty, and the emptiness somehow took over his body. It was anything but cleansing, as it still held a tight grip around his heart. He had to keep moving and not let it in, or else it would consume him again. He listened to Ben's footsteps five feet behind him as twigs and leaves gave way beneath the other man's feet. His own steps were silent. Coming to a fork in the stream, Tobias stopped. "Any suggestions?"

Ben looked around and pointed to the fork farthest from them. "I say we cross here, over to the other side, and follow it. There's twice as much water." He extended his arm to the fork closest to them and said, "This looks manmade, like someone is diverting it. There might be a farm ahead, people, or an ole dog." Ben snickered as he smiled at Tobias.

It was just like Ben to try to lighten the mood with a joke. Yes, the last thing they needed was to run into was another old dog. As they took a moment to catch their breath, Tobias studied both forks. Kneeling, he took a sip of water, which somehow dislodged the lump that had been in his throat for hours.

"Tobias . . . I thought you were amazin' back there with Pearl. It wasn't your fault. I've see many calves born dead. Ain't nothin' you can do sometimes, it just is. It ain't your fault."

"We should never have brought her." Tobias's words dropped off. There was no point in saying it again.

"You said yourself we ain't had no choice but to take her. What's done is done," Ben replied.

Tobias didn't feel the need or desire to say anything else. He began walking again, crossing the stream, as Ben had suggested, and continuing up the new fork.

As night fell upon them, Tobias could hear the sound of the stream change as the speed of the water increased and the stream widened.

"Do you hear the water?" Tobias asked. He stopped to allow Ben to catch up.

"What?" Ben halted next to him and turned his head, listening.

"The stream. I noticed that it was widening a little ways back. There's more streams feeding into it." Tobias didn't know what any of it meant; he was merely making conversation. He had to get out of his own head, to stop thinking.

Moving closer to the stream, they both kneeled down over the large rocks that bordered it and cupped a little bit of water to drink.

As they rehydrated their bodies, they also splashed the water across their faces, necks, and hair, rinsing the sweat from their bodies.

"It's cold," Ben announced as he took another sip. "Might be a good place to settle for the night. Before it gets too dark and we ain't able to see nothin'."

"Yeah, I guess it's as good as any." Tobias moved off the rocks and back onto the solid ground. Taking a seat on the dirt, he watched Ben, who continued to satisfy his thirst.

Thinking of Pearl's final few minutes, Tobias rubbed on the metal button that he had removed from the hem of her dress. In the same hand, he also had a leather shoestring that he had removed from her tattered boots. He threaded the leather through the buttonhole and tied it around his neck. Continuing to watch Ben from afar, he held his hand up to his throat and gently rubbed the button—the only thing left of Pearl.

When Ben sat down next to him, he looked twice either way along the embankment.

"What did you see?" Tobias asked.

"Just making sure we're alone." Ben leaned in and kissed him.

Ben's lips lingered on his. They were cool from the water. Tobias could feel Ben's warm breath and sensed that he wanted more than a kiss. But Tobias had nothing to give, and he turned his head away from Ben. He was tired and hungry and just wanted to lay his head down.

"It's okay," Ben murmured.

"I'm sorry." Tobias turned back to face him. He gently brushed his hand over Ben's wet hair and laid his head against Ben's shoulder. With no blankets, bedrolls, or roof over them, they made a little space in the tall grass to nestle down for the night.

"I love you." Tobias was the first to say.

"I love you too." Ben rolled over and kissed him goodnight. "Get some rest, sleepy head. I'll be right here when you open those big, beautiful brown eyes of yours in the mornin', okay?"

"Okay." Tobias knew that he would be asleep in no time. Spooning Ben's body, Tobias wrapped his arms around Ben and brought him even closer.

Sometime in the middle of the night, the roar of the water awakened Tobias as it cascaded over the rocks. Ben was still wrapped in his arms. Neither of them had moved an inch. Tobias pressed his erection against Ben's ass. Hours ago, sex had been the last thing on his mind; now, it was all he wanted. The sexual tension surged through his body, igniting a hunger—a need—to release a mountain of energy that had been building for days.

Listening to Ben's shallow breathing, Tobias wanted him more than ever before. Undoing his britches, he first freed himself. His heartbeat, the driving force of the momentum building within him, quickened. He deftly unsnapped each of Ben's buttons on his britches and slid his hand into the fly, lightly brushing Ben's soft skin until he found what he was looking for. Ben stirred, releasing a light moan as his body responded to Tobias's touch. Tobias listened as his lover's breathing picked up. Ben was awake and attempted to turn to kiss him.

"No . . . Roll over." Tobias didn't want to talk. An onslaught of raw physical desire had possessed him.

Without a word, Ben did as commanded, placing his arms under his own head as a pillow. Tobias lowered Ben's britches to the back of his knees.

"Mmm." Ben's buttocks stirred, a low moan emanating from him as Tobias straddled his backside.

From his neck all the way down his back, the tension pulled at him. He was like an animal ready to feast. Realizing that he had nothing to lubricate Ben with, he decided saliva would have to do. As Tobias spit into his hand, the world became an unimportant blur, banished into the far recesses of his mind.

Ben gasped for air as Tobias penetrated him. He was tight, really tight, forcing Tobias to be still. He heard the rasp of Ben's breathing subside, and the muscle relaxed, allowing him fully into the warmth of Ben's body.

What started as gentle and tender became a frenzy as Tobias released all his pent up emotions. He had never loved anyone such as Ben, a feeling that had now set his body ablaze. Within minutes, the dull ache changed into a hunger, each new thrust more powerful, bringing him closer. Grabbing Ben by the back of his hair, Tobias's vision went black as a shattering climax took over his body, spilling his seed deep within his lover.

Collapsing over the top of Ben, he savored the sea of pleasure that had stripped away every ounce of tension in his body. What had started as a dull ache in the tall grass under the stars had become a moment in which they were one.

His breathing returning to normal, Tobias still couldn't move. With barely the energy to kiss the back of Ben's neck, he closed his eyes and allowed himself to be present in the moment. Their heartbeats falling into sync, Tobias breathed a sigh seconds before drifting off to sleep.

Before the sun rose, Tobias felt Ben stir, pushing his buttocks up closer to him. Exhausted, Tobias figured that he had slept, at best, maybe an hour. The rest of the night, he had cradled Ben tight in his arms and listened to his breathing. He was comforted by the fact that this was the first time they had ever slept all night in one another's arms. He knew the sun would be up soon, and they had to choose whether to hide for the day or keep moving.

Ben stirred again, this time gently turning over to face Tobias. His eyes barely open, he smiled. "Good mornin'." He nuzzled against Tobias's neck, giving him delicate kisses.

Tobias's heart fluttered as Ben moved up his neck and their lips met, their breath mingled. He gasped with delight as Ben showered him with gentle, soft kisses, each with its own meaning. Tobias gazed up at him, feeling loved like he had never felt. Drawing back, their lips separated. Tobias studied Ben's face, the flat bridge of his nose, the almond shape of his beautiful brown eyes, the fullness of his lips and how they matched each other. He knew that they would never be apart. Ben gazed back at him, his long lashes touching as he blinked. His eyes told Tobias that, without a doubt, he felt the same.

"You know . . . I may not be able to walk today," Ben said, nibbling gently on Tobias's right ear.

"I'm sorry." Tobias's voice cracked. He felt guilty for taking Ben as he had.

"Are you kiddin' me? You can wake me up anytime like that." Ben rolled onto his back. "Damn, that was good, but I'm goin' to feel it all day, I reckon."

A sense of relief washed over Tobias, releasing him from the guilt. "I want to tell you something. I think about it every day, and I have to find a way to let it go. It torments me."

"What is it?" Ben sat up, his demeanor serious as his eyes focused on Tobias.

Tobias's tongue moistened his lips. He followed this with a heavy sigh. "The ship . . . I . . . we were chained like animals." He stopped. That wasn't where he wanted to start. "My people were deceived by poachers." That wasn't it, either. Tobias tried to collect his thoughts—the ones he couldn't speak about. "We heard stories for many years of the white men coming to get us, but we believed we were safe as we were over the mountain and far from the sea. After being captured, we were chained to each other by our hands and feet and made to march over the mountain towards the sea. I had seen the great water only once, as a small boy—it took many days to reach from our village.

"I heard one of the poachers say that we would be loaded onto the ship and taken to the "New World." I knew of this happening to others from my father's tales. The poachers did not know that I was one of the few who understood their language, and I listened to them talk to one another.

"On the fourth day of our journey to the sea, an older boy from a neighboring village was walking in front of me, chained. He fell to the ground, clutching his stomach in pain. The poachers knew he was sickly and shot him, leaving him on the side of the road to die. I knew that the Gods had answered this boy's prayers, rescuing him. They had taken him in their arms that stretched down from the skies, removing him from the evil around us. I prayed for the same."

Tobias fought back the tear that wanted to escape his eye. With the back of his hand, he brushed it away, giving it no chance of staining his face. "The weight of the chains around my neck and feet were unbearable. After many days of walking, we came to the ocean, where the temperature was much cooler and the winds blew wildly across the sand. I didn't see any ships and was confused about all that I had heard about them. We were held on the beach in cages for many days, and with each day, poachers brought more and more people from the villages.

"Within days, there were more people than I could count covering the entire beach. One morning, I saw it. Over the water, white, bigger than anything I had ever seen. I thought it was a sea God coming to rescue us. It was the opposite: it was the sails of the ship coming for us.

"White sails blew in the distance as they made their way to our shore. The white men and poachers rushed about the beach, gathering up camp and preparing to leave. The white men did not treat the poachers much more kindly than us. They barked orders to clean us up for the captain to inspect us.

"The poachers threw pails of seawater into our cages to wash the many days of dirt and grime from our skin. The salt water hit my raw skin, where the chains had worn holes, and the pain was immense. By that afternoon, they loaded us onto little boats and carried us out to the ship."

Tobias drew in a long breath. What had occurred on that ship were memories that he would likely never be rid of. The sound of the waves crashing against the ship, and the horrible smell of vomit, body secretions, and even death, came rushing back. He started to push the memories away, just as he'd done since leaving that torture chamber, but this time, he let them come. He had to talk about it— maybe that would free him of the constant nightmare. Staring at the ground, he felt Ben take his right hand and gently squeeze it.

"Those bastards betrayed you." Ben wiped a tear from his eye.

"They were never exactly our friends. But anyways, we were put into the belly of the ship and left in darkness." Tobias sniffled as he too took a swipe at his eyes. "We were chained down in rows and shackled four high in racks. I remember that I could feel the room rocking back and forth. It lasted for hours: water crashing in from the deck down onto us. We thrashed around. Many grew sick and could no longer keep what little food we had in our bellies.

"Within days, the smells of sweat, vomit, sickness, and the dead grew intolerable down in that dark chamber. One day, the hatch above our heads was opened. The sun poured in, and I thought I would go blind from its rays. They dumped more water on us and said that we were stinking up the ship. Although it was cold, the water chased away the flies that were eating at our skin, if just for a moment.

"More days passed, and some people were no longer moving. More grew sick, and others lay dead, some were left where they were for several days. When the hatch was opened again, I was so thirsty that I tried to prepare myself to catch the water in my mouth. Instead of the water raining down on us, though, we had a visitor. A man came down and examined us. He unchained the sick and the dead. The sick were pulled up to the deck first. I was then unshackled and ordered to help pull the dead up top. I did as I was told, careful not to anger them.

"I was in the sunshine now, and the air felt good as a salty mist brushed across my lips. Then I learned why I had been brought up on deck. I was ordered to help roll the dead into the water. I remember seeing the sick watch with horror as the dead bodies hit the water. Then the unspeakable happened. The sick were ordered to stand on the ships edge, where they were kicked into the water one by one. They soon stopped waiting to be kicked and jumped to their deaths. I knew many more would die before we reached land. I thought that, if I was lucky, I would be one of them. I will never forget the look in their eyes before they jumped."

Tobias couldn't hold back his tears any longer. He took another large breath, trying to cleanse his lungs. He couldn't tell what Ben was thinking. The color had drained from his face; the whites of his eyes were pink, and his lips were pressed together.

Silence lingered between them for several minutes before Ben reached out and clutched Tobias's cheeks with both hands. Placing a kiss on Tobias's forehead, their faces met, forehead to forehead and nose to nose. "You will never feel or see pain like that again. You will never again know such suffering. This I promise you!"

Lowering his head, Tobias wanted nothing more than to rid his soul of the pain. He attempted to get up, to break the unnatural stillness, but it felt as if a weight was on him, a force that wouldn't allow him to move.

"I love you." Ben slid his hand across Tobias's face before wrapping his arms around him. His head came to rest on Tobias's shoulder.

They sat quietly in the tall grass as the sun rose over them. The weight lifted from Tobias. His breathing was slow and even. The birds were somewhere close—he could hear them chirping. Although the terrain here was much different, the birds, the stream, and the morning air gave him visions of home. Tobias blew out a large breath. Looking up at the sun, he saw that it was time to go. "We have to decide if we should continue or find a safe place to hide until night fall." Traveling at night made more sense. It was cooler, and there was less chance of them being spotted.

Ben stood up, fastened his britches, and positioned his suspenders over both shoulders. Looking around for his hat, he located it several feet from where they had been sleeping. Picking it up, he dusted the top off with one hand before flipping it onto his head and bringing the brim down low over his eyes. "Well, if we sit here, the buzzards will be circling us in no time, waiting to pluck our eyeballs out. I say we head on up the embankment a little and head back into those trees. We can see anyone approaching that way. Come nightfall, we can come on back down and head up this here stream some more."

Tobias studied the stream: the sun shimmering off the rocks as the water cascaded over them, the tall grass that lined its shore, and the trees that stretched off into the distance. Where they stood was a beautiful spot. Calmness washed through his body as he took a big breath and quietly blew it away.

They made their way back up the embankment and into the woods, looking for a spot to bed down in for the day. It was going to be warm today, warmer than either of them was used to. Physically as well as emotionally, Tobias welcomed the decision to take cover for the day. After finding a spot far enough back in the woods, they both were fast asleep.

After several hours, Ben was the first to stir. His body snuggled next to Tobias's. He looked around, trying to remember where he was. As his memory filled in, he thought about the story Tobias had told him of being on the ship. It pained him to know that the sins of slavery went far beyond his own world and were every bit as brutal as what he had witnessed on the plantation. If the arms of slavery stretched out all the way to Africa, could he and Tobias really find a place where they could be together, to love one another? A place where fear was not a part of either of their lives? A nervousness grew in Ben's gut as he watched Tobias continue to sleep. There was no doubt in his mind that he loved Tobias more than he loved himself.

Sitting up, Ben squinted up through the trees at the sky. The clouds were moving in. It would be dark in a couple of hours. They would need to get moving soon. He went to shake Tobias, but stopped.

He would take a bath first. Clean up in the river below before waking up Tobias. He wanted to wash some of the grime off before Tobias had to look at him.

Carefully making his way down the embankment, Ben stopped at the edge of the tall grass, where he slowly begin to disrobe. Leaving his clothes in the weeds, he continued making his way over the rocks and entered the water, submerging his body in the cool water. The cold awakened every part of his body, and blood rushed through his veins, rejuvenating him. With another dunk under the water to ensure his hair was clean, he popped up and swiped the water from his eyes.

"I bet you didn't think I would ever find you did you?"

The familiar voice was so haunting. Ben's eyes sprung open.

Dexter stood on the shore, his feet spread apart as he rested his hands in front of his gun belt. The man looked every bit as evil as the devil himself, as his eyes bore into Ben.

The cool temperature of the water was no longer a pleasure for Ben, as he steadied his feet under him. Looking past Dexter at his own clothes, he saw there was no way he was making it to his own gun, which lay just on top of his britches. What was he supposed to do? The water behind him was swiftly moving downstream, so he could be gone in a flash if he allowed the river to take him. He was confident he could survive whatever the river threw at him, but he couldn't leave Tobias . . . *Tobias!* Had Dexter already found him? Did he have him already bound and gagged—or worse?

"Now, why don't you come on out of that water and let's bring some sense to this whole thing."

Struck with a sense of calmness, Ben had known this day would come. For so long, he had been tired of Dexter's merciless ways, and today was the day he cursed him for what he had done not only to Tobias, but to countless others before him. "Well, to be honest, I am a little surprised to see you. I figured you couldn't find your own butt, even if you had both hands in your back pockets. Just how much is my pa payin' you to track Tobias this far anyways?" Ben slowly moved to the shore, closer to his gun that lay just behind Dexter.

"It ain't the nigger I'm after. It's you and that money you stole." Dexter's eyes followed Ben as he moved closer to the shore.

As Ben's body lifted from the water, the nippy air attacked his bare skin. Wrapping his arms across his chest, he could feel the goosebumps on his arms as his hands ran across his wet skin. "Ok, so you found me, now what? I ain't goin' with you. You'll have to kill me if—."

"Killing you would be my preference. I know what you're doing with the nigger boy. Ain't right. Downright disgustin'."

Ben studied Dexter's face. His jaw muscles were tight; there was evil present in his eyes. "Does pa know?" Ben asked, as he stepped closer to Dexter. Cold licked at Ben's face as water dripped from his hair.

"Dunno, but between the two niggers and the money you stole, Mr. Lee's put a big enough bounty on your head, makes me think he really wantin' to have some words with you."

Ben stopped about five feet in front of Dexter. If not for the bounty, he knew Dexter would have no problem killing him; he could see it in his eyes. "So, just how do you suppose you're going to get to cash in on that there money?" Ben took a deep swallow. "You're 'bout the dimmest man I've ever known."

Ben licked his lips, as his eyes pierced into Dexter. He was not going with Dexter. They were going to have it out right here and now. He would make the man put a bullet in his chest, and then explain to his pa what happened. Love him or hate him, he knew his pa would have Dexter hanged if Dexter killed his only child.

Dexter withdrew his pistol from his holster and brought it up to his waist, pointing it directly at Ben. "Now, why don't we locate your clothes and go find your friends."

This told Ben that he hadn't seen his clothes or Tobias yet. Maybe there was a way out of this. His brain was firing on overload, and then he saw movement in the brush behind Dexter. "You alone?" Ben asked. "Heard you were travelin' with a real slave tracker." Ben's eye shifted back to Dexter.

"Yep, but that slave tracker was eating into my profits. Every day we spent lookin' for you was costing me money."

Ben released an ugly chuckle. "I see." Ben caught the movement again. This time, he saw that it was Tobias, silently crawling up behind Dexter. Not wanting to give Tobias away, Ben steadied his eyes on Dexter. "Well, I know my pa pretty well. Suspect the reward ain't nowhere as much as I took from him. What do you say I just hand over that money to you, and we both ride out into the sunset, never to be seen again? By this time next year, you could be sittin' high in the cotton on your own farm."

Dexter snickered before his mouth returned to a scowl. "And have Mr. Lee put a bounty on my head? I think not."

With everything Ben had in him, he avoided looking in Tobias's direction. He knew all too well that if he gave even the slightest glance, Dexter would pick up on it. Inhaling slowly, he steadied his breathing. He had to keep Dexter focused on the prize in front of him. "Well, I guess that really doesn't shock me. Too scared of my pa? I figured you for a yellow belly. Suppose I was right."

Dexter raised his pistol up to Ben's eye level and grinned. "You really do want to die, don't you?"

Tobias neared closer to Ben's clothes until he reached the gun. As silent as a panther, he rose to his feet behind Dexter.

"Well, if you're fixin' to shoot me, there's been somethin' I've been aiming to say for a while now." Ben's eyes narrowed in on Dexter's index finger as it quivered on the trigger. "You sorry son of a bitch, you're a nasty excuse for a human being. Those two . . ." Ben tried to steady his breathing, "that hung for guttin' your ma and pa? Well, I would have hung them too . . . for not finishing the job and stringin' your wimpy backside up next to them."

With fire in his eyes, Dexter leered. Just as he was about to say something, Tobias smashed his fist into the side of Dexter's head.

With a loud bang, Dexter's shot flew past Ben's head. The boom sent Dexter's horse off running. Ben watched as Dexter's body collapsed in the very spot that he stood. Falling to the ground, he was out.

"Good Lord, I think you killed him!" Ben's eyes were as big as saucers, as he stared at Dexter's lifeless body. "I can't believe you hit him with my pistol." Ben started laughing.

Tobias held the butt of the pistol up and smiled. Taking a deep breath, he kneeled down in front of Dexter and watched the man's chest. "He's not dead."

"Well, not yet, damn it! Give the man a minute." Ben jumped the two steps needed to be at Tobias's side. "How did you know he was here?"

Tobias continued watching Dexter's chest as it barely moved up and down. "I woke up and you were gone. When I stood up to see where you were, I saw Dexter ride up. I hid down in the grass until he passed. Then I saw you down by the river. I followed him. He never heard me."

"Well, I guess I don't have to show you how to use no gun. Like everything else, you did it your way." Ben grabbed Tobias's shoulder and squeezed firmly. "I ain't never seen the likes of someone like you."

Tobias handed Ben his pistol. "Come on. We need to get moving. Before he wakes up."

"Wakes up? That man is fixin' to take his last breath! He ain't never waking up, I can tell you that!" Ben dabbed a finger into the side of Dexter's head, where blood slowly oozed out onto the dirt.

Within minutes, Ben was dressed and the two raced as fast as they could to put some distance between them and Dexter.

For the next hour they ran, both famished and weak, until they couldn't run anymore. Slowing to a walk, they continued, the moon providing plenty of light to guide them.

They walked until their stream merged with a large river, Tobias led the way, finding a place to cross that put them on the west side of the river.

"I guess we'll see what's on this side now." Tobias stood looking at the river, which was now about a hundred feet across and moving faster than he had ever seen water move. "How deep is it?"

"Don't know. Imagine it's deep though," Ben said.

After they walked about a mile up the river, Tobias called for Ben to stop. "See it?" he said, pointing to a flickering glow about a hundred yards ahead of them.

Ducking into the trees, they kneeled in the brush. "I think it's a campfire," said Tobias. "I smell smoke." He held his nose up to take another whiff.

"I don't want to turn around. What should we do?" Ben could now smell the smoke, too.

Tobias stared at the campfire. "There looks to be a couple of them. Let's get closer."

The two quietly made their way toward the fire until Ben stopped them both. "I think its negroes," he whispered.

"You think they're runaways?"

"Don't know."

"Should we approach them? Maybe they can help us." Tobias studied the figures around the fire.

"Could be. If they're runaways, maybe," Ben whispered back.

They cautiously approached the men sitting around the fire. The last thing they wanted was to be mistaken for bandits and shot.

When they were closer, Tobias counted four men. He could smell fish being cooked. When he and Ben were about ten feet away, they stopped. "Good evening, gentleman," Tobias called out to them.

The men appeared unstartled by their presence. One of them stood. Taller than both Tobias and Ben, he stared out into the darkness.

Ben stepped up closer and removed his hat as a sign of respect. "Um, we—we're lost, might you be able to help us?" The men looked at him first and then at Tobias.

Another one of the men stood up. He too was a big fella. "Evenin'. You say you lost. Where you comin' from?"

"Warren, Warren County, Kentucky," Ben replied.

The men chuckled as the last two stood up. Tobias sized them up. They were giants, at least three or four inches taller than any man, he had ever seen. By the look of their nice clothes, they weren't slaves.

"Wells, you in Ohio now . . . Riley, Ohio."

Ohio? The words fell off Tobias's breath. They were in Ohio!

"This here is the Ohio River," one of them stated. "Where you want to be?"

"Canada." Tobias stuttered.

"Is you runnin'?" another of the negroes asked.

"Yes," Tobias answered. "We ran from Kentucky. We are trying to get to Canada and have lost our way. We're in need of some help—food, too, if you can spare some. We've been eating roots and berries all day."

"Runaways? That boy looks white to me. What you runnin' from?" another asked, looking directly at Ben.

"I ain't no runaway!" Ben's voice rose. "I'm white, pure white. Ain't got no negro blood in me." He took a couple of steps towards them, leaving Tobias in the shadow of the fire. "We come from my pa's farm. My friend here says he wanted to go to Canada, and I ain't never seen Canada either, so I reckon I'll go with him."

Tobias observed the strangers' height and size as he joined Ben at his side. The four giants appeared to have been fishing, and they looked as if they were about to eat. He examined the fire, looking for food.

"We's free, been free almost five years now here in Ohio. Gets into trouble though if we caught helpin' runaways from other states. My name is Samuel. These my brothers." He extended his hand to Ben.

Ben shook Samuel's hand. "So you can't help us is what you're sayin'?" Ben sounded irritated.

"Now, sir!" Samuel said, "I say we gets into trouble if we help, but didn't say we wouldn't help." Samuel whispered something to his brother on his left side and then turned his back on Ben and Tobias, continuing the conversation in a low whisper. It was several minutes before he turned and faced them. "I'll take you over to Willie's for the night until we can get a hold of Mr. Hall. Reckon he won't be put out to have two more." Samuel walked past them to his mule. "Okay, let's go get you boys taken care of."

"Wait!" Ben demanded. "Where are you takin' us? How do we know you ain't takin' us to a trap so you can collect reward money?"

Samuel stopped and turned back towards Ben. "Now, sir, I believe it was you who interrupted my dinner, and it was you who asked me to help you. And as much as I hate to say it, ain't no reward for you, I'm for damn sure. Now, you can come if you want, or you can keep followin' that star that led you to me in the first place." Samuel looked at Tobias and then started walking again.

He knows about the North Star, Tobias thought, as his eyes followed the man over to his mule. Ben and Tobias followed Samuel's mule, walking for about an hour in silence through trees and brush until they came to a small cabin. Cold, exhausted, and hungry, Tobias felt his legs tremble as he neared the building.

Samuel walked into the cabin first. "Willie, I got two that are lookin' for a good meal and a place to rest their heads for the night."

An older man came from around the corner. Tobias noticed that he, too, was a big man, his skin a honey brown marred with white blotches that covered the left side of his face. Unlike the others, his hair was completely grey, matching his full grey beard. Moving with a limp, he walked right up to them. "Wha's this?" His eyes shifted to Ben.

"Gots a runaway and his friend, the massa son no less. They headin' to Canada so this one can be free. I'll carry them over to Mr. Hall's in the mornin'. They hungry, and reckon they ready for a good night's sleep." Samuel removed his hat and coat and hung them on a peg on the wall.

Willie stepped uncomfortably close to Ben. Standing inches from his face, Willie sucked his teeth. "Your papa's his massa, you say? And you helpin' him to escape, to the land of the free? Why you do that? What are you gettin' in all this?" Willie's left eyebrow rose as he tilted his head to one side.

"Well, first of all, I'm his massa. Ain't never said pa was his massa. And I'm gettin' nothin' but seein' my friend live the life he was born to live." Ben's voice didn't waver, nor did his stare.

Willie backed down. Glancing at Tobias, he snarled before turning and walking back around the corner.

"Pay no mind to Willie. He ain't never met a white folk he liked, so take no offense," Samuel said.

"Relax. Take a seat." Over the banging of pots and pans coming from the kitchen, Samuel extended his hand, inviting them to sit on a cot in front of the fireplace. After disappearing for a couple of minutes, Samuel returned with a plate of grits, warm milk, and two biscuits left over from the morning meal.

The room was toasty as Ben and Tobias sat by the fire. Tobias watched Ben as he dipped his biscuit into his milk and chewed. Tobias spotted the light from the fire in Ben's eyes. His brown eyes and long beautiful lashes shone in the flames.

Willie and Samuel had walked outside, but their voices were still as clear as if they were sitting in the room.

"Do you trust he is who he say he is? Willie asked. "We been free almost five years and help free a whole lot of folks, but this don't smell right. A white man runnin' with a negro to Canada. Why he go with him? Tell me why!"

"Keep it down. They will hear you," Samuel replied.

"Wells, I ain't goin' to hang for helpin' no white man. One night . . . and then they go to Mr. Hall's in the mornin'. They can't stay here, nope, can't stay here. Ain't goin' be part of no underground railroad, you hear me?"

Stretching out across the cot, Ben brushed his hand over Tobias's as the two exchanged smiles. Minutes later, Ben's slow breathing indicated that he had drifted off to sleep. When Samuel came in, he tossed a blanket over each of them and took the rocker nearby.

The next morning, when Tobias woke up, Willie was stoking the fire and fussing. Tobias wondered whom he was talking to; there was no one else in the room. "Come now, them crops ain't goin' to pull themselves up out no ground. If you want to eat, then you got to work."

Tobias looked up, as the men he had seen the previous night by the fire climbed down from a loft above him.

Willie handed Tobias a plate of figs and walnuts, as well as a cup of chicory coffee, as he continued to fuss about the room.

After waking Ben up, Tobias stood to stretch his body. He saw Samuel through the front door, rushing about around a mule and wagon. Tobias felt relief upon seeing the wagon and knowing that they weren't walking this morning. The sole of his right boot had long ago fallen off at the toe, and at times, he had thought it would be easier to go without. As the brothers all made their way down from the loft, Tobias recognized them as the three who had been sitting by the campfire the previous night. He had been so tired that he hadn't heard them come in.

Sharing a plate of breakfast, Tobias and Ben sat side by side on the thin mattress. "I was proud of you yesterday." Ben said, as he slowly chewed on a mouth full of figs.

"Yeah?" Tobias really didn't know how he felt about it. It was clear he'd had to do something to stop Dexter. When he'd initially picked up the pistol, there had been no hesitation in the fact he was going to use it to stop Dexter. Seeing Ben defenseless, naked, and standing on the edge of the river, he had done what he had to do to save the one person who had already risked everything to save him.

"I know how your family and village felt about you not killin' that hog in the woods. That, somehow, it's a measurement of your manhood. But they're wrong. You're the strongest, bravest man I've come to know. All that you have suffered and you can still find room in your heart to love, that's incredible." Ben cautiously grabbed Tobias's hand and rubbed it lightly.

"Thank you. Thank you for saying that." Tobias thought about what Ben had said. Somehow, he had come to believe he wasn't a man because of tribal tradition, because someone said so, because of a single act. Tobias knew that on the previous day he had done what he had to do to protect what was important to him, and he had done it without hesitation. It didn't matter that he'd used the butt of the gun to knock Dexter out instead of firing it.

Tobias looked around the room before smiling at Ben. His smile continued to grow as he recalled the day he had failed to kill that hog. He had realized for the first time that he wasn't killing that hog because he had to, he was being asked to kill the animal to prove a point. It was a senseless killing, with no regard to life. Just like Ben's, that hog's life had value. "I am learning much about myself: that there is still so much to learn about life." Tobias stopped short and pulled his hand away from Ben's when Samuel walked into the cabin.

"You two about ready?" Samuel softly spoke, as if he knew he was interrupting something.

Tobias and Ben followed Samuel outside. "Go on and climb up there in that wagon. I'll cover you with this here canvas, then a layer of potatoes. Be a two-day trip up to Sandusky."

Ben's head whipped around to Samuel. "I ain't ridin' covered like that for two whole days!" His eyes shot back and forth between Samuel and Tobias.

Samuel's shoulders drooped as he shook his head. "Now, sir, I ain't never said you were ridin' like that for two days." Releasing an exasperated sigh, his head continued to shake. "We stoppin' in Columbus tonight. That is, if you ever get in."

Ben again looked at Tobias. Hesitating for a minute, he finally boarded the wagon and moved over so Tobias could squeeze in. "What's in Sandusky?" he asked.

"It ain't what, it's who," Samuel replied, as he tried to cover the two with a large tarp.

"Okay, who?" Ben pulled the canvas off of his head. The other three brothers, who were standing behind Samuel, laughed.

Samuel drew in a long breath. Crossing his arms, he shook his head. After a long pause, he grinned. "I bet ain't no one lookin' for you." The three brothers burst into hearty laughter.

Tobias didn't understand what was happening. What was so funny? He, too, wanted to know where they were going.

"Sandusky . . . We goin' to Sandusky, where I have a friend who can help you get to Canada." Samuel lowered his voice and looked at Tobias. "Please, sir, lie down, so we can go."

Ben nodded. His shoulders dropping, he laid down so Samuel could cover them. As the sacks of potatoes were placed on top of them, Ben reached out and took Tobias's hand.

24

The Halls' farm included a large home that stood in the middle of a walnut grove. Directly behind the house, about a mile away, was Lake Erie: the lake that they had to cross to make it to Canada. From the driver's bench, Samuel reached behind himself and shoved a couple of bags of potatoes out the way before uncovering the canvas. Revealing the two young men to Hall, Samuel threw his hands up in the air.

"This here is Judge Hall. He's goin' to help you from here," he said, directing his comment to Tobias.

Hall, a tall, distinguished white man in his forties, looked just as surprised as Willie and Samuel had when they first saw Ben. After hearing the visitors' story, he scratched his long grey beard and welcomed Ben and Tobias. "Well, come on in. The wife served supper already, but I suppose we can find something for you to eat."

"Hello." Tobias climbed out first and nodded to the stranger. "Pleased to meet you, Mr. Judge."

Judge Hall laughed. "No son, my name is Hall. I *am* the judge here in Erie County."

"You say you a judge, sir?" Ben made his way down from the wagon and joined Tobias. "I done seen everythin' now. Met lots of kind folks on our journey, but this is a first."

Tobias watched Ben, noticing how polite he was and how tall he was standing. Hall led them into the barn and then down into a tunnel that ran from the barn to the house. "Now, you'll be staying with us in the house until it's time to go. If slave trackers arrive during the night, I need you to quickly and quietly pick up your belongings and bedding and disappear down into this tunnel."

Tobias wasn't sure that he had heard the man correctly. They weren't staying out here in the barn? Following Hall and Ben, Tobias ran his hands along the dirt wall of the three-foot wide tunnel.

Hall continued to talk, his voice bouncing off the narrow passage. "If you hear the Misses singing "Wade in the water," this means you need to continue on through the tunnel, back to the barn, and out into the grove. You need to keep running until you reach the lake. There, you will find a boat and oars."

Tobias stopped behind Ben as they came to the end of the tunnel. Hall climbed a ladder and opened a hatch about twenty feet above their heads. Standing on the floor above, he helped Ben and then Tobias through before hiding the hatch with a rug and chaise lounge.

The man continued talking as he led them through the large house, across a hallway and into a dining room. "You will need to row out across the lake and keep rowing until you get to the other side. You'll be in Canada."

Walking into the dining room, they saw several negroes sitting around the table. They appeared to have just finished eating.

"Let's get you cleaned up first. Then we can come back, and I will introduce you to everyone." Hall waved for them to follow him. "They've been waiting to cross the river for about a week. We'll cross at night, when there is no moon, and the wind is blowing from the south. We have to have the wind, as it will aid us in moving faster across the water." He led them into a tiny room with a washtub in the middle of the floor. He handed them both washrags and said that he would return with clean clothes.

Within five minutes, Mrs. Hall returned and knocked on the door. "I have some clean clothes for you. Leave your old clothes in here, and I will darn them up in the morning. If you are satisfied with what I have here, you may keep them, or I can return these to you."

After shutting the door, Ben and Tobias stripped their clothes off and began the task of scrubbing the dirt from their bodies.

"Your skin was beginning to look as dark as mine." Tobias smiled as he watched Ben move his rag between his legs, revealing his beautiful, cream-colored thighs. Scrubbing and knocking at his balls and penis, Ben continued moving the rag up and down his legs as he scrubbed himself clean. When he bent over to clean the bottom of his legs and feet, he exposed his buttocks in all their glory to Tobias. Tobias had to look away as his own body responded. Seeing Ben's lean, naked body was driving him mad. He decided to use conversation to divert his attention. "Do you miss those fancy clothes you use to have?"

"No, but I sure in the heck miss bein' clean." Having turned the entire tub of clean water dirty, they were clean—cleaner than they had been in weeks.

When they returned to the dining room, everyone was gone. The table had been reset, with two place settings across from one another. They sat by Mr. Hall, and it wasn't long before Mrs. Hall appeared with a tray of food. Setting it down on the table, she smiled at them. "Sorry to keep you boys waiting. Now that you're clean, let me properly introduce myself. I am Mrs. Hall, but please, call me Tessie. This is my home, and you are my guests. Welcome."

With the proper introductions made, Mr. and Mrs. Hall left Ben and Tobias to dine on their black-eyed peas, a piece of fatback, and a pile of mustard greens.

Ben wasted no time starting in on the plate of food in front of him. "Mmm, this makes me think of Penny. Sure do miss her cookin'. I miss her mustard greens." Ben lifted his chin. "I think we are goin' to make it, Tobias. This is it. We've done it." Smiling, he held up his drinking glass for a toast.

Tobias smiled, but his stomach turned. He hoped it was from eating too fast, but his mind told him differently. The unknown waited. It was all so much to take in. "Not yet. You mustn't talk too soon."

After dinner, in their new clean clothes, they found Mr. and Mrs. Hall in the parlor, where the rest of the houseguests were sitting. Hall was reading a book to a negro child, and Tessie was teaching the runaway women how to crochet as they circled around her lap.

Hall stopped reading and stood up. "Come in, gentlemen. Let me introduce you to our other guests. This is Dorothy and Joseph; they're from Kentucky as well. And this is Rose, her husband Thomas, and their son Dada. And this beautiful lady is Momma Grace—she's from Tennessee. Everyone, this is Tobias and Ben Lee."

Rose looked up and smiled. "You're both Lees?" She was a petite woman with skin the color of light caramel. Her face was thin, and her green eyes were the color of emeralds. Tobias had long since learned that this skin tone and eye color indicated that she was of mixed heritage. Her father was most likely a white slave owner.

"Yes . . . We're both Lees." Ben stepped in front of Tobias, shaking everyone's hand as they greeted each of them.

Tobias could feel Rose watching him as they moved about the room.

Sitting by the fire, the others all shared with Ben and Tobias who they were and the stories of their journeys thus far. The young couple, Dorothy and Joseph, were both twenty and planned to marry once they arrived in Canada. They had fled upon discovering that Dorothy's master intended to use her as a broodmare on the farm due to her large size.

Rose said that she and Thomas had been married for fourteen years and that Dada was twelve. The boy was tall and skinny for his age and looked nothing like his parents. Once in Canada, he wanted to go to school and study.

And then there was Momma Grace, who, at the age of sixty-six, shared that when it was time for her to leave this earth, she wanted to take her last breath as a free woman. She resembled Miss Gee-gee, and this likeness brought sadness to Tobias when he looked at her.

Momma Grace had long grey hair that flowed down to the middle of her back. Her ancestors were from the West Indies, which explained her combination of European features and dark skin.

The women wept as Tobias shared the story of the day he was abducted from his village—the last day he had seen his mother, father, and little sister. He told them about Pearl, the bond they had shared as a new family, and how much he missed her. When the tightness in his throat prevented him from finishing the story of Pearl's death, Momma Grace wrapped her arms around him and hugged him securely.

They all talked about what they wanted to do with freedom—the new life that waited for them across Lake Erie. Tobias listened as the others talked about freedom, realizing that he was the only one in the room, other than Ben and the Halls, who had ever known what freedom was like.

As the sun set, Tobias couldn't remember the last time he had been this clean, well fed, and safe. He was in Ohio, a free state, and on his way to another country, called Canada. He had no idea what to expect, but it couldn't come fast enough.

He looked about the room. His village had been composed of huts with dirt floors. His father had been the medicine man, and life had been simple. He had never even seen a modern house until he came to America. Now, he was sitting in a parlor with a warm fire, next to the young man with whom he wanted to spend the rest of his life. He knew that Ben had risked everything, including his future.

Tobias couldn't believe how his life had changed in such a short time. Expressing his concern about Dexter, he was told by Mr. Hall that overseers rarely came this far looking for runaway slaves, though a good slave tracker seeking a big reward might. Since Ben was Master Lee's son, Ben might be the one whom they tracked the most persistently.

That night, bedrolls were fixed in the parlor, where all eight guests slept next to each other. Ben and Tobias fixed their beds side by side. As they faced each other, they drifted off to sleep.

After dinner each night, they all took to their own personal spaces in the large room. Again, Tobias eyed the beautiful, faded tapestries hanging from the reddish walls, which were draped with rich velvet curtains. Patterned carpets lay over the mahogany floor, and chairs were centered in front of the massive fireplace. Having only seen the parlor and the dining room, Tobias imagined that the rest of the rooms in the house were just as grand.

One evening, Tobias and Ben had settled on their bedrolls after dinner when Hall approached them. "I wanted to give you two time to settle in before I filled you in on the plan." He squatted, directing his words to Ben. "Within a couple of days, the moon will be at half. This is when we start looking for an opportunity to move. Ideally, the moon will be nothing more than a crest—the less light, the better."

"Yeah, less chance of bein' spotted." Ben mumbled, nodding.

"But we also need the right amount of wind. A storm out there will undoubtedly capsize the boats. They are small, and the waters are unforgiving." Hall's eyes shifted to Tobias.

They are small, and the waters are unforgiving. Their words rang in Tobias's ears. His pulse quickened as he thought of the small boats they had been loaded onto in Africa. He was overwhelmed by the feeling of being in the cargo hold of a large ship as it battled the sea— water rushing through the planks as the captain pushed through a storm. His lips pressed together; he breathed heavily through his nose, causing his nostrils to flare. He had questions, many questions, but his throat was too dry to speak.

"I will take Momma Grace, Rose, Thomas, and Dada first. Get them to safety. If we can go again, I will take you, Tobias, Dorothy, and Joseph the following night. Can you swim, Tobias?"

"Um—no, sir." Tobias's answer was nearly inaudible. The lack of oxygen in his lungs was beginning to squeeze his chest tight. Ben took his hand, but the touch did nothing to relieve the anxiety caused by Hall's words. Tobias sighed, reluctant to accept what he was hearing. He was filled with fear as Hall continued talking about the risks and dangers of the trip. His words were merely noise in Tobias's ears.

"Thank you," Ben said as Hall rose to his feet and stood over them, facing the entire group.

"I know you all have lots of questions, so please, please ask." Tessie moved from her chair and stood next to her husband.

"Where do negroes live in Canada?" Rose's voice was angelic; her back straight, her chin high, her eyes staring directly at their host.

Hall removed his glasses as he pondered her question. "Well, the shore of Lake Huron is about as far as I go. There will be people there to take you from the shores, settle you, and address your needs and desires. But I'm told you can get land up in Chatham. Do some farming."

"Can you fish there?" asked Thomas.

Tessie chimed in, "There is the Ausable River, about thirty-five miles up from Lake Huron, where you will be landing. This is country similar to ours but colder. Quite a few negroes are up in those parts, I am told."

Ben leaned close to Tobias and whispered, "I don't want to live around a bunch of people. We're goin' to find us some farm land." His look told Tobias that he was thinking naughty thoughts.

"Do you know any of these places they're speaking about?" Tobias couldn't picture anything—he had no vision of a farm. Twisting his knuckles, he couldn't shake the quiver in his stomach.

"No, but don't worry, we'll find us a place."

Tobias swallowed. The boats hung in the forefront of his mind. "Then why go? Let's stay here."

Ben's head turned to face him, his eyebrows squished together. "What—here?"

Tobias saw his look of confusion. "Ohio, let's just stay here. Why do we have to go and risk our lives again? They'll never find us here." Tobias had decided to persuade Ben that they could be okay here. They could find that same land here, be happy here. Tobias looked around to see if anyone was listening. He worried that they would know he was scared.

"You'll be fine. I'll protect you. Nothin' will happen." Ben's voice was relaxed as he looked back at Hall and his wife.

Ben *wasn't* hearing him. Tobias couldn't get in that boat.

Another day had passed. Tobias ate little of the chicken, corn, boiled potatoes, and biscuits that Tessie had prepared that evening. The walls of the house were closing in around him. He needed to get out of that house, get some air, and talk some sense into Ben before it was too late. He wasn't going to Canada.

After dinner, the group was exiting the dining room and crossing over into the parlor. This was Tobias's chance; he had to hold Ben back so they could have a moment to talk. Reaching out to take Ben's hand, Tobias jumped at the sudden alarm in Hall's voice.

"Quick, someone's coming!" Hall rushed everyone into the parlor. "Come, come!"

Tobias heard the sound of hoofs approaching. They had to be just outside the house.

"Into the tunnel, everyone! Tessie, clear that table! Come, we only have minutes!" Hall's voice was high, his eyes bulging as he pushed everyone along.

Coming to a stop, everyone waited their turn as they crammed down into the tunnel. Tobias watched as the women went first, Momma Grace moving at a speed that would surely get them all caught. Soon, they were all in the tunnel, and the hatch was sealed. Frightened, Tobias listened for the song that would tell them to run.

It was minutes before light appeared in the tunnel. Hall's face peered down from the hatch. "That was my secretary," he said, reaching down to help them climb out of the tunnel. "He came to warn us that the sheriff will be here in the morning. He has an Overseer from Kentucky who's tracking two negroes. The sheriff and I have history, and he doesn't care much for me."

One by one, they all exited the tunnel. Tobias and Ben stayed to the end to assist the others. Hall talked as each of them came up. "I'm not sure who the other fella is, but not to worry. Sheriff Casey has been here before and is not much smarter than that bug on the wall there. Still, we must be prepared. Pack your things, and be ready to move. Do not try to cross the lake during the day; there will be fishermen along the banks and on the lake. Wait in the woods until night, and then go. There are two boats down there. Use them both. I would rather you didn't make the trip without a guide, but if it comes down to that then you must." The distress in his voice was not lost on anyone, judging by the looks on their faces.

As they lay on their bedrolls that night, Tobias knew it was Dexter who was coming for them. He could feel it. That night, there was no fire in the fireplace. Tobias was lying on his back, and Ben's arm lay lightly pressed against his. But one arm wasn't enough. With the darkness of the room shielding him, Tobias reached down and took Ben's hands. Bringing their fingers together, he tried to control his breathing. He had no choice: he had to get in that boat. His breathing ragged, his lungs starved for air, he felt imprisoned in a living nightmare—get in the boat, or risk Dexter finding them. Both played on his deepest fears.

"I can hear you breathin'. It's goin' to be alright," Ben whispered. Grasping Tobias's hand, he tightly squeezed it. "It's goin' to be okay. We're almost there, a couple more days." He squeezed Tobias's hand again.

Tobias could think of no words to fill the void. The silence echoed throughout the dark room. His mind raced from one disastrous scenario to another.

"Tobias . . . What's the first thing you want to do when we get to Canada?" Ben whispered.

Tobias's jaw clenched. The last thing he wanted was to talk. "Um," he mumbled. "What do you mean, what do I want to do?" The question was too wide open for him. He knew Ben was just talking to be talking.

"We're goin' to find us a nice piece of land. Farm and live off that land. Raise some cattle. What do you think?" Ben asked.

Tobias was forced to speak. To come out of his head and be present. "I think I want to go to school. There is much for me to learn. I want to become a . . . doctor." He hadn't known that was what he wanted until the words came out of his mouth. "Yes, a doctor." He could learn about medicine. If there was a community of people such as him in Canada, they would need care. He thought of Pearl. He could make it right.

Ben let out a noise as if he was trying to contain laughter.

"Why do you laugh? Can't I be a doctor?" Tobias asked.

"Well I ain't never seen a negro doctor before, but then again, ain't nothin' normal any more. Of course, you can be a doctor." Ben's voice had a teasing tone. "Here you go." Ben's body shifted, and he put something in Tobias's hand.

It was cool to the touch. Bringing it close to his face, Tobias saw that it was Ben's gold pocket watch. He couldn't understand why in the world Ben would hand him his watch. He couldn't even tell time.

"If you goin' to be a doctor, you need a fancy watch. I ain't never had no use for such a thing. I want you to have it." Ben folded the watch into Tobias's hand and gently squeezed it.

Tobias had seen the watch a couple of times. He knew it was a gift from Ben's parents. Other than that, he had no understanding of the device.

They talked all night, until the morning light glowed from the edges of the covered windows. Tobias had talked himself past the boat, beyond the trip, and had arrived in an imaginary place somewhere in Canada. The sound of Ben's voice had quieted his fears.

Hall entered the room in a single step. "It's time! It's time! Everyone up, they're coming! Down into the tunnel!" He quickly explained that the sheriff and a slave tracker had been spotted at the neighbor's. A messenger had run through the grove to alert the judge.

"Good morning, Sheriff. What brings you out this far so early in the morning?" Hall asked, as he stood tall on his porch, staring down Dexter and the sheriff.

Sitting on his horse, the sheriff lowered his hat. "Now, you know that every now and again I gets these rumors that you got runaways sleeping up in there. Ain't never believed them rumors, but you knows I got to follow the law and check." He climbed off of his horse and looked over Hall's shoulders and into the house. "This fella has rode all the way from Kentucky tracking a nigger boy and girl, who may be traveling with a young Mr. Benjamin Lee. Say he's Mr. Emmett Lee's son, from the Oak Grove Plantation down in Kentucky.

Dexter, who had gotten off of his horse, stepped in front of Sheriff Casey. "I got little time to waste. I am this close to them. I know it! Do you got niggers up in there sleeping or not?"

"Well, I ain't never stopped a man from doing his job. Now, sir, you got quite the gash on the side of your head there. Suspect that hurt?" said Hall, as he straightened his back and lifted his shoulders. "But as the judge standing before you, I can honestly say I don't have any negroes in there sleeping." Hall chuckled.

Sheriff Casey joined Dexter as the two moved towards the porch. "Well, then, just like the last time, I'll be in and out and heading back to town in no time."

"I reckon you will be, right after you show me the proper paperwork for your search. As the judge of this town, I don't remember signing no warrant for you."

Both Sheriff Casey and Dexter stopped cold. "Well, no, sir, you didn't. I didn't have no warrant before, either."

"Yeah, and you caught me on a good day that day." Hall spit his tobacco over the rail. "But I ain't quite woke up yet, and I'm feeling a little sour at the moment."

"Didn't know it would come to this, Your Honor, but I could ride on over to Temple Hill and have Judge Fisher issue me one."

"Boy, don't you think if I had a runaway up in this house, he would be gone before you got back? How you were elected, I don't know. Good day, Sheriff!" Hall chuckled again, as he walked into the house.

Taking to the window, Hall and his wife watched as the sheriff and Dexter rode off the property. "Now, that was easier than I thought," Hall mumbled.

"They'll be back. I can feel it." Tessie caressed Hall's shoulder as they watched the dust settle.

25

Hall climbed down into the tunnel, his face grim, as he gathered everyone's attention. "You're going to have to spend the day down here. We'll leave tonight." Everyone gasped, causing Hall to pause. "The moon, it's not right, and there's a storm coming in a few days. I'm afraid if we don't go now, we'll have to wait until after the storm, and that's more days than we have. If we're rowing against the wind, it could make the journey tough." Hall exhaled a large breath. "I've never lost a single person."

Tobias peered over everyone's shoulders as he watched Hall's face. The tension there said what Hall wasn't saying. "So, we're all going in one trip? Is that what you're saying?"

Hall looked up at Tobias. "Yes. I fear it would be another twenty-eight days before you could get out, and we may not have twenty-eight days."

"Will you be coming with us?" Thomas asked, as he hugged his wife and child.

"Yes . . . Ben, can you captain the second boat? You'll have to stay close to me, close enough to hear my commands. Voices carry on the water. If anyone's around, they'll surely hear us."

Ben nodded. "Okay. I want Tobias in my boat."

"Can you do it?" Tobias asked.

Ben looked around the tunnel and knew there was only one answer he could give. "Yeah, I can do it."

"Everyone try to get some rest. It's going to be a long night." Hall looked over at Ben. "Ben, can I see you for a minute?" He pushed his way past everyone and led Ben a little ways down the tunnel. "How's your swimming?" Hall asked.

"Good, I'm a strong swimmer. Been swimmin' all my life."

"I'm concerned. If Momma Grace or anyone else goes overboard, I can't leave my boat, and neither can you. You can't save someone in those little boats without risking everyone in them. Do what you can, but maintain control of your boat."

Tobias watched as Hall and Ben talked just ten feet away. He knew that they would either be in Canada or dead by this time tomorrow.

When Hall returned to the tunnel hours later, they knew it was time to go. Ben and Tobias stood up and assisted Momma Grace in gathering her things. They said their good-byes to Tessie, with each of the women accepting a hug from her and a "God Be with You."

When they came out of the tunnel and passed through the barn, Tobias could feel the chill in the air. A storm was definitely coming, but the fresh air was exhilarating as it filled his lungs. They stayed in a tight group, as they walked the mile to the water.

When they reached the banks of the lake, the clouds had all but covered the moon. Ben moved to secure Tobias, Dorothy, and Joseph in his boat. Dorothy clung to Ben's arms as he steadied her in the middle of the boat.

"You'll be alright. It's okay." Ben's voice was soothing as he rubbed her hand. He then instructed Joseph to take the front and to sit on the left side. He put Tobias on the right side, between Dorothy and himself, as he checked out the rear of the boat.

Ben whispered to everyone in his boat that, under no circum-stances, should anyone stand up. "All our lives depend on this. If you see someone about to stand up, it's up to you to stop them, as your life depends on it."

Dorothy, who was sunk down as far as she could go into the bot-tom of the boat, turned to face Ben. "I can't swim."

"You won't have to." Ben walked over to Joseph and gave him one-on-one instructions on how to row a boat. "Tobias, did you get that?" Ben's face was stern as he looked at Tobias. He told them that, from the rear, he would keep the boat straight. They just needed to row at the same time, without stopping.

When Hall whispered to Ben that it was time to go, Ben, with all his strength, got behind the boat and pushed the rear of it into the water. Dorothy gasped as water splashed up over the side and into her lap. Tobias watched as she fidgeted.

"Tobias, Tobias . . . watch her, make sure she doesn't jump up," Ben whispered.

Tobias nodded at him and whispered to Dorothy, "See? We're floating, it's not going to sink. You're okay. You're okay." He repeated this until Dorothy's shoulders finally relaxed.

Ben remained behind Hall's boat as they rowed across the dark lake. The water was calm as the fog settled over the water. They used the fog to shield them as Hall navigated the two boats toward freedom.

Within an hour, Dorothy had settled and was sitting quietly be-hind her fiancé. Tobias watched her closely, doubting that she was as calm on the inside as she appeared to be.

The wind picked up, throwing up a light mist of water that splashed across the boats. Initially, Tobias thought the wind was good; he could feel the boat being pushed across the water with ease. Between Tobias and Joseph, every time they sank their oars into the water, the boat seemed to jump forward.

Tobias and Joseph paddled in perfect synchrony—it was as if they had been doing it their whole lives. Ben whispered that if they were not careful, they would overtake the other boat. "Save your strength, and we can row all night," he said.

When the wind increased, it cut across their faces like a knife, and the swells of water started to come over the sides of the boats. Ben yelled for Dorothy to bail the water out of the boat's bottom. He knew that, at some point, the extra water could weigh them down, but for right now, it was solely to keep her occupied. He thought his face was on fire each time the wind hit them, forcing them to keep their heads down, occasionally glancing up to ensure that they were on course and that the boats were still close to one another.

"I can't see!" Tobias screamed as he shielded his face from the wind.

"Keep paddling! Don't stop!" Ben called out to Tobias and Joseph, as he struggled to keep the boat on course.

The wind shifted. It was now attacking them from the side, rocking the boat. Tobias glanced up at one point and realized that he could no longer see the other boat. "Stop, Stop!" he cried out. "We lost them!" The boat slowed as the wind tried to capsize them. Looking through the fog, Tobias scanned the water for the other boat. Other than the wind, the lake was quiet. Tobias feared the worst. "Do you see them?"

"We have to keep paddling, or the wind will capsize us." Ben's voice shrieked, as the wind took it away.

"Slow!" Tobias shot back as he continued staring into the fog. He could hear Dorothy crying, but there wasn't enough of him to tend to her needs and row.

"I don't see them!" Ben's voice was barely audible as the wind ripped across their faces, whisking his words off into the darkness.

Then, about fifty feet to their right, they saw the other boat. "There they are!" Ben hollered. "Over there! Paddle, over there!"

Tobias could see that Dada, in the other boat, was struggling to keep his oar in the water as the wind ripped into their boat, which was barely moving. With a couple of strokes, Tobias and Joseph nearly slammed their boat into the side of Hall's.

Tobias prayed to the Gods for the winds to stop. Dorothy had stopped bailing the water. She sat crying and praying in the middle of the boat, fidgeting about in her seat, looking for somewhere to go.

The boats moved slowly and silently across the water for the next hour, cutting through the fog. Finally, the fog lifted, and the wind— once again gentle—grabbed the boats and softly propelled them through the water.

"It is the Gods! They have heard us!" Tobias cried out, mostly to himself.

By the time dawn was approaching, the waters had been calm for several hours, and the wind gently blew them to the north. Joseph was the first to see it, then Tobias and Ben. It was land. Dorothy had fallen asleep hours ago, but Tobias knew that they had to wake her up to share in this moment.

As the boat cut across the water towards land, Tobias wept. He tried to hold the tears back to avoid being heard, but this was his journey. As he rowed with all his might, Ben placed a hand on his shoulder and whispered to him, "I love you."

Tobias looked over into the other boat. Momma Grace was sitting in the middle of the boat, motionless, her head proudly up in the air and her beautiful grey hair blowing in the wind. She was about to have her first taste of freedom, and her facial expression said it all.

When the two boats washed up onto the quiet shores of Canada, the passengers all sat still in their seats, breathing as the cool morning air rushed into their lungs. Gripping the button tied to the leather necklace around his neck, Tobias brushed it with his hand and whispered to himself. "Oh, Pearl, I wish you were here. I am so sorry." Hearing a cry above his head, he looked up to see a white and grey seagull as it flew overhead, its wings allowing it to cut through the morning air, ever so gracefully.

They had arrived. After months of running, their skeletal frames rose from the boats. One by one, they parted, gathering in little groups along the shoreline. Tobias and Ben walked about twenty-five feet up the sandy white coastline before coming to a stop. Ben fell onto his knees and gripped the sand with his hands. "We made it, Tobias, we made it." His voice shook as he picked up a handful of warm sand. Letting the sand pour through his fingers, he smiled. "This is where we will make our new life together, a place we can call ours. They will know you as Mamadou, Mamadou Masamba." Smiling, his bright eyes held fast on Tobias.

Tobias hadn't heard his name emerge from someone's lips since being captured. He had to rest his hands on Ben's shoulders to steady himself. *Mamadou Masamba, Praiseworthy. The son of Babatunde Masamba, an Africa Healer.* His stomach tightened as a rush of emotions caused his chest to burn. A large lump formed in his throat, and his mouth was dry. The whisper of waves filled the silence.

His legs gave him no choice but to collapse onto the warm sand in front of Ben. They stared into each other's eyes. It was as if neither wanted to blink first.

Clearing his throat, Ben gave in first. "Can you be happy here? With just me?" There was an innocent, restless look in his eye. It was a display of vulnerability that Tobias had come to know well.

He knew what Ben was really asking him: will you stay here in Canada or return to your homeland? Tobias didn't know what tomorrow would bring, or even the next hour, but he knew he was safe. The thought of living in this world, without the one person who made him feel that way, was out of the question. He would be lying to himself if he denied that he hadn't thought of returning home. Of course he had. But Ben had brought him the emotional well-being and love to get through each passing day. "I can't say that the thought never occurred to me. To be free, to go home," he said.

Ben's face tensed. His chestnut eyes waited for Tobias's next word.

Tobias paused long enough to look to see who was within earshot of them. The smell of brine penetrated his nose. "I love you," he whispered, as he stared deeply into Ben's eyes. His mother's face flashed before him. He could see her as plain as day, her black hair pulled back out of her face, her warm brown eyes sparkling in the sunlight. She was here—he could feel her.

Mamadou, be happy. Love as I loved your father, she told him. The sun's rays warmed Tobias's back through his shirt. An overwhelming sense of peace struck him, like the waves against the boat just hours ago. He wanted to hug Ben, to kiss him, like he had never wanted to before. But there was still a barrier keeping them apart: the others around them. They were far enough away that their conversation could go unheard, but any display of affection would surely draw immediate attention.

Perhaps it would always be like this, having Ben only behind closed doors. His mouth too dry to speak, he gazed discreetly into Ben's eyes, hoping Ben could feel the love that poured from his soul. He knew little of the land that he would now call home. Most likely, there would be no safe haven for a love such as theirs. However, whenever he tried to imagine himself anywhere else, his heart always returned to Ben.

Something moved in the corner of Tobias's eye. Turning his head slightly, he saw that it was a wagon. It came to a stop about a hundred yards up, where the trees gave way to the shoreline and white sandy beach. Two older male Negroes were perched in the wagon's front, staring at them. Slowly, one of the men removed his hat and waved it at them.

Looking around, Tobias saw that Judge Hall was waving back. Within minutes, the two men were approaching the group. Tobias recalled that Judge Hall had told them that someone would be there to welcome them, to take them to a resting house, to help settle them. The light, salty mist rained upon Tobias's face as he noticed that the others were beginning to roam about. The two men hugged and greeted everyone and then slowly gathered all of them up. In a single file line, the group followed the men back to the wagon.

Tobias knew that he only had seconds to finish what he needed to say. "I know you left everything to be with me. For that, I will spend the rest of my life proving to you that I was worth it. I love you, but . . . the real question is: Will I be enough for you?"

Ben smiled as the color returned to his face. "You are more than I could've ever dreamed for my life. I can't wait to build our home." His words, faint over the sounds of waves breaking in the distance, made Tobias catch his breath.

Home. The word initially sounded odd to Tobias. "Home," he repeated under his breath. This was really to be. Months ago, they had left on a journey in which they thought they were seeking freedom for Tobias. In Africa, the story of Mamadou Masamba had been uncertain. He was not destined to marry; his life's path was to be chosen by the high priest. Once upon a time, he had been ready to accept this—but then, as Ben put it, he had realized why he was born. A ghastly turn of events had led him to Ben and to a life he had never known existed. It was a journey filled with sorrow and pain, yet rich in love and hope. Now, they were both in a place that they could call home.

Climbing into the wagon, Tobias moved in as close as he could next to Ben. He could feel Ben's breathing, the sensation of his pulse jumping from his body into Tobias's. Tobias closed his eyes and took in a long breath, feeling the rush of air as it penetrated his lungs, causing his head to swirl. Then he slowly exhaled. He felt Ben shift his weight and then saw him reach down between them. Their fingers joined. "Think of the oaks. Come, come to the oaks and be with me forever," Ben whispered in his ear.

Again, Tobias took in a breath as he closed his eyes. They would always be together. No one could keep them apart.

ABOUT THE AUTHOR

Bryan Thomas Clark is a funny, loving, family-oriented, and proud member of the LGBTQ community. After twenty-seven years in law enforcement, Bryan retired in 2015 to focus on his writing full time. He is the author of two previous Male/Male Romance novels: *Ancient House of Cards* and *Before Sunrise*. In his work, he is known to push the boundaries with brilliantly crafted stories of friendship, love, complicated relationships, and challenges all woven into a hard-earned happily-ever-after. In 2014, *Ancient House of Cards* was nominated for GOODREADS M/M ROMANCE 2014 Best Debut book of the year, and sold in seven countries its first year. *Before Sunrise* received a five-star review from USA Today, earning Bryan the high praise of a 'Master Storyteller'.

Behind his computer, working on his next novel, Bryan writes Male/Male Romance with an emphasis on *moral dilemma*. His multicultural characters and riveting plots embody real life, filled with challenges, personal growth, and, of course, what we all desire—love.

When Bryan isn't writing, he enjoys traveling, lying by a body of water soaking up the sun, and watching a good movie while snuggled up with his husband and their loyal companion (Nettie the Sheepadoodle) on the couch.

Born in Boston, Massachusetts, Bryan has made his home and life in the Central Valley of California.

E-mail-Bryanbrianx2@comcast.net
Website-www.btclark.com

If you've enjoyed *Come to the Oaks*, I'd love to hear about it. Honest reviews on Amazon, Barnes & Noble, and Goodreads are always appreciated. If you would like to explore some of my other novels, follow the links below.

Ancient House of Cards
http://www.amazon.com/dp/1494955172

Before Sunrise:
http://www.amazon.com/dp/0997056207

Made in United States
Orlando, FL
03 August 2023

35716602R00150